ROBOT TALK

"Have you ever thought you would like to be a man?" Andrew asked.

The surgeon hesitated a moment, as though the question fitted nowhere in his allotted positronic pathways. "But I am a robot, sir."

"Would it be better to be a man?"

"It would be better, sir, to be a better surgeon. I would be pleased to be a more advanced robot."

"It does not offend you that I can order you about?"

"It is my pleasure to please you, sir. Now, upon whom am I to perform this operation?"

"Upon me," Andrew said.

"But that is impossible, according to the First Law. It is patently a damaging operation, interfering with human safety."

"That does not matter," said Andrew, calmly.

"I must not inflict damage," said the surgeon.

"On a human being, you must not," said Andrew, "but I, too, am a robot."

NEBULA
WINNERS
TWELVE

EDITED BY GORDON R. DICKSON

*This low-priced Bantam Book
has been completely reset in a type face
designed for easy reading, and was printed
from new plates. It contains the complete
text of the original hard-cover edition.*
NOT ONE WORD HAS BEEN OMITTED.

NEBULA WINNERS TWELVE

*A Bantam Book / published by arrangement with
Harper & Row Publishers, Inc.*

PRINTING HISTORY

*Harper & Row edition published March 1978
2nd printing .... December 1978
Bantam edition / April 1979*

*Grateful acknowledgment is hereby made for permission to re-
print the following:*

"A Crowd of Shadows" by Charles L. Grant. © 1976 by C. L.
Grant. First appeared in The Magazine of Fantasy and Science
Fiction.
"Breath's a Ware That Will Not Keep" by Thomas F. Monte-
leone. From Dystopian Visions by Roger Elwood, Prentice
Hall, 1975. Copyright © 1975 by Roger Elwood. Reprinted by
permission of the author and the author's agent, Kirby Mc-
Cauley.
"Tricentennial" by Joe Haldeman. Copyright © The Condé
Nast Corp., 1977. First appeared in Analog.
"In the Bowl" by John Varley. Copyright © 1975 Mercury
Press, Inc. First appeared in The Magazine of Fantasy and
Science Fiction. Reprinted by permission of the author and his
agent, Kirby McCauley.
"The Bicentennial Man" by Isaac Asimov. Copyright © 1976
by Random House, Inc. First appeared in Stellar 2, edited by
Judy-Lynn Del Ray.
"Houston, Houston, Do You Read?" by James Tiptree, Jr.
Copyright © 1976 by Fawcett Publications, Inc. First appeared
in Aurora: Beyond Equality, edited by Vonda N. McIntyre
and Susan Janice Anderson.

*Bantam Books are published by Bantam Books, Inc. Its trade-
mark, consisting of the words "Bantam Books" and the por-
trayal of a bantam, is Registered in U.S. Patent and Trademark
Office and in other countries. Marca Registrada. Bantam
Books, Inc., 666 Fifth Avenue, New York, New York 10019.*

To Clifford D. Simak, Grand Master,
by Award of the Science Fiction Writers
of America, April 30, 1977

Contents

NEBULA WINNERS
TWELVE

Introduction

This is the twelfth annual edition of the Nebula Awards winners, a volume containing the winning novella, novelette, and short story, and some of the runners-up for the Nebula Awards in 1977. The stories published here, as with those in the anthologies of previous years, are remarkable for their quality; and the question arises, as it has before, how long such a standard can be maintained. Regarded with a slightly pessimistic eye, this string of winners and runners-up over the twelve-year period since the Awards were begun could look to be a result of a series of favorable accidents—accidents so favorable, in fact, that it would seem to be flying in the face of statistics to expect they would continue.

Well, is this twelve-year list of Award winners and nominees indeed the result of a series of lucky accidents? Or is it perhaps the result of factors that may provide for such a list to continue, supplying more good writers and more good stories in the future?

There are at least some specific factors that not only tend to explain the long line of worthy pieces of writing we have had in the past, but indicate their probable continuance into the future. These factors have their roots in the very nature of twentieth-century science fiction itself. First, and most important, of these is the fact that the field of science fiction has always had one outstanding characteristic. That is that its readers have always welcomed an unusual amount of freedom on the part of its writers, freedom from any single idea, pattern, attitude, or style. The result has been that traditionally science fiction has tended to produce writers who were unique and experimental—in a word, pioneers.

This is the more remarkable in that the field originally emerged from a tight classification which imprisoned it along with the mystery story, the western, and even the historical and adventure stories, back in the days of pulp fiction. All the factors were in existence at that time which could have been expected to keep science fiction permanently in a literary straitjacket. Instead, it has spent the last forty years gaining and maintaining its independence from just that sort of restriction; and it has been able to succeed in this primarily because it has developed not merely its own writers, but its own editors and—finally, now—its own publishers, people who grew up in the field and are today in a position to see published what they know from experience the readers will want to read.

In point of fact, the urge to break loose from artificial restrictions on story and substance showed up in science fiction writers very early. The trend to plow new territory appeared in the magazines of the late thirties and the early forties. Science fiction, by definition, was always future-conscious—sometimes even future-self-conscious. There is no point here in rehearsing once more what John Wood Campbell did for the independence of the field in those early years. There were other editors as well, also with the courage to publish what they liked, even though it did not conform to the category pattern that was then being impressed on pulp fiction generally.

Literally, from the beginning, this field broke taboos. Literally, even from the beginning, it produced writers who created the field by what they wrote. One of the most stubborn misconceptions about this area of fiction on the part of those who do not read it has always been the notion that there was a particular, describable literary animal known as science fiction, and what did not fit the description, was not.

Of course, there was and is no such description. Instead, there is a growing collection of works by a number of authors over a period of nearly fifty years which by its existence has defined the term "science fiction." Every successful writer who emerges in this area clears new territory out of the virgin literary wilderness and adds it to the territory already recognized to lie under the flag of the genre. Until the new lands are laid open to view, their possible existence is unimagined. Who, for example, could have foreseen the stories Frederik Pohl, James Tiptree, Jr., Isaac Asimov, and Charles Grant would create to win the awards they have won this year?

The answer is that none of these writers or the kinds of writing they do could have been predicted before they had made their appearance. Looking at the four Award winners mentioned above, we can recognize at least four types of science fiction. But what have even these four authors in common that makes what they all write science fiction? This is the hardest question in the world to answer; and writers and publishers within the field have struggled with it for many years without coming up with a really workable definition. Damon Knight's "science fiction is what I point at" remains about the only unassailable—if not very helpful—yardstick that the field has produced for defining itself. We tend to recognize science fiction, as we recognize genius, only after it has made its appearance. Nonetheless, freedom remains an essential element of it, whatever form it takes—freedom from previously recognized patterns, even from the pattern of current literary fashion.

It seems, then, that if we must have a hallmark for the field, we will have to return to the image of the science fiction writer as a literary pioneer. Literature by pioneers tends to appeal to other pioneers—and science fiction does tend to appeal to research scientists, to futurists, to readers at odds with or in revolt against some establishment of the present. It appeals because in literature, as in history, a pioneer needs and is necessarily concerned with courage, determination, and a great desire for freedom and independence, and whatever the form or style of the science fiction concerned, it tends to deal with such things.

In a literary sense, these elements translate into the work of a writer who has something for his or her own to say unlike anything that has ever been said before; and who wishes to say it not only in his or her own way, but in his or her own voice and words. Work of such kind is difficult to censor or regiment; and this difficulty has made it a practical impossibility for a common and inhibiting form to develop in science fiction. That there is no such common form has sometimes been very difficult for some observers outside the professional boundaries of the field to believe. It is human nature for the individual to think that good literature is what that particular individual approves of, and all else should be outside the canon. Unfortunately, this aspect of human nature has shown itself to tend toward a blindness to the virtues of what is not approved, and a tendency to condemn what it does not understand, or finds too different for comfort. Consequently, science fiction, as a self-defining genre, has had to resist the impulses of some of its best friends to put it into different bags at different times in its history, right down to the present one—bags which in every case would have excluded work that properly belonged within its canon. The efforts continue; not merely on the part of some publishers and booksellers, but on the part of some scholars, academics, critics, and others without and within the field itself. Human nature being what it is, they can be expected to so continue into the future.

Still, so far, all such assaults upon the essential and necessary freedom of the field have been defeated. Pioneers, historically, are not easy to conquer. Because this is so, and the freedom remains, there is every reason to expect that the field will go on, as it has, to attract more and more new writers of merit and independence. So that what we have enjoyed for nearly half a century we may continue to enjoy in continually new and different forms, as new and different authors emerge to comment upon the unrolling page of time, running ahead without fear of being shut out from their readers, to point out the hills and valleys, the mountains and caverns—indeed, the worlds—that lie ahead.

GORDON R. DICKSON

Twin City Airport, Minnesota
July, 1977

had taken only a few steps before they too were struck down by the Martians. Pitiful forms . . .

Clinton had . . . their dead through a narrow path through the corridor. Suddenly people were stumbling . . . dazzled men from . . . came out into the broken Tank Area and were also brought down screaming and . . .

CHARLES L. GRANT

A Crowd of Shadows

One of the characteristics not mentioned in the introduction to this volume is the fact that those who end up being successful in this field tend to have one particular virtue before all others. This is the characteristic of being able and willing to work very hard indeed at their writing.

Charlie Grant is a worker and, in a few short years, has compiled an impressive record as a young author. He was born in 1942, and was raised and lived in New Jersey. On his way to becoming a full-time writer and after graduating from Trinity College, Hartford, with a B.A. in history, he taught English, drama, and history in public high schools in New Jersey.

He is married, has a son named Ian, and is still living in the East. He is now, however, a full-time writer with just over three dozen stories sold, as well as five novels in the science fiction and fantasy field. He has edited both nonfiction and fiction, and he has been the Executive Secretary of the Science Fiction Writers of America for four years now.

"A Crowd of Shadows," the story that follows, is interestingly much more of a piece of writing than its surface action seems to indicate—which is reflected in the fact that it won the Nebula Award for short stories this year. Charlie Grant tends to be a strongly thematic writer and this, together with his capability for hard work, promises a great deal more remarkable writing to be seen under his name in the future.

Of all the means of relaxation that I have devised for myself over the years, most required nothing more strenuous than driving an automobile, and not one of them had anything remotely to do with murder. Yet there it was, and now here I am—alone, though not always lonely, and wondering, though not always puzzled. I'm neither in jail nor exile, asylum nor hospital. Starburst is where I am and, unless I can straighten a few things out, Starburst is where I'm probably going to stay.

I had long ago come to the conclusion that every so often the world simply had to thumb its nose at me and wink obscenely as if it knew what the hell was making things tick and for spite wasn't about to let me in on the secret. When that happens, I succumb to the lure of Huck Finn's advice and light out for the territory: in my case, that turns out to be Starburst. Where the luncheonette is called The Luncheonette, the hotel is The Hotel, and so on in understated simplicity. Where the buildings, all of them, rise genteelly from well-kept lawns on full-acre lots, painted sunrise-new and no two the same shape or shade—a half-moon-fashioned com-

3

munity that prides itself on its seclusion and its ability to sponge out the world from transients like me. It's a place that not many can stand for too long, but it's a breather from every law that anyone ever thought of.

At least that's what I thought when I came down last May.

It was a bit warm for the season, but not at all uncomfortable. Wednesday, and I was sitting on the grey sand beach that ribboned the virtually waveless bay they had christened Nova. The sun was pleasantly hot, the water cool, and the barest sign of a breeze drifted down from the misted mountains that enclosed the town. I had just dried myself off and was about to roll over onto my stomach to burn a little when a thin and angular boy about fifteen or so dashed in front of me, kicking up crests of sand and inadvertently coating me and my blanket as he pursued some invisible swift quarry. I was going to protest when there was a sudden shout and he stumbled to a halt, turning around immediately, his arms dejectedly limp at his sides. Curious, I followed his gaze past me to a middle-aged couple huddled and bundled under a drab beach umbrella. The woman, hidden by bonnet, dark glasses and a black, long-sleeved sweater, beckoned sharply. The boy waved in return and retraced his steps at a decidedly slower pace. As he passed me, looking neither left nor right, I only just happened to notice the tiny and blurred sequence of digits tattooed on the inside of his left forearm.

I'm sure my mouth must have opened in the classic gesture of surprise, but though I've seen them often enough in the city, for some reason I didn't expect to see an android in Starburst.

I continued to stare rather rudely until the boy reached the couple and flopped face-down on the sand beside them, his lightly tanned skin pale against the grey. The beach was quietly deserted, and the woman's voice carried quite easily. Though her words were indistinct, her tone was not: boy or android, the lad was in trouble. I supposed he was being told to stay close, paying for his minor act of rebellion.

I smiled to myself and lay back with my cupped hands serving as a pillow. Poor kid, I thought, all he wanted was a little fun. And then I had to smile at myself for thinking the boy human. It was a common mistake, though one I usually don't make, and I forgot about it soon enough as I dozed. And probably would never have thought of it again if I hadn't decided to indulge myself in a little fancy dining that evening.

Though my stays are irregular, they have been frequent enough to educate the hotel staff to my unexciting habits, and I had little difficulty in reserving my favorite table: a single affair by the dining room window overlooking the park, overlooking, in point of fact, most of the town, since the hotel was the only structure in Starburst taller than two stories, and it was only six. The unadorned walls of the circular room were midnight-green starred with white, a most relaxing, even seductive combination, and its patrons were always suitably subdued. I was just getting into my dessert when I noticed the boy from the beach enter with the couple I had assumed were his parents. They huddled with the maitre d' and were escorted to a table adjacent to my own. The boy was exceptionally polite, holding the chair for mother, shaking hands with father before sitting down himself. When he happened to glance my way, I smiled and nodded, but the gesture quickly turned to a frown when I heard someone mutter, "Goddamned humie."

The threesome were apparently ignoring the remark, but I was annoyed enough to scan the neighboring tables. Nothing. I was going to shrug it off to bad manners when suddenly an elderly man and his wife brusquely pushed back their chairs and left without any pretense of politeness. As they threaded between me and the boy, the old man hissed "robie" just loud enough. Perhaps I should have said something in return, or made overtures, gestures, something of an apology to the boy. But I didn't. Not a thing.

Instead, I ordered a large brandy and turned to watch the darkness outside the uncurtained window.

And in the reflection of the room, I saw the boy glaring at his empty plate.

In spite of the ground that fact and fiction have covered in exploring the myriad possibilities of societies integrated with the sometimes too-human android, the reality seemed to have come as a surprise to most people. For some it was a pleasant one: androids were androids; pleasant company, tireless workers, expensive but economical. Their uses were legion, and their confusion with actual humans minimal. For others, however, and predictably, androids were androids: abominations, blasphemies, monsters and all the horrid rest of it.

They had become, in fact, the newest minority that nearly everyone could look down upon if they were close-minded enough. Ergo, the tattoos and serial numbers. For people not sensitive enough to detect the subtle differences, the markings served as some sort of self-gratifying justification, though for what I've never been able to figure out exactly. I have a friend in London who has replaced all his servants with androids and has come to love them almost as brothers and sisters. Then, too, there's another friend who speaks of them as he would of his pets.

It's true they haven't brought about the Utopia dreamed of in centuries past; they are strictly regulated in the business community—always clannish, job preference still goes to the human, no matter how much more efficient the simulacrum might be. Still and all, I thought as I emptied my glass and rose to leave, there's something to be said for them: at least they have unfailing manners.

So I smiled as graciously as I could as I passed their table. The boy smiled back, the parents beamed. The lad was obviously their surrogate son, and I was slightly saddened and sorry for them.

I spent the rest of the evening closeted in my room, alternately reading and speculating on the reasons for their choice. Death, perhaps, or a runaway: as I said, the androids' uses are legion. It puzzled me, however, why the parents hadn't kept the boy covered on the beach. It would have at least avoided the scene in the dining room. Then I told myself to mind my own stupid business, and for the last time I slept the sleep of the just.

The following morning my door was discreetly knocked upon, and I found myself being introduced to the local detective-in-chief by Ernie Wills, the manager. I invited them in and sat myself on the edge of the still-unmade bed. "So. What can I do for you, Mr. Harrington?"

The policeman was a portly, pale-faced man with a hawk nose and unpleasantly dark eyes. Somehow he managed to chew tobacco throughout the entire interview without once looking for a place to spit. I liked the man immediately.

"Did you know the Carruthers family very well?" His voice matched his size, and I was hard put not to wince.

I looked blank. "Carruthers? I don't know them at all. Who are they?"

Harrington just managed a frown. "The couple sitting next to you last night at dinner. The boy. I was under the impression that you knew them."

"Not hardly," I said. "I saw them once on the beach yesterday afternoon, and again at dinner." I spread my hands. "That's all."

"Some of the other guests said you were rather friendly to them."

By that time I was completely puzzled and looked to Ernie for some assistance, but he only shrugged and tipped his head in Harrington's direction. It's his show, the gesture said. And for the first time, I noticed how harassed he seemed.

"In a detective novel," I said as lightly as I could, "the hero usually says, 'You have me at a disadvantage.' I'm sorry, Mr. Harrington, but I haven't the faintest idea what in God's name you're talking about."

Harrington grinned. His teeth were stained. "Touché. And I apologize, okay? I didn't mean to be so damned mysterious, but sometimes I like to play the role. I read those books too." He settled himself more deeply into the only armchair in the room and reached into a coat pocket for a handkerchief which he used to wipe his hands. "You see, there's been a murder in the hotel."

I looked at him patiently, but he didn't say anything else, apparently waiting for my reaction. I almost said, So what?, but I didn't. "Am I supposed to guess who was murdered, or who did it? My God, it wasn't one of the Carruthers, was it?"

Harrington shook his head.

Ernie swallowed hard.

"Well, surely you don't suspect one of them?"

"Wish I knew," Harrington said. "An old man was found outside his door on the third floor about three o'clock this morning. His throat was, well, not exactly torn . . . more like yanked out. Like somebody just grabbed hold and pulled."

That I understood, and the unbidden image that flashed into my mind was enough to swear me off breakfast, and probably lunch. I shuddered.

"Some people," the detective continued, "said they heard this old guy call the boy 'robie.' Did you hear it?"

"Yes," I answered without thinking. "And I heard someone else, I don't know who, call him a 'humie.' There were other remarks, I guess, but I didn't hear them all. That kind of talk isn't usual, you know. The Carruthers may have been offended, but I hardly think they'd have murdered for it. I smiled as nicely as I could because I felt sorry for them, and the boy."

Harrington kept wiping his hands; then, with a flourish, deposited the cloth back into his pocket and stood. "Okay," he said brusquely. "Thanks for the information."

As he turned to leave, I couldn't help asking if he really believed the boy or his parents had done it. "After all," I said, "the boy is an android. He can't kill anyone."

Harrington stopped with his hand on the door knob. He actually looked sorry for me. "Sir, either you read too much, or you watch too much TV. Andy or not, if ordered, that kid could kill as easily as I could blink."

And then he left, with silent Ernie trailing apologetically behind. Slowly I walked to the window and gazed out toward the bay. The sun was nearing noon, and the glare off the water partially blinded me to the arms of the coast that came within a hundred meters of turning Nova into a lake. Below was the single block of business that squatted between me and the beach. Leaning forward, I spotted a milling group of people and a squad car. I watched, trying to identify some of them, until Harrington strolled from the building and drove away. The crowd, small as it was, disturbed me. Starburst wasn't supposed to deal in murder.

"Christ," I said. "And I wanted to punch that old guy in the face."

I shook myself and dressed quickly. At least Harrington didn't tell me not to leave town. Not that I would have. I still had four days of vacation left, and though I was sorry for the old nameless man, and sorrier for the shroud the crime must have placed on the Carruthers, I still intended to soak up as much sun as possible.

And so I did until a shadow blocked the heat, and I looked up from my blanket into the face of the boy: the face turned black by the sun behind him. Specter. Swaying. I imagine I appeared startled because he said, "Hey, I'm sorry, mister. Uh, can I talk with you a minute?"

"Why, sure, why not?" I shifted to one side and sat up. Today the boy was fully dressed in sweat shirt, jeans and sockless sneakers. His dark hair was uncombed. He squatted next to me and began to draw nothings in the sand. Since I'm single, I guess I haven't developed whatever special rapport a man can have with a younger version of himself; and when that youthful image isn't even human, well, I just sat there, waiting for someone to say something.

"You were nice to me and my people last night," he said finally, his voice just this side of quavering. "I think I should thank you."

My mind was still not functioning properly. Part of me kept up a warning that this kid was suspected of murder, and my throat tightened. The other parts kept bumping into each other searching for something to say that sounded reasonably intelligent.

"They, uh, treated you rather unkindly, son."

He shrugged and wiped the sand from his doodling finger. "We get used to it. It happens all the time, though I guess that's not really true. Not all the time, anyway. Maybe it just seems bad here because it's so small. I'm . . . we're not used to small places."

He began digging into the sand, tossing the fill up to be caught and scattered by a sharp, suddenly cool breeze.

"People can be cruel at times," I said unoriginally. "You shouldn't let it bother you and your folks. Small people, you know, and small minds."

The boy stared at me from the corner of his eyes, his face still in shadow. "Aren't you afraid of me?"

"Why? Should I be?"

He shrugged again and worried the hole with the heel of his hand. "I think that detective thinks I killed that old man. He talked with us nearly two hours this morning. He said he was satisfied. I don't think so."

I shifted around to face him, but he continued to avert his face. I couldn't remember seeing such a shy boy before, though I supposed that the shock of the crime wasn't the easiest thing in the world to accept with nonchalance, especially when he was on the receiving end of the suspicion. I made a show of searching the beach, stretching my neck and gawking like a first-time tourist. "I don't see your, uh, parents. Are they as unconcerned as you?"

"My people are inside. They don't want anyone staring at them."

My people. That was the second time he'd used that wording, and I wondered. In the silence I found myself trying to place his accent, thinking it was perhaps a custom of wherever he came from, but there was nothing to it. Curiously so. He could have lived anywhere. On impulse I asked if he and his mother and father would care to join me for dinner. He shook his head.

"Thank you, but no. We'll eat in our room until

something happens to change their minds. The doorman almost slammed the door in my face."

That figures, I thought as the boy struggled to his feet. He looked down at me and said, "Thank you again," and was gone as abruptly as he had come. It was then that I noticed the few sunbathers staring at me, their hostility radiating clearly. I grinned back at them and lay face-down, hoping they hadn't seen the grin twist to grimace.

As I lay there, I considered: unlike members of most minorities, androids had no recourse to courts, education or native human talent to drag them out of their social ghetto. They were as marked as if their skin had been black or brown, only worse because whatever rights they had stopped at the factory entrance. And I wasn't at all pleased to have to admit to myself that even I couldn't see handing them the same rights and privileges as I had. I was beginning to wonder just how far above the crowd I really was for all my ideas. I thought of the people who'd glared at me: you'd better stop casting stones, I told myself. Don't feel sorry for the boy, feel sorry for the parents.

And then I dozed off, which, for my skin, is tantamount to stretching out on a frying pan. When I awoke again, my back felt as if it had been dragged over hot coals. And in feeling the burning pain, I surprised myself at the foul language I could conjure. I tried to put on my shirt, gave it up as the second worst idea I'd had that day, next to sunbathing, and gathered my things together. I walked across the sand and between the buildings that had their backs to the bay. When I reached the street, I stopped dead at the curb. There was the squad car again and an ambulance. A crowd getting noisy. And the flashing red lights. I spotted Detective Harrington staring at me, and I waved and crossed. He met me by the police car.

"Heart attack?" I asked, indicating the ambulance.

"You could say that," he said dryly. "A man has had his head bashed in."

I found it difficult to believe. It was as if someone had drilled a pipeline directly from the outside world into

Starburst and was pumping in that which we were all here to get away from. Some wonder the people milling around us were in such a foul mood. I tried a sympathetic smile on Harrington, received no reaction and turned to go. I hadn't taken a single step when he placed a gently detaining hand on my arm.

"Somebody said you were talking to the boy."

"Somebody?" Suddenly I was very mad. "Just who the hell are these somebodies that seem to know everything, every goddamned thing that I do or say?"

"Concerned citizens," he said with a slight trace of bitterness, as if he'd had his fill of concerned citizens. "Were you?"

"Yes, as a matter of fact, I was." I looked at my watch. "About an hour ago. On the beach."

"For how long?"

I tried to ignore the people trying very hard not to appear as if they were eavesdropping. "Hell, I don't know. Fifteen minutes, maybe twenty, twenty-five."

I looked at Harrington closely, trying to snare a clue as to what he was thinking. I did know that, for some reason, he still felt the boy had to be involved with these two appalling crimes. Yet, if the boy had committed them, he would have had to have been ordered to do so. And that meant the Carruthers. Somehow I couldn't see those two becoming entangled in something quite so lurid. I was about to say as much when a flower-shirted man shoved through the crowd and confronted us. The stereotypes come crawling out of the woodwork, I thought and immediately wished there was something I could do for the big detective.

"If you're the police," the man demanded in a voice as shrill as a woman's, "why aren't you doing something about this?"

"Sir, I am doing what I can."

"I don't like it."

Harrington shrugged. The man was evidently a tourist, and the detective obviously felt as if he had more important people, like the natives, to be answerable to. "I'm sorry you feel that way, sir, but unless we can—"

"I want some protection!" the man said loudly and was instantly echoed by several of the crowd who had paused to listen.

Harrington smiled wryly. "Now how do you expect me to manage that with the force I have here? Did you know the man?"

"Of course not. I only arrived yesterday."

"Then what exactly are you worried about?"

"Well, that killer's obviously a maniac. He could kill anyone next."

The detective stared at him, then glanced at me. "No," he said quietly. "I don't think so."

"Well, what about that andy," someone else demanded. "Why the hell don't you lock it up? It's dangerous."

With that bit of melodramatic tripe, Harrington's patience finally reached its end. "Lady," he said with exaggerated calm, "if you can give me the proof, I'll snap that kid's tape faster than you can blink. But he belongs to someone, and there isn't anything I can do without proof. So why don't you, and all the rest of you, why don't you just go about your business and leave us alone. You want me to catch this man, boy, woman, whatever, I can't stand around here answering your hysterical, stupid questions."

For a moment I was tempted to applaud. In fact, one or two people did. But I just stood aside while the crowd dispersed, far more rapidly than I thought it would. Most of the people disappeared into the hotel, muttering loudly. The rest scattered and were gone within a minute's time. When it was quiet, Harrington signaled the ambulance driver, then slid into his own car. He rolled down the window, chewing his tobacco slowly. He spat. "Middle-class backbone of the race," he said to me and drove off. The ambulance followed and I was alone on the sidewalk. I don't remember how long I stood there, but staring passers-by reminded me that I was dressed only in my bathing trunks and still carrying my beach paraphernalia. Embarrassed, I darted inside and rushed up to my room. In the bathroom was a first-aid kit, and after many painful contortions, I managed to empty the can of aerosol sunburn medication onto my back.

I felt flushed.

Feverish, nearly groggy as if in a nightmare.

Despite the air conditioning, the room felt warm, but I didn't want to go out again. Not for a while. A long while. In spite of some of the other hotel guests' fears, I realized I hadn't once felt as though I were in the slightest danger, and when that fact sunk in, I was horrified. I didn't believe I was in danger because I knew I had never been anything more than polite to the Carruthers and their son. *Guilty*. Jesus Christ, I thought they were guilty.

You son of a bitch, I told myself. You're as bad as the rest of them. Would a grown man murder for an insult as common as the ones Carruthers must have been getting for as long as he'd had the android? To strike back so drastically was too immature for the owner of a simulacrum—he would be too vulnerable.

Hell! It was not a pleasant day. It had not been a pleasant vacation. I hesitated and finally tossed my things into my bag. I decided to wait until after dinner to leave. Until then, I lay on my bed, and it wasn't long before I fell asleep.

I dreamt, but I'd just as soon not remember what it was I saw in those dreams.

In Starburst, the dark is not quite the same as in the rest of the world. Because of the mist on the hills, the slate and stone roofs, the moonlight and starlight glinted off more than just water, and the result was a peculiar shimmer that slightly distorted one's vision. When I awoke to the unnatural light, I had a splitting headache. Groping around on the nightstand, I found my watch and saw it was close to ten o'clock. Hurriedly I swung off the bed, thinking that if I were as good a patron as the hotel led me to believe, I might be able to squeeze in a meal before the kitchen closed for the night. The clothes I was going to wear home were laid out on a chair, and without turning on the lamp, I dressed, standing in front of the window. The moon was hazed, and what stars there were challenged my schoolboy knowledge of constellations. I was staring out over the building at the bay when I caught movement on the beach. All I could see was a group of shadows. Struggling.

I leaned forward, straining to make out details, curious as to who would be playing games this time of night, since Starburst was definitely not noted for its evening festivities. As I clipped on my tie, the shadows merged into a single black patch, then separated and merged again. But not fast enough to prevent me from spotting one of them lying on the ground. The figure didn't move, and for no reason other than an unpleasant hunch, I dashed from the room and, not wanting to wait for the elevators, ran down the fire stairs and outside.

Once on the sidewalk, I hesitated for the first time, realizing I could very likely be making a complete ass of myself. There were no sounds but the evening wind in the park trees. As I crossed the street, my heels sounded like nails driven into wood and I self-consciously lightened my step. I became more cautious, though feeling no less silly, when I entered an alley and could see the beach and bay beyond. By the time I reached the far end, I was almost on hands and knees, and now I could hear: grunting, and the dull slap of body blows, struggling feet scraping against the sand. It didn't take a mastermind to figure out what was happening, and, for all my professed cowardice, I burst from the alley shouting, just a split second before I heard someone gasp, "Oh my God, look at that!"

The group of people were close to fifty meters from me, and when they heard my racket, they scattered, leaving me behind, motionless on the beach.

I vacillated, then ran to the fallen body. Closer, and in the dim moonlight I could see it was the boy.

Standing next to him, I could see he was bleeding.

And kneeling, I knew he was dead.

A boy.

I panted, my breath shuddering.

A boy.

I'm not sure exactly what I felt at the moment. Shock,

anger, sorrow. Anger, I suppose, the greatest of these. Not so much for the shadows who had killed him, but for the ruse he had perpetrated on us all. Callously I stared at his bloodied face and thought: you tricked me. Damn it, you tricked me.

Slowly I rose. I brushed the sand from my knees and walked swiftly back to the hotel. Just before I stepped into the lobby, I saw the whirling red light on a squad car, and I was glad I wasn't the one who had made the call.

The fourth floor, like the lobby and elevator, was deserted. I walked to the end of the hall and knocked on the Carruthers' door. When there was no answer, I knocked again and turned the knob. The door opened to a darkened room, and I stepped in.

The man and woman were sitting motionless in identical chairs facing the room's only window.

"Mr. Carruthers?" I didn't expect an answer, and I received none.

I moved closer and gathered what nerve I had left to reach down and touch the woman's cheek, poised to snap my hand back should she flinch. The skin was cold. She didn't move, didn't react. She and the man stared directly into the moonlight without blinking. Carefully I rolled up her sleeve, and though the light was dim, I found the markings easily. There was no need to do the same to the man.

I was still standing there when the lights flicked on and Harrington lumbered in, followed by a covey of police photographers and fingerprint men. The detective waited until my eyes adjusted to the bright light, then pulled me to one side, away from the strangely silent activities. It was as if they were investigating a morgue. Harrington watched for a while, pulling out his handkerchief and again wiping his hands. I never did learn how he'd picked up that habit, but at that particular time it seemed more than apropos.

"You, uh, saw the boy, I take it?" he said.

I nodded dumbly.

"Didn't happen to see who did it, I suppose."

"Only some shadows, Harrington. They were gone before I got close enough to identify them. Any of them."

One of the men coughed and immediately apologized.

"Would it be too much to ask who called you?" I said.

"What call? I was coming over here to question the kid." He pulled a slip of wrinkled paper from his jacket pocket and squinted at some writing. "I checked on the, uh, parents, just for the hell of it, just to keep those people off my back. Seems he was fairly well off—the kid, I mean. He is, was eighteen and from the time he was six was shunted back and forth between aunts and uncles like a busted Ping-Pong ball." He shook his head and pointed a stubby finger at some line on the paper. "When he reached majority and claimed his money, he bought himself some guardians. Parents, I guess they were supposed to be. According to some relative of his, this was the first place he brought them. Trial run." He shoved the paper back into his pocket as though it were filth. "I'm surprised nobody noticed."

I had nothing to say. And Harrington didn't stop me when I left.

My people.

He had deliberately exposed the false identification on his arm and had never once looked me straight in the eye. It was all there, but who would have thought to look for it? He had been challenging me and everyone else, using the simulacra to strike back at the world. Maybe he wanted to be exposed; maybe he was looking for someone as real as I to stop the charade and give him a flesh-and-blood hand to shake. Maybe—but when I think of going back to a city filled with androids and angry people, I get afraid.

And worse . . . my own so-called liberal, humanitarian, live-and-let-live armor had been stripped away, and I don't like what I see. As much as I feel sorry for the boy, I hate him for what he's done to me.

That crowd of shadows could have easily held one more.

THOMAS F. MONTELEONE

Breath's a Ware That Will Not Keep

Thomas F. Monteleone is a newer writer of the hard-working school to which Charles Grant also belongs. He is also an extremely sensitive writer, as he has been proving since 1972, when he sold his first story to AMAZING SCIENCE FICTION, and with his first novel in 1974. In person, he is a deceptively quiet man with an amazingly quick perception that tends to be obscured by the gentleness of his speech. The story that follows, "Breath's a Ware That Will Not Keep," takes its title from a poem called "Rebellion" by A. E. Houseman, and it has a poetry of its own. The story is part of Tom Monteleone's "Chicago" series, which will be published later this year as a novel, THE TIME-SWEPT CITY, by Popular Library.

Benjamin Cipriano sat down at his console, casting a quick glance outward to the Breeder Tank below him. He switched his attention to the controls and opened up a communications channel to the Tank. He pulled the psi-helmet over his head and pressed the throat mike close to his larynx. "Good morning, Feraxya. Feeling okay today?"

His scalp tingled as invisible fingers slipped into his skull to massage his brain. The helmet fed her psi-words into him: "Good morning to you, too, Benjamin." The "voice" sounded just vaguely feminine to him, and his imagination reinforced the conceptualization. "I'm feeling fine. Everything is normal. You know I always feel comfortable when you are on the console."

"Thank you," said Cipriano, pausing for a moment. "Now, I have some tests to run this morning, so we'd better get started." He flipped several toggles as he continued speaking to her. "It's all routine stuff . . . blood sugar, enzyme scans, placental balance quotients . . . things like that. Nothing to worry about."

There was a short silence before she touched his

mind again: "I never worry when you're on. Perhaps we'll have time to talk, later on?"

"If you want to. I'll have some time in a few minutes. Bye now." He switched off the communications channel and stared at the protoplasmic nightmare on the other side of his console-booth window. Stretched out before him were all the Breeder Tanks for his Sector of the City. They were Chicago's symbols of deliverance from misery and deprivation for all the City's members. Except, perhaps, the Host-Mothers themselves. Cipriano wondered about them in general, Feraxya in particular, and what their lives must be like.

Technically speaking, Feraxya was human. Visually, however, she was an amorphous, slithering, amoeba-like thing. She was tons of genetically cultured flesh, a human body inflated and stretched and distended until it was many times its normal size. Lost beneath her abundant flesh was a vestigial skeleton which floated disconnected and unmoving in a gelatinous sea. Her bioneered organs were swollen to immense proportions and hundreds of liters of blood pumped through her extensive circulatory system.

Yet he knew, even as he activated the probes that plunged into her soft flesh, that she was still a woman to him. A very special kind of woman. From her earliest moments of consciousness, she had spent her life contained within the glassteel walls of the Breeder Tank. It was an immense cube, ten meters on each side, the back wall covered with connecting cables and tubes which carried her life-support systems, monitoring devices, and biomedical elements that were necessary for her continued maintenance.

To Cipriano, she *was* the glassteel tube. Feraxya had no face, no arms, no legs; all those things were buried beneath the folds of swollen flesh that rippled with life-fluids. And yet she was a person, a Citizen of Chicago, who had received the standard education by means of special input programs piped through her sensory nerves and into her brain, bypassing her useless eyes and ears. She also represented several basic changes from previous Host-Mothers. Feraxya was a third-generation mutant; careful genetic selection and programming had given her primary-level psi-powers, which were used in communication and eventually for education. Chicago's Central Computers postulated that the quiet, undisturbed environ of the Breeder Tank would be an ideal atmosphere for the development of psi.

Ben looked away from the giant Tank, leaned back in his chair, and watched the monitoring data come clicking into the tapes at his console. As he waited for the data to accumulate, his gaze wandered down the long row of other consoles like his own, where many other Breeder Monitors sat reading their indicators and print-outs. Each Monitor was charged with his own Host-Mother; each Host-Mother held within her an enlarged uterus that was filled with thirty human fetuses.

It was in this way that the Host-Mothers provided the City with every desired type of Citizen. There were no outcasts, no misfits, now that society was shaped by the benevolent but highly efficient Central Computers of Chicago. An entire hierarchy was cybernetically conceived and programmed, then handed down through the bureaucratic chain until it reached the Bioneers and Eugenicists. In Chicago's massive Eugenic Complex, hundreds of Host-Mothers like Feraxya carried the fetuses of the next generation of Citizens. Laborers, artists, scientists, bureaucrats, and technicians—all pre-coded and expected.

A message suddenly flashed on Cipriano's console which reminded him to check the night-shift Monitor's report. He did so and found it satisfactory. Feraxya had only recently received her first uterine implant and there was little for him to do at this point except routine systems-checks. Later when her brood of fetuses grew and began to crowd her great womb, Cipriano's tasks would also grow. A Host-Mother nearing the end of gestation required much attention.

He replaced the psi-helmet on his head and signaled to her. A tingling sensation touched his mind as she was raised from her inner thoughts: "Yes, Ben?"

"The databanks are still filling," he said. "I've some

free time. Thought you might want to talk for a little while."

"Yes, I would. Thank you. I wanted to tell you about the dream I had. . . ."

"A dream?" he asked. "About what?"

"About you. I think about you a lot."

"I didn't know that," said Ben, smiling self-consciously. His words were only a half-truth.

"Yes, it's true . . ." She paused and his mind leapt at the emptiness she created there. "Ben?" she began again.

"Yes?"

"Do you ever think about me? When you're not here, working?"

"Well, yes. I guess I do. Sometimes."

"I'm glad," she said. "You're different from my other Monitors. Of course I'm sleeping most of that time, anyway."

"Different?" The word did not sit well in his mind. The Monitors were planned to be quite similar. "How do you mean?"

"You're kinder," she said. "More understanding, I think. It's just easier to talk with you."

"Thank you, Feraxya. I'm just trying to be myself, though."

"Your mate is very lucky to have someone like you," she said candidly. "I guess I should tell you that I've thought about having you myself. Even though I know it's impossible."

Ben paused for a moment, stirred and somewhat shaken by the mental image her suggestion brought to mind. "You could use your Id-Tapes if you really wanted—" He tried to be helpful but she interrupted him.

"That's little more than masturbation."

"I'm sorry," he said. "I was just trying to suggest something that might help, that's all."

"You're sweet. But that's not what I want from you. If I could have it my way it would be like the dream. I had a *real* body, like you, and we were going through the City at night. It was bright and beautiful. Sometimes I wish it could have been like that."

She paused, and Cipriano searched for any subliminal meaning in her words. There were people who would interpret them as dangerous. He wondered what she meant by them. "It wasn't meant to be," he said finally, shallowly.

"I know. And the Host-Mothers are needed. Someone must serve," she said slowly, as if she were contemplating the implications of what she was saying.

"That's true," he said. "Besides—"

Cipriano was interrupted by the chatter of his console. The results from the morning's test began to flash upon his grid. A large graph appeared and flickered violently; superimposed over the graph was a one-word message: CRITICAL.

"Just a minute, Feraxya," he said, staring at the alarm signal in semi-shock. "Uh, . . . some of the results have just come in and I've got to check them out. I'll get back to you as soon as I can, okay?"

"All right, Ben. We can talk later."

He threw off the helmet and depressed several digital keys, requesting clarification of the warning signal. Cipriano read through the figures, double-checked them, and started an entire new series of tests to ensure against errors.

As the console began to click and chatter with the new instructions, he called his Superior, Faro Barstowe. Several seconds passed before the man's lean, foxlike face appeared on the screen: "Yes, what is it?"

"Cipriano here. Breeder Tank 0078-D. Generic name: Feraxya. My routine monitoring has picked up what looks like a nucleotide dysfunction. Probable cause is an inadequate enzyme transfer. Too early to tell yet. Just calling to let you know that I'm running a double-check."

Barstowe's face seemed tense. "Let's see . . . You've got a litter of thirty. RNA Code 45a7c. Superior Range. Administrator Class. That sound right?"

"Yes, sir. That's right," said Cipriano, watching the

man's small shining eyes burn into him, even through the screen.

"All right, Cipriano. It's been sixty-four days since implantation. That makes it too late for an *in vitro* injection to change or rectify the enzyme transfer. Collect all the data you can from the second scan. I'll call Bioneering and send some men over there to see what's up. That's all for now." The screen blacked out, leaving Ben with the cool sounds of the console.

When he read through the second test results, he knew that they only confirmed what he had first imagined. There was indeed a dysfunction in Feraxya's system; but he could do nothing until the Bioneers arrived. His first thought was to contact her, so that she would be aware of what was happening inside her great body. But he knew that would not be possible until he received word from Barstowe.

It was several minutes before the white uniformed specialists from Bioneering entered his booth. One of them read over the data collected from his console while the other two adjusted their white, antiseptic, helmeted suits as they prepared to enter the Breeder Tank Area itself. Cipriano looked past them, through the glass window to Feraxya, who floated within her prison still ignorant of her problems.

Later, as he watched the Bioneers scurrying about Feraxya's Tank, he wondered if she could, somehow, sense their nearness, their insensitive prying into the secrets of her grotesque body. He wanted to talk to her, and he entertained the notion of contact as his eyes fell upon the psi-helmet by the console.

One of the Bioneers returned to the booth, quickly removing his helmet and wiping some perspiration from his forehead. He looked at Cipriano and shook his head.

"What's that mean?" said Ben.

"Not good," said the man in white. "There hasn't been any reaction between the DNA/enzyme interface. The 'blueprint injections' didn't copy at all. That's why you were getting the alarms."

"Which means . . . ?" asked Cipriano.

"Which means her fetuses would be completely variable if we brought them to term." The man paused and gestured out towards Feraxya's Tank. "*Randoms* —that's what we're growing in that one."

"What do we do now?"

"You'd better call Barstowe," said the Bioneer. "My men'll be making an official report, but I think he'd appreciate knowing about it now."

Cipriano knew what Barstowe would say: they would have to remove her brood. He wondered what Feraxya's reaction to the decision would be. Remembering how pleased she had been to receive her first implantation, Cipriano did not look forward to the moment when he would have to confront her with the news.

After he had contacted Barstowe and relayed the results of the Bioneers' inspection, the Superior shook his head, grimacing. "That's too bad. Going to throw us off schedule. I'll arrange for Stander to prepare for a scrape as soon as possible. Tomorrow morning, hopefully."

"I was wondering when I should tell Feraxya about it," said Cipriano.

The foxlike features stared at him for a moment. "You'll have plenty of time in the morning. Don't worry about it. You really don't have anything else to do today; why don't you get out of here?"

"All right," said Cipriano. "But I hope she understands why." Barstowe didn't answer; the screen had already blacked. Ben shook his head slowly and shut down his console. He left the Eugenic Complex and took the Rapids home to his con-apt, hoping that the following day would be less difficult than this one.

That night, Jennifer wanted him.

She was warm and young and fashionably lean; and he wanted her, too. He always did. She was something of a romantic, since she always used candles to illuminate their lovemaking, but Cipriano didn't mind.

Jennifer helped him attach the electrodes to his forehead; she had already hooked herself into the machine. They lay side by side, naked, in the candlelight as the machine beneath their bed hummed and touched their pleasure centers. Physiological feedback was encoded from each of them, amplified, and routed into each other as mutual stimuli. Their orgasms were reached simultaneously with the aid of the machine. Never touching each other, not needing to do so, there was no chance of a nonapproved conception. Afterwards, they lay in silence, smiling from the rush of moist satisfaction. Jennifer arose in the semi-darkness and unhooked the electrodes. Cipriano was asleep before she even turned off the machine.

When he reached his console the next morning, he sensed there was something different about the Eugenic Complex. He hoped that it was merely his imagination. Through the glass, he could see several technicians and a Bioneer working on Feraxya's Tank.

Cipriano placed the psi-helmet on his head and flipped the transmission switch. "I've been expecting you," said Feraxya, instantly crowding his mind; the transmission was almost aggressive.

"What do you mean?" he said quickly.

"When you never came back yesterday, I began to worry about you. Then I felt them fumbling around my Tank. I knew something was wrong."

"I'm sorry," he said. "I was very busy yesterday. I didn't have time to—"

"Don't try to explain. I already know what they're getting ready to do."

"What? What're you talking about. How?" He looked out at the great mass of flesh, seeing it for the first time as something that could be very different from what he had always imagined.

"The night-shift Monitor told me what had happened. I forced him to do it. I wanted to know why they were tampering with me. And when he told me, I was hurt by it. Why couldn't *you* tell me, Benjamin? I didn't want that other man to tell me, but I had no choice."

"I'm sorry," was all he could manage to say.

"It hurt to know that you had run out of the Complex without telling me, Benjamin."

"Please," he said. "I understand what you're saying. And I'm sorry. I shouldn't have done it."

"Why do they call it a 'scrape'?"

"It's just slang, that's all. It doesn't mean anything. They don't do abortions that way anymore."

"Will they be coming soon?" she asked.

"I think so. Don't worry. It won't take long. You won't even feel—"

"No, Benjamin. I don't want them to do it. You've got to tell them not to do it."

Cipriano suppressed a laugh, although it was more from anxiety than from humor. "You don't want it? There isn't anything you can do about it. It's the law, Feraxya! Chicago doesn't allow random births. You know that."

"The only thing I know is that they want to destroy my brood. They want to cut me open and rip them from my flesh. It is wrong," she said slowly.

"There was a mistake in the gene-printing," said Cipriano, trying to explain things in the only way he understood. "Your fetuses aren't perfect constructs."

"But they're human beings, Benjamin. They want to murder them. I can't let them do it."

Cipriano tried to understand her feelings, her reasons for talking such nonsense to him. He began to fear that maybe she was losing control of her senses. "Why are you telling me this?" he asked finally. "You know there isn't anything I can do about it."

"You can tell them not to try. I want to give them a chance."

"They won't listen to me, Feraxya. Barstowe's already scheduled the surgery for this morning. There's nothing you can do but accept what's happening. Face the truth: you're getting an abortion." He regretted the last sentence as soon as he had said it. He could almost feel the pain he was inflicting in her.

"I can't believe that's really you talking. I always thought you were *different* from the rest of them. You acted like you had more understanding, more compassion . . ."

"You make it sound like I'm against you," he said defensively.

"Perhaps you're not. But you've got to tell them that I'll stop anybody who tries to get near me. Even kill them if necessary." Feraxya's voice in his mind was sharp, cutting deeply into his skull like a bright razor.

"And you're telling me about understanding, about compassion? Feraxya, what's happening to you?" Inwardly, he reviewed her last words. What was this talk about *killing?* If her mind was going, Barstowe would have to know about it.

"I can't help it, Benjamin. It's something that I feel deep inside. Something that we've almost forgotten about. The instincts, the drive that a mother feels to protect her children."

"They're not your children," he said vindictively.

"They were given to me. They're *mine.*" There was a long pause. "I don't want to argue with you. Please, go tell them what I've said."

Cipriano exhaled slowly. "All right. I'll see Barstowe, but I don't think it'll do any good."

He waited for her to reply, but when she didn't, he switched off the communications channel and pulled the helmet from his head. He keyed in Barstowe's office, but the lines were all jammed with other calls. Wanting to get the matter finished as quickly as possible, he left the booth and walked to the elevators that would take him to Barstowe's office level.

After the Superior was given a reconstruction of the conversation, he shook his head as if in disbelief. "Nothing like this has ever happened before," the man said.

"Well, what do we do about it?" asked Cipriano.

"Do!" cried Barstowe. "We don't have to do anything about it. We just ignore that crap and go on with the operation. You can tell her she'll be getting a new implantation as soon as possible."

Cipriano paused, still thinking about what she had said to him. He looked at Barstowe and spoke again: "What about that bit about 'killing' people?"

Barstowe laughed. "Just a threat . . . a very stupid one at that."

"You don't think she's more powerful than we've imagined, do you?"

"What're you getting at?" Barstowe stared at him with cold, penetrating eyes that looked like oiled ball bearings.

"*I* don't know," said Cipriano. "I just can't figure out why she'd talk like that. It's not like her."

"Well, we don't have time to worry about it. For now—" Barstowe was interrupted by the buzzer on his communicator. He answered it, and saw a white-helmeted Bioneer on the screen. They spoke for several seconds, then the screen darkened out. "That was Stander. They're about ready to get started. I want you down there. You can tell her what was said up here."

Cipriano nodded and left the office. When he returned to his console, he could see the surgical team approaching Feraxya's Tank. He put on the helmet and opened the channel to her mind. "They wouldn't listen," he said. "They're coming now. Pretty soon you'll be going under anesthesia. I'm sorry, Feraxya."

"Don't be sorry, Benjamin," was all she said. There was something chilling in the way she had touched his mind. The familiar warmness had vanished, and Cipriano felt the first twinges of terror icing in his spinal cord.

A Bioneer approached the console and prepared to administer the anesthesia. Outside the booth, Cipriano could see the surgical team as they reached the glassteel wall of the Tank. Suddenly the man next to him threw back his head and uttered a brief scream. The man tried to press his hands to his head just as blood began to stream from his nose and the corners of his mouth; his eyes bulged out, unseeing, and he slumped over the console, dead from a massive cerebral hemorrhage. Cipriano rushed over to him, but there was nothing that could be done.

Next to the Breeder Tank, the three men of the surgical team were waiting for the anesthesia to take effect. One of them had begun scaling the wall of the

Tank, but he never made it. Falling backward, the man landed on his back as he struggled with his suit's helmet, he convulsed for several seconds and then lay still. The remaining two surgeons rushed to his aid, but had taken only a few steps before they too were struck down by some unseen, killing force.

Cipriano watched their death throes as alarms wailed through the corridors. Suddenly people were scrambling all around him. Two parameds ran into the Breeder Tank Area and were also brought down screaming and convulsing. Benjamin stepped back from the booth window, feeling a pit form at the base of his stomach. He flipped on the screen and punched for Barstowe's office. "Something's happened to the team!" he yelled before the picture materialized. "Barstowe! Can you hear me?"

The Superior's face appeared on the screen. "I know! What's going on down there? The intercom's going crazy!"

"I don't know," said Cipriano. "I don't know!"

"Who's in there with you?"

"I'm not sure. There's a lot of noise . . . confusion. Some technicians, a medic."

"Put one of the techs on," said Barstowe, regaining some of his usual composure.

Cipriano called the closest man over to the communicator. Barstowe said something to the technician, who nodded and reached for the anesthesia switch. Before he threw it, blood spurted from his nose and ears, and he fell away from the console. He was dead before he hit the floor.

Backing away from the console, Benjamin looked out to the Tank of pink flesh. Now the massiveness of the thing took on a new meaning. Within its walls lurked a powerful and angry intelligence.

The screen was signaling, but there was no one close enough to answer it. Wiping the perspiration from his face, Cipriano edged close to the screen and saw Barstowe's searching eyes. "Get out of there!" the Superior screamed. "I'm calling back all the emergency units. Get up here right now." The screen blacked out.

Quickly, Cipriano shouldered his way through the crowd of Complex guards and Bioneers and headed for the nearest elevator. When he reached Barstowe's office, he found the man in animated conversation in front of his communicator. Seeing Cipriano, the Superior flicked off the screen and spoke to him: "Chicago Central Computer postulates some kind of limited-range telekinetic power—an unexpected variable of the psi-training."

"I thought it would be something like that," said Benjamin. "What do you want with me?"

"You seem to have gotten along with her reasonably well in the past," said Barstowe, pausing for dramatic effect. "And she seemed to leave you alone down there just now."

"And . . . ?"

"Get in touch with her again. Try to reason with her. Calm her down. Tell her anything. Tell her that we've capitulated, that we won't abort her brood. Anything, I don't care what."

"I don't understand," said Cipriano.

"You don't have to understand it. Just do what you're told." Barstowe stood up from his desk and faced him squarely. "We want you to divert her attention, keep her occupied until we can rig up a bypass away from your console to the Breeder Tank."

"A bypass? What're you talking about?" Cipriano asked, although he already had an idea of what Barstowe intended.

"We're going to try and shut her down from outside the Complex. Shunt from the Central Computer."

"You mean you're going to *kill* her?"

"You're goddamn right we are!" Barstowe screamed. "Listen, Chicago has postulated what would happen if that thing downstairs could somehow communicate with the other Host-Mothers. If the combined psi-powers of the entire Breeder Tank Area could be coordinated, their power would be awesome. We can't let some kind of matrix like that materialize. Now get out of here."

Cipriano rode down to his level and returned once more to the console. The entire area was deserted and his footsteps echoed down the corridor adjoining his booth. Barstowe's words were also echoing through his mind. Thought of Feraxya, of the other Host-Mothers, of the men who'd been killed, of the entire nightmarish scene all swarmed through his mind like a cloud of devouring insects. He felt helplessly trapped in the middle of a conflict that he wanted no part of.

He sat down and put on the helmet. As he threw on the proper switch, he could feel her mind lurking nearby, waiting for him to speak. "You've changed, Feraxya," he said finally.

"Why did you come back?" she said.

"I don't know," he lied. "There was nothing else to do."

"What are they going to do with me, Benjamin?"

"I . . . don't know." Again, he lied. And this time it was painful. Adrenaline pumped through him; his hands were trembling. He was glad that she could not see him.

"Do you understand why I had to do it?" she asked. "You know I didn't want it this way."

"No, I don't understand. You've become a murderer, Feraxya."

"I didn't want to do it. I just wanted to protect my brood. They have as much right to live as you or me. I won't let them be killed." Her voice in his mind seemed strained, tense. Perhaps her mind *was* going. He shuddered as he thought of what an insane horror she could become.

"What are you going to do now?" he asked. "They've evacuated the entire Complex. But they'll be back. You can't hold out like this forever, you know."

"I don't know, Benjamin. I'm scared. You know I'm scared. If they would promise to leave me alone, to leave my brood alone, I won't hurt them. My duty to the Society is to produce new Citizens. That's what I want to do. That's all. You believe me, don't you?"

"Yes, I believe you," said Cipriano just as he was distracted by several flashing lights on his console. He hadn't touched any of the switches; the technicians must be activating the controls through the recently rigged bypass circuits. He knew what was going to happen.

"Benjamin, are you still there . . . ? What's wrong?"

"I'm sorry," he said quickly, while his mind raced ahead, envisioning what would come next. He was of two minds, one of which wanted to cry out, to warn her of what was planned, the other that was content to sit back and witness her execution. He heard himself talking: ". . . and you've got to trust us, Feraxya. You can't keep killing everybody. There would be no one to maintain your systems. Everyone would lose in the end." Watching the console, Cipriano recognized the symbols that now blazed in bright scarlet on the message grid. They were planning to terminate.

"All right, Benjamin . . ." Feraxya's words were echoing through his brain. "I'll—"

Her words were cut short. Cipriano jumped up from the chair, his eyes on the great Breeder Tank. The console chattered and flickered as it processed the remote commands being fed into it. "Feraxya!" he screamed as he realized what was happening, what she must now know. A life-support systems graph appeared on the grid; the plot lines all began dropping towards the y-coordinate. His mind was flooded with her last thoughts—surprise, panic, loathing, and pain. For a moment he thought he felt her icy, telekinetic grip reaching out to him, enclosing cold fingers about his brain. The seconds ticked by with glacierlike slowness. His mind lay in a dark pit of fear as he awaited her retribution.

The life-fluids and the oxygen were cut off, and the great amorphous body convulsed within the Breeder Tank. She reached out and touched his mind for the last time, but in fear rather than anger or hate. She forced him to experience death. Cipriano closed his eyes against this vicarious pain, unable to wrench the helmet from his head.

Then suddenly it was over. A gathering darkness filled him. The console had begun force-feeding acid through her circulatory system, bubbling away the flesh, insuring that she was gone.

The communicator screen grew into brightness and Barstowe's face appeared there. The Superior was smiling, but Benjamin ripped off the helmet and left the console before the man spoke. The corridor outside his booth was again filled with people, their voices loud with celebration and relief. He ignored their back-slapping and shouldered past them to the descent elevators.

He kept wondering why she had touched him like that, at the end. Had she known? Did she think it was he that was killing her?

He left the Complex under the weight of his thoughts. Outside, Chicago sparkled under the night sky. Its slidewalks and transit systems were filling up with work-wearied crowds who sought entertainment in the City. Cipriano stepped onto a slidewalk that carried him through the midsection of the urban Complex. He was in no hurry to go home now.

Ahead of him, the walk snaked through a kaleidoscopic forest of color and light, through the pleasure-center of the City—Xanadu. The crowds were heavy here, each seeking the mindless relief that was always to be found in this Sector. Cipriano studied them as he threaded his way through the mobs. They were all born of Host-Mothers, like Feraxya, all laughing and playing their games of escape, oblivious to their grotesque origins. He passed a series of Fantasy Parlors, where the lines were already long. The patrons were mostly lower-level Citizens—nontechs, laborers, and drones—that filled this Sector. They were all eager to use the City's computers to immerse themselves in imaginary worlds. Sexual fantasies were a major part of the catalog. Cipriano knew this as he passed the other opiate-dispensing centers: the mind-shops, elec-drug centers, and other pleasure domes. The brightness of the lights assaulted him with their vulgar screams, the polished steel and reflecting glass shimmered with a special kind of tawdriness. For the first time, perhaps, Cipriano realized a terrible truth: the City was unable to provide for all of man's needs. There was something missing, something primal and liberating, something that was now only a desiccated memory out of man's dark history.

Perhaps Feraxya, too, was aware of the deficiency, he thought. Perhaps that would help to explain what he had first thought to be her irrational action. He closed his eyes against the argon-brightness, frustrated because his questions would forever be unanswered.

The slidewalk moved on, taking him away from the entertainment Sector. He entered a corridor of glassteel spires—Chicago's con-apt Sectors. Cipriano untangled the matrix of walks and ramps and lifts which led to his building, and reluctantly ascended to his con-apt level. Before he could palm the homeostatic lock, Jennifer was at the door, her face a portrait of concern. All the media had been blurting out the news of the near-catastrophe at the Eugenic Complex; she already knew what he had been forced to do.

During dinner she pressed him for details, which he produced grudgingly in short clipped sentences. Even Jennifer could perceive his lack of enthusiasm. "Perhaps I can help," she said.

At first he did not understand, for his mind was not really listening to her. Only after she stood up from the table and took a few steps towards the bedroom did he fully comprehend: she wished to console him in the only manner that she knew.

He felt cold. The memory of Feraxya's last moments of life passed through him like winter's breath. He could feel her reaching through the darkness, trying until the very end to make him *know* her, choosing him to be cursed with her memory.

Jennifer called his name.

Feraxya's image shattered like broken glass, and he felt himself rising from his chair, entering the bedroom.

A solitary candle burned there, where Jennifer sat making cursory adjustments on the machine. Turning, she reached out and began to undress him. Mechanically, he did the same for her.

As her clothes fell away, revealing her warm, silky flesh, he suddenly saw her differently. Instead of reaching for the wired bands and electrodes, Cipriano extended his hand and touched one of her breasts. For a moment, she was transfixed, frozen by his action. His hand slowly moved, cupping the fullness in his hand, brushing her nipple with his fingers.

He felt it swell and become rigid as she spoke: "No . . . no! Oh, please Benjamin . . . don't. Please . . ."

"But why?" he asked as he removed his hand. Inwardly he was still marvelling at the softness of her.

"Not like that," she was saying. "The machine. We *can't*. Not without the machine."

Something dark and ugly roiled inside his mind. He wanted to challenge her, to break through her defenses with his reckless anomie. But when he looked into her haunted eyes and saw the fear and disbelief that lay there, he knew that he could not.

She could not be touched. In either sense.

Lying down, he let her attach the electrodes, felt her recline beside him. The humming of the machine rose in intensity, crowding out his thoughts. Sensations seeped into him, sending slivers of pleasures into the maelstrom of his mind's center. Vaguely, he was aware of Jennifer writhing beside him, arching her body upwards as the simulations increased. His own desires, finally awakened, snaked through him, radiating out from his groin, threatening to strangle him with their grasp. He resisted the electronic impulses, and focused his mind's eye upon the Breeder Tank where Feraxya floated in the jellied sea, where she had been able to touch him, perhaps even love him, like no one had ever done before.

Jennifer increased the accentuator, forcing the machine to drive them to unusual, even for her, frenzy. The energy-burst overwhelmed him as he finally succumbed to the wave of pleasure collapsing over him.

Feraxya faded from his consciousness as he tripped through a series of orgasms.

wait, but I didn't. "Am I supposed to guess who was murdered, or who did it? My God, it wasn't one of the Cannigers, was it?"

rington shook his head.

swallowed. "well?"

"Well, surely you don't suspect one of them?"

"Wish I knew," Harrington said. "An old man was

Tricentennial

Joe Haldeman is a public relations department's dream.

Handsome, with a dashing beard, and in his early
thirties, he is not only a world traveler, a teacher, a
lecturer, a former senior editor of ASTRONOMY magazine, guitar player, and skin diver, but in addition to his
science fiction he has written adventure novels, nonfiction books, short stories, articles, poems, and songs. In
1976 he won a Nebula Award for his novel THE FOR-
EVER WAR, which also that year won a Hugo, the
award given out by the World Science Fiction Convention annually. This year he is nominated in two catego-
ries for the Hugo—both his novel MINDBRIDGE and
"Tricentennial," the short story that follows.

You would think that this would be enough for anyone.
Add, however, the fact that Joe Haldeman's university
degree is in astrophysics, with postgraduate work in
mathematics, computer science, statistics, and art, and
the further fact that he is a decorated Vietnam War
veteran who was severely wounded in combat, and you
have, as I said, a package that a public relations department—even one that deals with authors year in and year
out—tends to find almost embarrassingly rich in interesting details.

Nonetheless, all these things are as true and real as
Joe Haldeman himself is real. And you will see as you
read "Tricentennial," on the pages that follow, that this
is one of his geniuses as a writer—his writing also has
a rare element of reality within it.

December 1975

Scientists pointed out that the Sun could be part of a double star system. For its companion to have gone undetected, of course, it would have to be small and dim, and thousands of astronomical units distant.

They would find it eventually; "it" would turn out to be "them"; they would come in handy.

January 2075

The office was opulent even by the extravagant standards of twenty-first-century Washington. Senator Connors had a passion for antiques. One wall was lined with leatherbound books; a large brass telescope symbolized his role as Liaison to the Science Guild. An intricately woven Navajo rug from his home state covered most of the parquet floor. A grandfather clock. Paintings, old maps.

The computer terminal was discreetly hidden in the top drawer of his heavy teak desk. On the desk: a blotter, a precisely centered fountain pen set, and a century-old sound-only black Bell telephone. It chimed.

His secretary said that Dr. Leventhal was waiting to see him.. "Keep answering me for thirty seconds," the Senator said. "Then hang it and send him right in."

He cradled the phone and went to a wall mirror. Straightened his tie and cape; then with a fingernail evened out the bottom line of his lip pomade. Ran a hand through long, thinning white hair and returned to stand by the desk, one hand on the phone.

The heavy door whispered open. A short thin man bowed slightly. "Sire."

The Senator crossed to him with both hands out. "Oh, blow that, Charlie. Give ten." The man took both his hands, only for an instant. "When was I ever 'Sire' to you, heyfool?"

"Since last week," Leventhal said, "Guild members have been calling you worse names than 'Sire.' "

The Senator bobbed his head twice. "True, and true. And I sympathize. Will of the people, though."

"Sure." Leventhal pronounced it as one word: "Willathapeeble."

Connors went to the bookcase and opened a chased panel. "Drink?"

"Yeah, Bo." Charlie sighed and lowered himself into a deep sofa. "Hit me. Sherry or something."

The Senator brought the drinks and sat down beside Charlie. "You shoulda listened to me. Shoulda got the Ad Guild to write your proposal."

"We have good writers."

"Begging to differ. Less than two percent of the electorate bothered to vote: most of them for the administration advocate. Now you take the Engineering Guild—"

"*You* take the engineers. And—"

"They used the Ad Guild." Connors shrugged. "They got their budget."

"It's easy to sell bridges and power plants and shuttles. Hard to sell pure science."

"The more reason for you to—"

"Yeah, sure. Ask for double and give half to the Ad

boys. Maybe next year. That's not what I came to talk about."

"That radio stuff?"

"Right. Did you read the report?"

Connors looked into his glass. "Charlie, you know I don't have time to—"

"Somebody read it, though."

"Oh, righty-o. Good astronomy boy on my staff: he gave me a boil-down. Mighty interesting, that."

"There's an intelligent civilization eleven light-years away—that's 'mighty interesting'?"

"Sure. Real breakthrough." Uncomfortable silence. "Uh, what are you going to do about it?"

"Two things. First, we're trying to figure out what they're saying. That's hard. Second, we want to send a message back. That's easy. And that's where you come in."

The Senator nodded and looked somewhat wary.

"Let me explain. We've sent messages to this star, 61 Cygni, before. It's a double star, actually, with a dark companion."

"Like us."

"Sort of. Anyhow, they never answered. They aren't listening, evidently: they aren't sending."

"But we got—"

"What we're picking up is about what you'd pick up eleven light-years from Earth. A confused jumble of broadcasts, eleven years old. Very faint. But obviously not generated by any sort of natural source."

"Then we're already sending a message back. The same kind they're sending us."

"That's right, but—"

"So what does all this have to do with me?"

"Bo, we don't want to whisper at them—we want to *shout!* Get their attention." Leventhal sipped his wine and leaned back. "For that, we'll need one hell of a lot of power."

"Uh, righty-o. Charlie, power's money. How much are you talking about?"

"The whole show. I want to shut down Death Valley for twelve hours."

The Senator's mouth made a silent O. "Charlie, you've been working too hard. Another Blackout? On purpose?"

"There won't be any Blackout. Death Valley has emergency storage for fourteen hours."

"At half capacity." He drained his glass and walked back to the bar, shaking his head. "First you say you want power. Then you say you want to turn off the power." He came back with the burlap-covered bottle. "You aren't making sense, boy."

"Not turn it off, really. Turn it around."

"Is that a riddle?"

"No, look. You know the power doesn't really come from the Death Valley grid; it's just a way station and accumulator. Power comes from the orbital—"

"I know all that, Charlie. I've got a Science Certificate."

"Sure. So what we've got is a big microwave laser in orbit, that shoots down a tight beam of power. Enough to keep North America running. Enough—"

"That's what I mean. You can't just—"

"So we turn it around and shoot it at a power grid on the Moon. Relay the power around to the big radio dish at Farside. Turn it into radio waves and point it at 61 Cygni. Give 'em a blast that'll fry their fillings."

"Doesn't sound neighborly."

"It wouldn't actually be that powerful—but it would be a hell of a lot more powerful than any natural 21-centimeter source."

"I don't know, boy." He rubbed his eyes and grimaced. "I could maybe do it on the sly, only tell a few people what's on. But that'd only work for a few minutes . . . what do you need twelve hours for, anyway?"

"Well, the thing won't aim itself at the Moon automatically, the way it does at Death Valley. Figure as much as an hour to get the thing turned around and aimed.

"Then, we don't want to just send a blast of radio waves at them. We've got a five-hour program, that first builds up a mutual language, then tells them about us, and finally asks them some questions. We want to send it twice."

Connors refilled both glasses. "How old were you in '47, Charlie?"

"I was born in '45."

"You don't remember the Blackout. Ten thousand people died . . . and you want me to suggest—"

"Come on, Bo, it's not the same thing. We know the accumulators work now—besides, the ones who died, most of them had faulty fail-safes on their cars. If we warn them the power's going to drop, they'll check their fail-safes or damn well stay out of the air."

"And the media? They'd have to take turns broadcasting. Are you going to tell the People what they can watch?"

"Fuzz the media. They'll be getting the biggest story since the Crucifixion."

"Maybe." Connors took a cigarette and pushed the box toward Charlie. "You don't remember what happened to the Senators from California in '47, do you?"

"Nothing good, I suppose."

"No, indeed. They were impeached. Lucky they weren't lynched. Even though the real trouble was 'way up in orbit.

"Like you say: people pay a grid tax to California. They think the power comes from California. If something fuzzes up, they get pissed at California. I'm the Lib Senator from California, Charlie; ask me for the Moon, maybe I can do something. Don't ask me to fuzz around with Death Valley."

"All right, all right. It's not like I was asking you to wire it for me, Bo. Just get it on the ballot. We'll do everything we can to educate—"

"Won't work. You barely got the Scylla probe voted in—and that was no skin off nobody, not with L-5 picking up the tab."

"Just get it on the ballot."

"We'll see. I've got a quota, you know that. And the Tricentennial coming up, hell, everybody wants on the ballot."

"Please, Bo. This is bigger than that. This is bigger than anything. Get it on the ballot."

"Maybe as a rider. No promises."

March 1992:

From *Fax & Pix,* 12 March 1992:

ANTIQUE SPACEPROBE
ZAPPED BY NEW STARS

1. Pioneer 10 sent first Jupiter pix Earthward in 1973 (see pix upleft, upright).

2. Left solar system 1987. First man-made thing to leave solar system.

3. Yesterday, reports NSA, Pioneer 10 begins AM to pick up heavy radiation. Gets more and more to max about 3 PM. Then goes back down. Radiation has to come from outside solar system.

4. NSA and Hawaii scientists say Pioneer 10 went through disk of synchrotron (sin kro tron) radiation that comes from two stars we didn't know about before.

  A. The stars are small "black dwarfs."

  B. They are going round each other once every 40 seconds, and take 350,000 years to go around the Sun.

  C. One of the stars is made of *antimatter.* This is stuff that blows up if it touches real matter. What the Hawaii scientists saw was a dim circle of invisible (infrared) light, that blinks on and off every twenty seconds. This light comes from where the atmospheres of the two stars touch (see pic downleft).

  D. The stars have a big magnetic field. Radiation comes from stuff spinning off the stars and trying to get through the field.

  E. The stars are about 5000 times as far away from the Sun as we are. They sit at the wrong angle, compared to the rest of the solar system (see pic downright).

5. NSA says we aren't in any danger from the stars. They're too far away, and besides, nothing in the solar system ever goes through the radiation.

6. The woman who discovered the stars wants to call them Scylla (*skill*-a) and Charybdis (ku-*rib*-dus).

7. Scientists say they don't know where the hell those two stars came from. Everything else in the solar system makes sense.

February 2075

When the docking phase started, Charlie thought, that was when it was easy to tell the scientists from the baggage. The scientists were the ones who looked nervous.

Superficially, it seemed very tranquil—nothing like the bonehurting skinstretching acceleration when the shuttle lifted off. The glittering transparent cylinder of L-5 simply grew larger, slowly, then wheeled around to point at them.

The problem was that a space colony big enough to hold 4000 people has more inertia than God. If the shuttle hit the mating dimple too fast, it would fold up like an accordian. A spaceship is made to take stress in the *other* direction.

Charlie hadn't paid first class, but they let him up into the observation dome anyhow; professional courtesy. There were only two other people there, standing on the Velcro rug, strapped to one bar and hanging on to another.

They were a young man and woman, probably new colonists. The man was talking excitedly. The woman stared straight ahead, not listening. Her knuckles were white on the bar and her teeth were clenched. Charlie wanted to say something in sympathy, but it's hard to talk while you're holding your breath.

The last few meters are the worst. You can't see over the curve of the ship's hull, and the steering jets make a constant stutter of little bumps: left, right, forward, back. If the shuttle folded, would the dome shatter? Or just pop off.

It was all controlled by computers, of course. The pilot just sat up there in a mist of weightless sweat.

Then the low moan, almost subsonic shuddering as the shuttle's smooth hull complained against the friction pads. Charlie waited for the ringing *spang* that would mean they were a little too fast: friable alloy plates under the friction pads, crumbling to absorb the energy of their forward motion; last-ditch stand.

If that didn't stop them, they would hit a two-meter wall of solid steel, which would. It had happened once. But not this time.

"Please remain seated until pressure is equalized," a recorded voice said. "It's been a pleasure having you aboard."

Charlie crawled down the pole, back to the passenger area. He walked rip,rip,rip back to his seat and obediently waited for his ears to pop. Then the side door opened and he went with the other passengers through the tube that led to the elevator. They stood on the ceiling. Someone had laboriously scratched a graffito on the metal wall:

> Stuck on this lift for hours, perforce:
> This lift that cost a million bucks.
> There's no such thing as centrifugal force:
> L-5 sucks.

Thirty more weightless seconds as they slid to the ground. There were a couple of dozen people waiting on the loading platform.

Charlie stepped out into the smell of orange blossoms and newly-mown grass. He was home.

"Charlie! Hey, over here." Young man standing by a tandem bicycle. Charlie squeezed both his hands and then jumped on the back seat. "Drink."

"Did you get—"

"Drink. Then talk." They glided down the smooth macadam road toward town.

The bar was just a rain canopy over some tables and chairs, overlooking the lake in the center of town. No bartender: you went to the service table and punched in your credit number, then chose wine or fruit juice; with or without vacuum-distilled raw alcohol. They talked about shuttle nerves awhile, then:

"What you get from Connors?"

"Words, not much. I'll give a full report at the meeting tonight. Looks like we won't even get on the ballot, though."

"Now isn't that what we said was going to happen? We shoulda gone with Francois Petain's idea."

"Too risky." Petain's plan had been to tell Death Valley they had to shut down the laser for repairs. Not tell the groundhogs about the signal at all, just answer it. "If they found out they'd sue us down to our teeth."

The man shook his head. "I'll never understand groundhogs."

"Not your job." Charlie was an Earth-born, Earth-trained psychologist. "Nobody born here ever could."

"Maybe so." He stood up. "Thanks for the drink; I've gotta get back to work. You know to call Dr. Bemis before the meeting?"

"Yeah. There was a message at the Cape."

"She has a surprise for you."

"Doesn't she always? You clowns never do anything around here until I leave."

All Abigail Bemis would say over the phone was that Charlie should come to her place for dinner; she'd prep him for the meeting.

"That was good, Ab. Can't afford real food on Earth."

She laughed and stacked the plates in the cleaner, then drew two cups of coffee. She laughed again when she sat down. Stocky, white-haired woman with bright eyes in a sea of wrinkles.

"You're in a jolly mood tonight."

"Yep. It's expectation."

"Johnny said you had a surprise."

"Hooboy, he doesn't know half. So you didn't get anywhere with the Senator."

"No. Even less than I expected. What's the secret?"

"Connors is a nice-hearted boy. He's done a lot for us."

"Come on, Ab. What is it?"

"He's right. Shut off the groundhogs' TV for twenty

minutes and they'd have another Revolution on their hands."

"Ab . . ."

"We're going to send the message."

"Sure. I figured we would. Using Farside at whatever wattage we've got. If we're lucky—"

"Nope. Not enough power."

Charlie stirred a half-spoon of sugar into his coffee. "You plan to . . . defy Connors?"

"Fuzz Connors. We're not going to use radio at all."

"Visible light? Infra?"

"We're going to hand-carry it. In Daedalus."

Charlie's coffee cup was halfway to his mouth. He spilled a great deal.

"Here, have a napkin."

June 2040

From *A Short History Of the Old Order* (Freeman Press, 2040):

. . . and if you think *that* was a waste, consider Project Daedalus.

This was the first big space thing after L-5. Now L-5 worked out all right, because it was practical. But Daedalus (named from a Greek god who could fly)— that was a clear-cut case of throwing money down the rat-hole.

These scientists in 2016 talked the bourgeoisie into paying for a trip to another *star!* It was going to take over a hundred years—but the scientists were going to have babies along the way, and train *them* to be scientists (whether they wanted to or not!).

They were going to use all the old H-bombs for fuel—as if we might not need the fuel some day right here on Earth. What if L-5 decided they didn't like us, and shut off the power beam?

Daedalus was supposed to be a spaceship almost a kilometer long! Most of it was manufactured in space, from Moon stuff, but a lot of it—the most expensive part, you bet—had to be boosted from Earth.

They almost got it built, but then came the Breakup

and the People's Revolution. No way in hell the People were going to let them have those H-bombs, not sitting right over our heads like that.

So we left the H-bombs in Helsinki and the space freeks went back to doing what they're supposed to do. Every year they petition to get those H-bombs, but every year the Will of the People says no.

That spaceship is still up there, a skytrillion dollar boondoggle. As a monument to bourgeoisie folly, it's worse than the Pyramids!!

February 2075

"So the Scylla probe is just a ruse, to get the fuel—"

"Oh no, not really." She slid a blue-covered folder to him. "We're still going to Scylla. Scoop up a few megatons of degenerate antimatter. And a similar amount of degenerate matter from Charybdis.

"We don't plan a generation ship, Charlie. The hydrogen fuel will get us out there; once there, it'll power the magnetic bottles to hold the real fuel."

"Total annihilation of matter," Charlie said.

"That's right. Em-cee-squared to the ninth decimal place. We aren't talking about centuries to get to 61 Cygni. Nine years, there and back."

"The groundhogs aren't going to like it. All the bad feeling about the original Daedalus—"

"Fuzz the groundhogs. We'll do everything we said we'd do with their precious H-bombs: go out to Scylla, get some antimatter, and bring it back. Just taking a long way back."

"You don't want to just tell them that's what we're going to do? No skin off . . ."

She shook her head and laughed again, this time a little bitterly. "You didn't read the editorial in *Peoplepost* this morning, did you?"

"I was too busy."

"So am I, boy; to busy for that drik. One of my staff brought it in, though."

"It's about Daedalus?"

"No . . . it concerns 61 Cygni. How the crazy scientists want to let those boogers know there's life on Earth."

"They'll come make people-burgers out of us."

"Something like that."

Over three thousand people sat on the hillside, a "natural" amphitheatre fashioned of moon dirt and Earth grass. There was an incredible din, everyone talking at once: Dr. Bemis had just told them about the 61 Cygni expedition.

On about the tenth "Quiet, please," Bemis was able to continue. "So you can see why we didn't simply broadcast this meeting. Earth would pick it up. Likewise, there are no groundhog media on L-5 right now. They were rotated back to Earth and the shuttle with their replacements needed repairs at the Cape. The other two shuttles are here.

"So I'm asking all of you—and all of your brethren who had to stay at their jobs—to keep secret the biggest thing since Isabella hocked her jewels. Until we lift.

"Now Dr. Leventhal, who's chief of our social sciences section, wants to talk to you about selecting the crew."

Charlie hated public speaking. In this setting, he felt like a Christian on the way to being catfood. He smoothed out his damp notes on the podium.

"Uh, basic problem." A thousand people asked him to speak up. He adjusted the microphone.

"The basic problem is, we have space for about a thousand people. Probably more than one out of four want to go."

Loud murmur of assent. "And we don't want to be despotic about choosing . . . but I've set up certain guidelines, and Dr. Bemis agrees with them.

"Nobody should plan on going if he or she needs sophisticated medical care, obviously. Same toke, few very old people will be considered."

Almost inaudibly, Abigail said, "Sixty-four isn't very old, Charlie. I'm going." She hadn't said anything earlier.

He continued, looking at Bemis. "Second, we must

leave behind those people who are absolutely necessary for the maintenance of L-5. Including the power station." She smiled at him.

"We don't want to split up mating pairs, not for, well, nine years plus . . . but neither will we take children." He waited for the commotion to die down. "On this mission, children are baggage. You'll have to find foster parents for them. Maybe they'll go on the next trip.

"Because we can't afford baggage. We don't know what's waiting for us at 61 Cygni—a thousand people sounds like a lot, but it isn't. Not when you consider that we need a cross-section of all human knowledge, all human abilities. It may turn out that a person who can sing madrigals will be more important than a plasma physicist. No way of knowing ahead of time."

The four thousand people did manage to keep it secret, not so much out of strength of character as from a deep-seated paranoia about Earth and Earthlings.

And Senator Connors' Tricentennial actually came to their aid.

Although there was "One World," ruled by "The Will of the People," some regions had more clout than others, and nationalism was by no means dead. This was one factor.

Another factor was the way the groundhogs felt about the thermonuclear bombs stockpiled in Helsinki. All antiques: mostly a century or more old. The scientists said they were perfectly safe, but you know how that goes.

The bombs still technically belonged to the countries that had surrendered them, nine out of ten split between North America and Russia. The tenth remaining was divided among forty-two other countries. They all got together every few years to argue about what to do with the damned things. Everybody wanted to get rid of them in some useful way, but nobody wanted to put up the capital.

Charlie Leventhal's proposal was simple. L-5 would provide bankroll, materials, and personnel. On a barren rock in the Norwegian Sea they would take apart the old bombs, one at a time, and turn them into uniform fuel capsules for the Daedalus craft.

The Scylla/Charybdis probe would be timed to honor both the major spacefaring countries. Renamed the *John F. Kennedy,* it would leave Earth orbit on America's Tricentennial. The craft would accelerate halfway to the double star system at one gee, then flip and slow down at the same rate. It would use a magnetic scoop to gather antimatter from Scylla. On May Day, 2077, it would again be renamed, being the *Leonid I. Brezhnev* for the return trip. For safety's sake, the antimatter would be delivered to a lunar research station, near Farside. L-5 scientists claimed that harnessing the energy from total annihilation of matter would make a heaven on Earth.

Most people doubted that, but looked forward to the fireworks.

January 2076

"The *hell* with that!" Charlie was livid. "I—I just won't do it. Won't!"

"You're the only one—"

"That's not true, Ab, you know it." Charlie paced from wall to wall of her office cubicle. "There are dozens of people who can run L-5. Better than I can."

"Not better, Charlie."

He stopped in front of her desk, leaned over. "Come on, Ab. There's only one logical person to stay behind and run things. Not only has she proven herself in the position, but she's too old to—"

"That kind of drik I don't have to listen to."

"Now, Ab . . ."

"No, you listen to me. I was an infant when we started building Daedalus; worked on it as a girl and a young woman.

"I could take you out there in a shuttle and show you the rivets that I put in, myself. A half-century ago."

"That's my—"

"I earned my ticket, Charlie." Her voice softened.

"Age is a factor, yes. This is only the first trip of many —and when it comes back, I *will* be too old. You'll just be in your prime . . . and with over twenty years of experience as Coordinator, I don't doubt they'll make you captain of the next—"

"I don't want to be captain. I don't want to be Coordinator. I just want to *go!*"

"You and three thousand other people."

"And of the thousand that don't want to go, or can't, there isn't one person who could serve as Coordinator? I could name you—"

"That's not the point. There's no one on L-5 who has anywhere near the influence, the connections, you have on Earth. No one who understands groundhogs as well."

"That's racism, Ab. Groundhogs are just like you and me."

"Some of them. I don't see you going Earthside every chance you can get . . . what, you like the view up here? You like living in a can?"

He didn't have a ready answer for that. Ab continued: "Whoever's Coordinator is going to have to do some tall explaining, trying to keep things smooth between L-5 and Earth. That's been your life's work, Charlie. And you're also known and respected here. You're the only logical choice."

"I'm not arguing with your logic."

"I know." Neither of them had to mention the document, signed by Charlie, among others, that gave Dr. Bemis final authority in selecting the crew for Daedalus/ Kennedy/Brezhnev. "Try not to hate me too much, Charlie. I have to do what's best for my people. All of my people."

Charlie glared at her for a long moment and left.

June 2076

From *Fax & Pix,* 4 June 2076:

**SPACE FARM LEAVES FOR
STARS NEXT MONTH**

1. The *John F. Kennedy,* that goes to Scylla/Char-
ybdis next month, is like a little L-5 with bombs up
its tail (see pix up left, up right).

   A. The trip's twenty months. They could either take
a few people and fill the thing up with food, air,
and water—or take a lot of people inside a
closed ecology, like L-5.

   B. They could've gotten by with only a couple hundred people, to run the farms and stuff. But almost all the space freeks wanted to go. They're
used to living that way, anyhow (and they never
get to go anyplace).

   C. When they get back, the farms will be used as
a starter for L-4, like L-5 but smaller at first,
and on the other side of the Moon (pic down
left).

2. For other Tricentennial fax & pix, see bacover.

July 2076

Charlie was just finishing up a week on Earth the day
the *John F. Kennedy* was launched. Tired of being interviewed, he slipped away from the media lounge at
the Cape shuttleport. His white clearance card got
him out onto the landing strip alone.

The midnight shuttle was being fueled at the far end
of the strip, gleaming pink-white in the last light from
the setting sun. Its image twisted and danced in the
shimmering heat that radiated from the tarmac. The
smell of the soft tar was indelibly associated in his mind
with leave-taking, relief.

He walked to the middle of the strip and checked
his watch. Five minutes. He lit a cigarette and threw
it away. He rechecked his mental calculations: the
flight would start low in the southwest. He blocked out
the sun with a raised hand. What would 150 bombs
per second look like? For the media they were called
fuel capsules. The people who had carefully assembled
them and gently lifted them to orbit and installed them
in the tanks, they called them bombs. Ten times the
brightness of a full moon, they had said. On L-5 you
weren't supposed to look toward it without a dark filter.

No warm-up: it suddenly appeared, an impossibly brilliant rainbow speck just over the horizon. It gleamed for several minutes, then dimmed slightly with a haze, and slipped away.

Most of the United States wouldn't see it until it came around again, some two hours later, turning night into day, competing with local pyrotechnic displays. Then every couple of hours after that, Charlie would see it once more, then get on the shuttle. And finally stop having to call it by the name of a dead politician.

September 2076

There was a quiet celebration on L-5 when *Daedalus* reached the mid-point of its journey, flipped, and started decelerating. The progress report from its crew characterized the journey as "uneventful." At that time they were going nearly two tenths of the speed of light. The laser beam that carried communications was red-shifted from blue light down to orange; the message that turn-around had been successful took two weeks to travel from *Daedalus* to L-5.

They announced a slight course change. They had analyzed the polarization of light from Scylla/Charybdis as their phase angle increased, and were pretty sure the system was surrounded by flat rings of debris, like Saturn. They would "come in low" to avoid collision.

January 2077

Daedalus had been sending back recognizable pictures of the Scylla/Charybdis system for three weeks. They finally had one that was dramatic enough for groundhog consumption.

Charlie set the holo cube on his desk and pushed it around with his finger, marvelling.

"This is incredible. How did they do it?"

"It's a montage, of course." Johnny had been one of the youngest adults left behind: heart murmur, trick knees, a surfeit of astrophysicists.

"The two stars are a strobe snapshot in infrared.

Sort of. Some ten or twenty thousand exposures taken as the ship orbited around the system, then sorted out and enhanced." He pointed, but it wasn't much help, since Charlie was looking at the cube from a different angle.

"The lamina of fire where the atmospheres touch, that was taken in ultraviolet. Shows more fine structure that way.

"The rings were easy. Fairly long exposures in visible light. Gives the star background, too."

A light tap on the door and an assistant stuck his head in. "Have a second, Doctor?"

"Sure."

"Somebody from a Russian May Day committee is on the phone. She wants to know whether they've changed the name of the ship to *Brezhnev* yet."

"Yeah. Tell her we decided on 'Leon Trotsky' instead, though."

He nodded seriously. "Okay." He started to close the door.

"Wait!" Charlie rubbed his eyes. "Tell her, uh . . . the ship doesn't have a commemorative name while it's in orbit there. They'll rechristen it just before the start of the return trip."

"Is that true?" Johnny asked.

"I don't know. Who cares? In another couple of months they won't *want* it named after anybody." He and Ab had worked out a plan—admittedly rather shaky—to protect L-5 from the groundhogs' wrath: nobody on the satellite knew ahead of time that the ship was headed for 61 Cygni. It was a decision the crew arrived at on the way to Scylla Charybdis; they modified the drive system to accept matter-antimatter destruction while they were orbiting the double star. L-5 would first hear of the mutinous plan via a transmission sent as *Daedalus* left Scylla/Charybdis. They'd be a month on their way by the time the message got to Earth.

It was pretty transparent, but at least they had been careful that no record of *Daedalus'* true mission be left on L-5. Three thousand people did know the truth, though, and any competent engineer or physical scientist would suspect it.

Ab had felt that, although there was a better than even chance they would be exposed, surely the ground-hogs couldn't stay angry for 23 years—even if they were unimpressed by the antimatter and other wonders. . . .

Besides, Charlie thought, it's not their worry anymore.

As it turned out, the crew of *Daedalus* would have bigger things to worry about.

June 2077

The Russians had their May Day celebration—Charlie watched it on TV and winced every time they mentioned the good ship *Leonid I. Brezhnev*—and then things settled back down to normal. Charlie and three thousand others waited nervously for the "surprise" message. It came in early June, as expected, scrambled in a data channel. But it didn't say what it was supposed to:

> *"This is Abigail Bemis, to Charles Leventhal.*
>
> *"Charlie, we have real trouble. The ship has been damaged, hit in the stern by a good chunk of something. It punched right through the main drive reflector. Destroyed a set of control sensors and one attitude jet.*
>
> *"As far as we can tell, the situation is stable. We're maintaining acceleration at just a tiny fraction under one gee. But we can't steer, and we can't shut off the main drive.*
>
> *"We didn't have any trouble with ring debris when we were orbiting since we were inside Roche's limit. Coming in, as you know, we'd managed to take advantage of natural divisions in the rings. We tried the same going back, but it was a slower, more complicated process, since we mass so goddamn much now. We must have picked up a piece from the fringe of one of the outer rings.*
>
> *"If we could turn off the drive, we might have a chance at fixing it. But the work pods can't keep up*

*with the ship, not at one gee. The radiation down
there would fry the operator in seconds, anyway.*

*"We're working on it. If you have any ideas, let us
know. It occurs to me that this puts you in the clear—
we were headed back to Earth, but got clobbered.
Will send a transmission to that effect on the regular
comm channel. This message is strictly burn-before-
reading.*

"Endit."

It worked perfectly, as far as getting Charlie and L-5
off the hook—and the drama of the situation precipitated a level of interest in space travel unheard-of since
the 1960's.

They even had a hero. A volunteer had gone down
in a heavily-shielded work pod, lowered on a cable,
to take a look at the situation. She'd sent back clear
pictures of the damage, before the cable snapped.

> *Daedalus:* A.D. 2081
> Earth: A.D. 2101

The following news item was killed from *Fax & Pix,*
because it was too hard to translate into the "plain
English" that made the paper so popular:

SPACESHIP PASSES 61 CYGNI—
SORT OF
(L-5 Stringer)

A message received today from the spaceship *Daedalus* said that it had just passed within 400 astronomical units of 61 Cygni. That's about ten times as far as
the planet Pluto is from the Sun.

Actually, the spaceship passed the star some eleven
years ago. It's taken all that time for the message to get
back to us.

We don't know for sure where the spaceship actually is, now. If they still haven't repaired the runaway
drive, they're about eleven light-years past the 61
Cygni system (their speed when they passed the
double star was better than 99% the speed of light).

The situation is more complicated if you look at it from the point of view of a passenger on the spaceship. Because of relativity, time seems to pass more slowly as you approach the speed of light. So only about four years passed for them, on the eleven light-year journey.

L-5 Coordinator Charles Leventhal points out that the spaceship has enough antimatter fuel to keep accelerating to the edge of the Galaxy. The crew then would be only some twenty years older—but it would be twenty *thousand* years before we heard from them. . . .

(*Kill this one. There's more stuff about what the ship looked like to the people on 61 Cygni, and how-cum we could talk to them all the time even though time was slower there, but its all as stupid as this.*)

Daedalus: A.D. 2083
Earth: A.D. 2144

Charlie Leventhal died at the age of 99, bitter. Almost a decade earlier it had been revealed that they'd planned all along for *Daedalus* to be a starship. Few people had paid much attention to the news. Among those who did, the consensus was that anything that got rid of a thousand scientists at once, was a good thing. Look at the mess they got us in.

Daedalus: 67 light-years out, and still accelerating.

Daedalus: A.D. 2085
Earth: A.D. 3578

After over seven years of shipboard research and development—and some 1500 light-years of travel—they managed to shut down the engine. With sophisticated telemetry, the job was done without endangering another life.

Every life was precious now. They were no longer simply explorers; almost half their fuel was gone. They were colonists, with no ticket back.

The message of their success would reach Earth in fifteen centuries. Whether there would be an infrared telescope around to detect it, that was a matter of some conjecture.

Daedalus: A.D. 2093
Earth: ca. A.D. 5000

While decelerating, they had investigated several systems in their line of flight. They found one with an Earth-type planet around a Sun-type sun, and aimed for it.

The season they began landing colonists, the dominant feature in the planet's night sky was a beautiful blooming cloud of gas that astronomers had named the North American Nebula.

Which was an irony that didn't occur to any of these colonists from L-5—give or take a few years, it was America's Trimillennial.

America itself was a little the worse for wear, this three thousandth anniversary. The seas that lapped its shores were heavy with a crimson crust of anaerobic life; the mighty cities had fallen and their remains, nearly ground away by the never-ceasing sandstorms.

No fireworks were planned, for lack of an audience, for lack of planners; bacteria just don't care. May Day too would be ignored.

The only humans in the Solar System lived in a glass and metal tube. They tended their automatic machinery, and turned their backs on the dead Earth, and worshiped the constellation Cygnus, and had forgotten why.

JOHN VARLEY

In the Bowl

John Varley is from Texas. He lived in California most of his adult life and now makes his home in Oregon with his family. He started writing science fiction in 1973, is thirty years old, and one of the most interesting of the newer writers. A large number of people have been predicting great things for John Varley. He has the narrative gift—which is to say that it is impossible to start reading him without getting caught up in the action behind his words. This, by itself, has always been an ability much prized among story tellers. But John Varley has something else. His thinking is the thinking of the seventies; and the ideas, the themes and concepts of his stories are those of the 1970's. "In the Bowl"—the story by him that follows—is a thematic story, but in typical Varley fashion, it is a thematic story that will pick you up by the ears and carry you away.

Never buy anything at a secondhand organbank. And while I'm handing out good advice, don't outfit yourself for a trip to Venus until you *get* to Venus.

I wish I had waited. But while shopping around at Coprates a few weeks before my vacation, I happened on this little shop and was talked into an infraeye at a very good price. What I should have asked myself was what was an infraeye doing on Mars in the first place?

Think about it. No one wears them on Mars. If you want to see at night, it's much cheaper to buy a snooperscope. That way you can take the damn thing off when the sun comes up. So this eye must have come back with a tourist from Venus. And there's no telling how long it sat there in the vat until this sweet-talking old guy gave me his line about how it belonged to a nice little old schoolteacher who never . . . ah, well. You've probably heard it before.

If only the damn thing had gone on the blink before I left Venusburg. You know Venusburg: town of steamy swamps and sleazy hotels where you can get mugged

67

as you walk down the public streets, lose a fortune at
the gaming tables, buy any pleasure in the known universe, hunt the prehistoric monsters that wallow in the
fetid marshes that are just a swampbuggy ride out of
town. You do? Then you should know that after hours
—when they turn all the holos off and the place reverts
to an ordinary cluster of silvery domes sitting in darkness and eight hundred degree temperature and pressure enough to give you a sinus headache just *thinking*
about it, when they shut off all the tourist razzle-dazzle
—it's no trouble to find your way to one of the rental
agencies around the spaceport and get medicanical
work done. They'll accept Martian money. Your Solar
Express Card is honored. Just walk right in, no waiting.

However . . .

I had caught the daily blimp out of Venusburg just
hours after I touched down, happy as a clam, my infraeye working beautifully. By the time I landed in
Cui-Cui Town, I was having my first inklings of trouble.
Barely enough to notice; just the faintest hazing in the
right-side peripheral vision. I shrugged it off. I had
only three hours in Cui-Cui before the blimp left for
Last Chance. I wanted to look around. I had no intention of wasting my few hours in a bodyshop getting
my eye fixed. If it was still acting up at Last Chance,
then I'd see about it.

Cui-Cui was more to my liking than Venusburg.
There was not such a cast-of-thousands feeling there.
On the streets of Venusburg the chances are about ten
to one against meeting a real human being; everyone
else is a holo put there to spice up the image and help
the streets look not quite so *empty*. I quickly tired of
zoot-suited pimps that I could see right through trying
to sell me boys and girls of all ages. What's the *point?*
Just try to touch one of those beautiful people.

In Cui-Cui the ratio was closer to fifty-fifty. And the
theme was not decadent corruption, but struggling
frontier. The streets were very convincing mud, and the
wooden storefronts were tastefully done. I didn't care
for the eight-legged dragons with eyestalks that con-
stantly lumbered through the place, but I understand

they are a memorial to the fellow who named the town.
That's all right, but I doubt if he would have liked to
have one of the damn things walk through him like a
twelve-ton tank made of pixie dust.

I barely had time to get my feet "wet" in the "pud-
dles" before the blimp was ready to go again. And the
eye trouble had cleared up. So I was off to Last Chance.

I should have taken a cue from the name of the town.
And I had every opportunity to do so. While there, I
made my last purchase of supplies for the bush. I was
going out where there were no air stations on every
corner, and so I decided I could use a tagalong.

Maybe you've never seen one. They're modern
science's answer to the backpack. Or maybe to the
mule train, though in operation you're sure to be reminded of the safari bearers in old movies, trudging
stolidly along behind the White Hunter with bales of
supplies on their heads. The thing is a pair of metal
legs exactly as long as your legs, with equipment on
the top and an umbilical cord attaching the contraption
to your lower spine. What it does is provide you with
the capability of living on the surface for four weeks
instead of the five days you get from your Venus-lung.

The medico who sold me mine had me laying right
there on his table with my back laid open so he could
install the tubes that carry air from the tanks in the
tagalong into my Venus-lung. It was a golden opportunity to ask him to check the eye. He probably would
have, because while he was hooking me up he inspected
and tested my lung and charged me nothing. He wanted
to know where I bought it, and I told him Mars. He
clucked, and said it seemed all right. He warned me
not to ever let the level of oxygen in the lung get too
low, to always charge it up before I left a pressure
dome, even if I was only going out for a few minutes.
I assured him that I knew all that and would be careful.
So he connected the nerves into a metal socket in the
small of my back and plugged the tagalong into it. He
tested it several ways and said the job was done.

And I didn't ask him to look at the eye. I just wasn't
thinking about the eye then. I'd not even gone out on

the surface yet. So I'd no real occasion to see it in action. Oh, things looked a little different, even in visible light. There were different colors and very few shadows, and the image I got out of the infraeye was fuzzier than the one from the other eye. I could close one eye, then the other, and see a real difference. But I wasn't thinking about it.

So I boarded the blimp the next day for the weekly scheduled flight to Lodestone, a company mining town close to the Fahrenheit Desert. Though how they were able to distinguish a desert from anything else on Venus was still a mystery to me. I was enraged to find that, though the blimp left half-loaded, I had to pay two fares: one for me, and one for my tagalong. I thought briefly of carrying the damn thing in my lap but gave it up after a ten-minute experiment in the depot. It was full of sharp edges and poking angles, and the trip was going to be a long one. So I paid. But the extra expense had knocked a large hole in my budget.

From Cui-Cui the steps got closer together and harder to reach. Cui-Cui is two thousand kilometers from Venusburg, and it's another thousand to Lodestone. After that the passenger service is spotty. I did find out how Venusians defined a desert, though. A desert is a place not yet inhabited by human beings. So long as I was still able to board a scheduled blimp, I wasn't there yet.

The blimps played out on me in a little place called Prosperity. Population seventy-five humans and one otter. I thought the otter was a holo playing in the pool in the town square. The place didn't look prosperous enough to afford a real pool like that with real water. But it was. It was a transient town catering to prospectors. I understand that a town like that can vanish overnight if the prospectors move on. The owners of the shops just pack up and haul the whole thing away. The ratio of the things you see in a frontier town to what really is there is something like a hundred to one.

I learned with considerable relief that the only blimps I could catch out of Prosperity were headed in the di-

rection I had come from. There was nothing at all going
the other way. I was happy to hear that and felt it was
only a matter of chartering a ride into the desert. Then
my eye faded out entirely.

I remember feeling annoyed; no, more than annoyed.
I was really angry. But I was still viewing it as a nuisance
rather than a disaster. It was going to be a matter of
some lost time and some wasted money.

I quickly learned otherwise. I asked the ticket seller
(this was in a saloon-drugstore-arcade; there was no
depot in Prosperity) where I could find someone who'd
sell and install an infraeye. He laughed at me.

"Not out here you won't, brother," he said. "Never
have had anything like that out here. Used to be a
medico in Ellsworth, three stops back on the local
blimp, but she moved back to Venusburg a year ago.
Nearest thing now is in Last Chance."

I was stunned. I knew I was heading out for the
deadlands, but it had never occurred to me that any
place would be lacking in something so basic as a
medico. Why, you might as well not sell food or air as
not sell medicanical services. People might actually *die*
out here. I wondered if the planetary government knew
about this disgusting situation.

Whether they did or not, I realized that an incensed
letter to them would do me no good. I was in a bind.
Adding quickly in my head, I soon discovered that the
cost of flying back to Last Chance and buying a new
eye would leave me without enough money to return
to Prosperity and still make it back to Venusburg. My
entire vacation was about to be ruined just because I
tried to cut some corners buying a used eye.

"What's the matter with the eye?" the man asked
me.

"Huh? Oh, I don't know. I mean, it's just stopped
working. I'm blind in it, that's what's wrong." I grasped
at a straw, seeing the way he was studying my eye.

"Say, you don't know anything about it, do you?"

He shook his head and smiled ruefully at me. "Naw.
Just a little here and there. I was thinking if it was the

muscles that was giving you trouble, bad tracking or something like that—"

"No. No vision at all."

"Too bad. Sounds like a shot nerve to me. I wouldn't try to fool around with that. I'm just a tinkerer." He clucked his tongue sympathetically. "You want that ticket back to Last Chance?"

I didn't know what I wanted just then. I had planned this trip for two years. I almost bought the ticket, then thought what the hell. I was here, and I should at least look around before deciding what to do. Maybe there was someone here who could help me. I turned back to ask the clerk if he knew anyone, but he answered before I got it out.

"I don't want to raise your hopes too much," he said, rubbing his chin with a broad hand. "Like I say, it's not for sure, but—"

"Yes, what is it?"

"Well, there's a kid lives around here who's pretty crazy about medico stuff. Always tinkering around, doing odd jobs for people, fixing herself up; you know the type. The trouble is she's pretty loose in her ways. You might end up worse when she's through with you than when you started."

"I don't see how," I said. "It's not working at all; what could she do to make it any worse?"

He shrugged. "It's your funeral. You can probably find her hanging around the square. If she's not there, check the bars. Her name's Ember. She's got a pet otter that's always with her. But you'll know her when you see her."

Finding Ember was no problem. I simply back-tracked to the square and there she was, sitting on the stone rim of the fountain. She was trailing her toes in the water. Her otter was playing on a small water-slide, looking immensely pleased to have found the only open body of water within a thousand kilometers.

"Are you Ember?" I asked, sitting down beside her.

She looked up at me with that unsettling stare a Venusian can inflict on a foreigner. It comes of having one blue or brown eye and one that is all red, with no white. I looked that way myself, but I didn't have to look at it.

"What if I am?"

Her apparent age was about ten or eleven. Intuitively, I felt that it was probably very close to her actual age. Since she was supposed to be handy at medicanics, I could have been wrong. She had done some work on herself, but of course there was no way of telling how extensive it might have been. Mostly it seemed to be cosmetic. She had no hair on her head. She had replaced it with a peacock fan of feathers that kept falling into her eyes. Her scalp skin had been transplanted to her lower legs and forearms, and the hair there was long, blonde, and flowing. From the contours of her face I was sure that her skull was a mass of file marks and bone putty from where she'd fixed the understructure to reflect the face she wished to wear.

"I was told that you know a little medicanics. You see, this eye has—"

She snorted. "I don't know who would have told you *that*. I know a hell of a lot about medicine. I'm not just a backyard tinkerer. Come on, Malibu."

She started to get up, and the otter looked back and forth between us. I don't think he was ready to leave the pool.

"Wait a minute. I'm sorry if I hurt your feelings. Without knowing anything about you I'll admit that you must know more about it than anyone else in town."

She sat back down, finally had to grin at me.

"So you're in a spot, right? It's me or no one. Let me guess: you're here on vacation, that's obvious. And either time or money is preventing you from going back to Last Chance for professional work." She looked me up and down. "I'd say it was money."

"You hit it. Will you help me?"

"That depends." She moved closer and squinted into my infraeye. She put her hands on my cheeks to hold my head steady. There was nowhere for me to look but her face. There were no scars visible on her; at least she was that good. Her upper canines were about five millimeters longer than the rest of her teeth.

"Hold still. Where'd you get this?"

"Mars."

"Thought so. It's a Gloom Piercer, made by Northern Bio. Cheap model; they peddle 'em mostly to tourists. Maybe ten, twelve years old."

"Is it the nerve? The guy I talked to—"

"Nope." She leaned back and resumed splashing her feet in the water. "Retina. The right side is detached, and it's flopped down over the fovea. Probably wasn't put on very tight in the first place. They don't make those things to last more than a year."

I sighed and slapped my knees with my palms. I stood up, held out my hand to her.

"Well, I guess that's that. Thanks for your help."

She was surprised. "Where you going?"

"Back to Last Chance, then to Mars to sue a certain organbank. There are laws for this sort of thing on Mars."

"Here, too. But why go back? I'll fix it for you."

We were in her workshop, which doubled as her bedroom and kitchen. It was just a simple dome without a single holo. It was refreshing after the ranch-style houses that seemed to be the rage in Prosperity. I don't wish to sound chauvinistic, and I realize that Venusians need some sort of visual stimulation, living as they do in a cloud-covered desert. Still, the emphasis on illusion there was never to my liking. Ember lived next door to a man who lived in a perfect replica of the Palace at Versailles. She told me that when he shut his holo generators off the residue of his *real* possessions would have fit in a knapsack. Including the holo generator.

"What brings you to Venus?"

"Tourism."

She looked at me out of the corner of her eye as she swabbed my face with nerve deadener. I was stretched out on the floor, since there was no furniture in the room except a few work tables.

"All right. But we don't get many tourists this far out. If it's none of my business, just say so."

"It's none of your business."

She sat up. "Fine. Fix your own eye." She waited with a half smile on her face. I eventually had to smile, too. She went back to work, selecting a spoon-shaped tool from a haphazard pile at her knees.

"I'm an amateur geologist. Rock hound, actually. I work in an office, and weekends I get out in the country and hike around. The rocks are an excuse to get me out there, I guess."

She popped the eye out of its socket and reached in with one finger to deftly unhook the metal connection along the optic nerve. She held the eyeball up to the light and peered into the lens.

"You can get up now. Pour some of this stuff into the socket and squint down on it." I did as she asked and followed her to the workbench.

She sat on a stool and examined the eye more closely. Then she stuck a syringe into it and drained out the aqueous humor, leaving the orb looking like a turtle egg that's dried in the sun. She sliced it open and started probing carefully. The long hairs on her forearms kept getting in the way. So she paused and tied them back with rubber bands.

"Rock hound," she mused. "You must be here to get a look at the blast jewels."

"Right. Like I said, I'm strictly a small-time geologist. But I read about them and saw one once in a jeweler's shop in Phobos. So I saved up and came to Venus to try and find one of my own."

"That should be no problem. Easiest gems to find in the known universe. Too bad. People out here were hoping they could get rich off them." She shrugged. "Not that there's not some money to be made off them. Just not the fortune everybody was hoping for. Funny; they're as rare as diamonds used to be, and to make it even better, they don't duplicate in the lab the way diamonds do. Oh, I guess they could make 'em, but it's way too much trouble." She was using a tiny device to staple the detached retina back onto the rear surface of the eye.

"Go on."

"Huh?"

"Why can't they make them in the lab?"

She laughed. "You *are* an amateur geologist. Like I said, they could, but it'd cost too much. They're a blend of a lot of different elements. A lot of aluminum, I think. That's what makes rubies red, right?"

"Yes."

"It's the other impurities that make them so pretty. And you have to make them in high pressure and heat, and they're so unstable that they usually blow before you've got the right mix. So it's cheaper to go out and pick 'em up."

"And the only place to pick them up is in the middle of the Fahrenheit Desert."

"Right." She seemed to be finished with her stapling. She straightened up to survey her work with a critical eye. She frowned, then sealed up the incision she had made and pumped the liquid back in. She mounted it in a caliper and aimed a laser at it, then shook her head when she read some figures on a readout by the laser.

"It's working," she said. "But you really got a lemon. The iris is out of true. It's an ellipse, about .24 eccentric. It's going to get worse. See that brown discoloration on the left side? That's progressive decay in the muscle tissue, poisons accumulating in it. And you're a dead cinch for cataracts in about four months."

I couldn't see what she was talking about, but I pursed my lips as if I did.

"But will it last that long?"

She smirked at me. "Are you looking for a six-month warranty? Sorry, I'm not a member of the VMA. But if it isn't legally binding, I guess I'd feel safe in saying it ought to last that long. Maybe."

"You sure go out on a limb, don't you?"

"It's good practice. We future medicos must always be on the alert for malpractice suits. Lean over here and I'll put it in."

"What I was wondering," I said, as she hooked it up

and eased it back into the socket, "is whether I'd be safe going out in the desert for four weeks with this eye."

"No," she said promptly, and I felt a great weight of disappointment. "Nor with any eye," she quickly added. "Not if you're going alone."

"I see. But you think the eye would hold up?"

"Oh, sure. But you wouldn't. That's why you're going to take me up on my astounding offer and let me be your guide through the desert."

I snorted. "You think so? Sorry, this is going to be a solo expedition. I planned it that way from the first. That's what I go out rock hunting for in the first place: to be alone." I dug my credit meter out of my pouch. "Now, how much do I owe you?"

She wasn't listening but was resting her chin on her palm and looking wistful.

"He goes out so he can be alone, did you hear that, Malibu?" The otter looked up at her from his place on the floor. "Now take me, for instance. Me, I know what being alone is all about. It's the crowds and big cities I crave. Right, old buddy?" The otter kept looking at her, obviously ready to agree to anything.

"I suppose so," I said. "Would a hundred be all right?" That was about half what a registered medico would have charged me, but like I said, I was running short.

"You're not going to let me be your guide? Final word?"

"No. Final. Listen, it's not you, it's just—"

"I know. You want to be alone. No charge. Come on, Malibu." She got up and headed for the door. Then she turned around.

"I'll be seeing you," she said, and winked at me.

It didn't take me too long to understand what the wink had been all about. I can see the obvious on the third or fourth go-around.

The fact was that Prosperity was considerably bemused to have a tourist in its midst. There wasn't a rental agency or hotel in the entire town. I had thought of that but hadn't figured it would be too hard to find someone willing to rent his private skycycle if the price

was right. I'd been saving out a large chunk of cash for
the purpose of meeting extortionate demands in that
department. I felt sure the locals would be only too willing to soak a tourist.

But they weren't taking. Just about everyone had a
skycycle, and absolutely everyone who had one was
uninterested in renting it. They were a necessity to anyone who worked out of town, which everyone did, and
they were hard to get. Freight schedules were as spotty
as the passenger service. And every person who turned
me down had a helpful suggestion to make. As I say,
after the fourth or fifth such suggestion I found myself
back in the town square. She was sitting just as she
had been the first time, trailing her feet in the water.
Malibu never seemed to tire of the waterslide.

"Yes," she said, without looking up. "It so happens
that I *do* have a skycycle for rent."

I was exasperated, but I had to cover it up. She had
me over the proverbial barrel.

"Do you always hang around here?" I asked. "People
tell me to see you about a skycycle and tell me to look
here, almost like you and this fountain are a hyphenated
word. What else do you do?"

She fixed me with a haughty glare. "I repair eyes for
dumb tourists. I also do body work for everyone in town
at only twice what it would cost them in Last Chance.
And I do it damn well, too, though those rubes'd be the
last to admit it. No doubt Mr. Lamara at the ticket
station told you scandalous lies about my skills. They
resent it because I'm taking advantage of the cost and
time it would take them to get to Last Chance and pay
merely inflated prices, instead of the outrageous ones
I charge them."

I had to smile, though I was sure I was about to
become the object of some outrageous prices myself.
She was a shrewd operator.

"How old are you?" I found myself asking, then
almost bit my tongue. The last thing a proud and independent child likes to discuss is age. But she surprised
me.

"In mere chronological time, eleven Earth years.

That's just over six of your years. In real, internal time, of course, I'm ageless."

"Of course. Now about that cycle. . . ."

"Of course. But I evaded your earlier question. What I do besides sit here is irrelevant, because while sitting here I am engaged in contemplating eternity. I'm diving into my navel, hoping to learn the true depth of the womb. In short, I'm doing my yoga exercises." She looked thoughtfully out over the water to her pet. "Besides, it's the only pool in a thousand kilometers." She grinned at me and dived flat over the water. She cut it like a knife blade and torpedoed out to her otter, who set up a happy racket of barks.

When she surfaced near the middle of the pool, out by the jets and falls, I called to her.

"What about the cycle?"

She cupped her ear, though she was only about fifteen meters away.

"I said what about the cycle?"

"I can't hear you," she mouthed. "You'll have to come out here."

I stepped into the pool, grumbling to myself. I could see that her price included more than just money.

"I can't swim," I warned.

"Don't worry, it won't get much deeper than that." It was up to my chest. I sloshed out until I was on tiptoe, then grabbed at a jutting curlicue on the fountain. I hauled myself up and sat on the wet Venusian marble with water trickling down my legs.

Ember was sitting at the bottom of the waterslide, thrashing her feet in the water. She was leaning flat against the smooth rock. The water that sheeted over the rock made a bow wave at the crown of her head. Beads of water ran off her head feathers. Once again she made me smile. If charm could be sold, she could have been wealthy. What am I talking about? Nobody ever sells anything *but* charm, in one way or another. I got a grip on myself before she tried to sell me the north and south poles. In no time at all I was able to see her as an avaricious, cunning little guttersnipe again.

"One billion Solar Marks per hour, not a penny less," she said from that sweet little mouth.

There was no point in negotiating from an offer like that.

"You brought me out here to hear *that?* I'm really disappointed in you. I didn't take you for a tease, I really didn't. I thought we could do business. I—"

"Well, if that offer isn't satisfactory, try this one. Free of charge, except for oxygen and food and water." She waited, threshing the water with her feet.

Of course there would be some teeth in that. In an intuitive leap of truly cosmic scale, a surmise worthy of an Einstein, I saw the string. She saw me make that leap, knew I didn't like where I had landed, and her teeth flashed at me. So once again, and not for the last time, I had to either strangle her or smile at her. I smiled. I don't know how, but she had this knack of making her opponents like her even as she screwed them.

"Are you a believer in love at first sight?" I asked her, hoping to throw her off guard. Not a chance.

"Maudlin wishful thinking, at best," she said. "You have *not* bowled me over, Mister—"

"Kiku."

"Nice. Martian name?"

"I suppose so. I never really thought of it. I'm not rich, Ember."

"Certainly not. You wouldn't have put yourself in my hands if you were."

"Then why are you so attracted to me? Why are you so determined to go with me, when all I want from you is to rent your cycle? If I was that charming, I would have noticed it by now."

"Oh, I don't know," she said, with one eyebrow climbing up her forehead. "There's *something* about you that I find absolutely fascinating. Irresistible, even." She pretended to swoon.

"Want to tell me what it is?"

She shook her head. "Let that be my little secret for now."

I was beginning to suspect she was attracted to me

by the shape of my neck—so she could sink her teeth into it and drain my blood. I decided to let it lie. Hopefully she'd tell me more in the days ahead. Because it looked like there would be days together, many of them.

"When can you be ready to leave?"

"I packed right after I fixed your eye. Let's get going."

Venus is spooky. I thought and thought, and that's the best way I can describe it.

It's spooky partly because of the way you see it. Your right eye—the one that sees what's called visible light—shows you only a small circle of light that's illuminated by your hand torch. Occasionally there's a glowing spot of molten metal in the distance, but it's far too dim to see by. Your infraeye pierces those shadows and gives you a blurry picture of what lies outside the torchlight, but I would have almost rather been blind.

There's no good way to describe how this dichotomy affects your mind. One eye tells you that everything beyond a certain point is shadowy, while the other shows you what's in those shadows. Ember says that after a while your brain can blend the two pictures as easily as it does for binocular vision. I never reached that point. The whole time I was there I was trying to reconcile the two pictures.

I don't like standing in the bottom of a bowl a thousand kilometers wide. That's what you see. No matter how high you climb or how far you go, you're still standing in the bottom of that bowl. It has something to do with the bending of the light rays by the thick atmosphere, if I understand Ember correctly.

Then there's the sun. When I was there it was night time, which means that the sun was a squashed ellipse hanging just above the horizon in the east, where it had set weeks and weeks ago. Don't ask me to explain it. All I know is that the sun never sets on Venus. Never, no matter where you are. It just gets flatter and flatter and wider and wider until it oozes around to the north

or south, depending on where you are, becoming a
flat, bright line of light until it begins pulling itself
back together in the west, where it's going to rise in a
few weeks.

Ember says that at the equator it becomes a complete circle for a split second when it's actually directly
underfoot. Like the lights of a terrific stadium. All
this happens up at the rim of the bowl you're standing
in, about ten degrees above the theoretical horizon. It's
another refraction effect.

You don't see it in your left eye. Like I said, the
clouds keep out virtually all of the visible light. It's in
your right eye. The color is what I got to think of as
infrablue.

It's quiet. You begin to miss the sound of your own
breathing, and if you think about that too much, you
begin to wonder why you *aren't* breathing. You know,
of course, except the hindbrain, which never likes it
at all. It doesn't matter to the automatic nervous system that your Venus-lung is dribbling oxygen directly
into your bloodstream; those circuits aren't made to
understand things; they are primitive and very wary
of improvements. So I was plagued by a feeling of
suffocation, which was my medulla getting even with
me, I guess.

I was also pretty nervous about the temperature
and pressure. Silly, I know. Mars would kill me just
as dead without a suit, and do it more slowly and
painfully into the bargain. If my suit failed here, I
doubt if I'd have felt anything. It was just the thought
of that incredible pressure being held one millimeter
away from my fragile skin by a force field that, physically speaking, isn't even there. Or so Ember told
me. She might have been trying to get my goat. I mean,
lines of magnetic force have no physical reality, but
they're *there,* aren't they?

I kept my mind off it. Ember was there and she
knew about such things.

What she couldn't adequately explain to me was
why a skycycle didn't have a motor. I thought about
that a lot, sitting on the saddle and pedaling my ass

off with nothing to look at but Ember's silver-plated buttocks.

She had a tandem cycle, which meant four seats; two for us and two for our tagalongs. I sat behind Ember, and the tagalongs sat in two seats off to our right. Since they aped our leg movements with exactly the same force we applied, what we had was a four-human-power cycle.

"I can't figure out for the life of me," I said on our first day out, "what would have been so hard about mounting an engine on this thing and using some of the surplus power from our packs."

"Nothing hard about it, lazy," she said, without turning around. "Take my advice as a fledgling medico; this is much better for you. If you *use* the muscles you're wearing, they'll last you a lot longer. It makes you feel healthier and keeps you out of the clutches of money-grubbing medicos. I *know*. Half my work is excising fat from flabby behinds and digging varicose veins out of legs. Even out here, people don't get more than twenty years' use of their legs before they're ready for a trade-in. That's pure waste."

"I think I should have had a trade-in before we left. I'm about done in. Can't we call it a day?"

She tut-tutted, but touched a control and began spilling hot gas from the balloon over our heads. The steering vanes sticking out at our sides tilted, and we started a slow spiral to the ground.

We landed at the bottom of the bowl—my first experience with it, since all my other views of Venus had been from the air where it isn't so noticeable. I stood looking at it and scratching my head while Ember turned on the tent and turned off the balloon.

The Venusians use null fields for just about everything. Rather than try to cope with a technology that must stand up to the temperature and pressure extremes, they coat everything in a null field and let it go at that. The balloon on the cycle was nothing but a standard globular field with a discontinuity at the bottom for the air heater. The cycle body was protected with the same kind of field that Ember and I wore, the kind that follows the surface at a set distance. The tent was a hemispherical field with a flat floor.

It simplified a lot of things. Airlocks, for instance. What we did was to simply walk into the tent. Our suit fields vanished as they were absorbed into the tent field. To leave one need merely walk through the wall again, and the suit would form around you.

I plopped myself down on the floor and tried to turn my hand torch off. To my surprise, I found that it wasn't built to turn off. Ember turned on the campfire and noticed my puzzlement.

"Yes, it is wasteful," she conceded. "There's something in a Venusian that hates to turn out a light. You won't find a light switch on the entire planet. You may not believe this, but I was shocked silly a few years ago when I heard about light switches. The idea had never occurred to me. See what a provincial I am?"

That didn't sound like her. I searched her face for clues to what had brought on such a statement, but I could find nothing. She was sitting in front of the campfire with Malibu on her lap, preening her feathers.

I gestured at the fire, which was a beautifully executed holo of snapping, crackling logs with a heater concealed in the center of it.

"Isn't that an uncharacteristic touch? Why didn't you bring a fancy house, like the ones in town?"

"I like the fire. I don't like phony houses."

"Why not?"

She shrugged. She was thinking of other things. I tried another tack.

"Does your mother mind you going into the desert with strangers?"

She shot me a look I couldn't read.

"How should I know? I don't live with her. I'm emancipated. I think she's in Venusburg." I had obviously touched a tender area, so I went cautiously.

"Personality conflicts?"

She shrugged again, not wanting to get into it.

"No. Well, yes, in a way. She wouldn't emigrate

from Venus. I wanted to leave and she wanted to stay. Our interests didn't coincide. So we went our own ways. I'm working my way toward passage off-planet."

"How close are you?"

"Closer than you might think." She seemed to be weighing something in her mind, sizing me up. I could hear the gears grind and the cash register bells cling as she studied my face. Then I felt the charm start up again, like the flicking of one of those nonexistent light switches.

"See, I'm as close as I've ever been to getting off Venus. In a few weeks, I'll be there. As soon as we get back with some blast jewels. Because you're going to adopt me."

I think I was getting used to her. I wasn't rocked by that, though it was nothing like what I had expected to hear. I had been thinking vaguely along the lines of blast jewels. She picks some up along with me, sells them, and buys a ticket off-planet, right?

That was silly, of course. She didn't need *me* to get blast jewels. She was the guide, not I, and it was her cycle. She could get as many jewels as she wanted, and probably already had. This scheme had to have something to do with me, personally, as I had known back in town and forgotten about. There was something she wanted from me.

"That's why you had to go with me? That's the fatal attraction? I don't understand."

"Your passport. I'm in love with your passport. On the blank labeled 'citizenship' it says 'Mars.' Under age it says, oh . . . about seventy-three." She was within a year, though I keep my appearance at about thirty.

"So?"

"So, my dear Kiku, you are visiting a planet which is groping its way into the stone age. A medieval planet, Mr. Kiku, that sets the age of majority at thirteen—a capricious and arbitrary figure, as I'm sure you'll agree. The laws of this planet state that certain rights of free citizens are withheld from minor citizens. Among these are liberty, the pursuit of hap-

piness, and the ability *to get out of the goddam place!*"
She startled me with her fury, coming so hard on the
heels of her usual amusing glibness. Her fists were
clenched. Malibu, sitting in her lap, looked sadly up
at his friend, then over to me.

She quickly brightened and bounced up to prepare
dinner. She would not respond to my questions. The
subject was closed for the day.

I was ready to turn back the next day. Have you
ever had stiff legs? Probably not; if you go in for that
sort of thing—heavy physical labor—you are probably
one of those health nuts and keep yourself in shape. I
wasn't in shape, and I thought I'd die. For a panicky
moment I thought I *was* dying.

Luckily, Ember had anticipated it. She knew I was
a desk jockey, and she knew how pitifully under-con-
ditioned Martians tend to be. Added to the sedentary
life styles of most modern people, we Martians come
off even worse than the majority because Mars' gravity
never gives us much of a challenge no matter how
hard we try. My leg muscles were like soft noodles.

She gave me an old-fashioned massage and a new-
fangled injection that killed off the accumulated poisons. In an hour I began to take a flickering interest
in the trip. So she loaded me onto the cycle and we
started off on another leg of the journey.

There's no way to measure the passage of time. The
sun gets flatter and wider, but it's much too slow to
see. Sometime that day we passed a tributary of the
Reynolds Wrap River. It showed up as a bright line in
my right eye, as a crusted, sluggish semiglacier in my
left. Molten aluminum, I was told. Malibu knew what
it was, and barked plaintively for us to stop so he
could go for a slide. Ember wouldn't let him.

You can't get lost on Venus, not if you can still see.
The river had been visible since we left Prosperity,
though I hadn't known what it was. We could still see
the town behind us and the mountain range in front
of us and even the desert. It was a little ways up the
slope of the bowl. Ember said that meant it was still

about three days' journey away from us. It takes practice to judge distance. Ember kept trying to point out Venusburg, which was several thousand kilometers behind us. She said it was easily visible as a tiny point on a clear day. I never spotted it.

We talked a lot as we pedaled. There was nothing else to do and, besides, she was fun to talk to. She told me more of her plan for getting off Venus and filled my head with her naive ideas of what other planets were like.

It was a subtle selling campaign. We started off with her being the advocate for her crazy plan. At some point it evolved into an assumption. She took it as settled that I would adopt her and take her to Mars with me. I half believed it myself.

On the fourth day I began to notice that the bowl was getting higher in front of us. I didn't know what was causing it until Ember called a halt and we hung there in the air. We were facing a solid line of rock that sloped gradually upward to a point about fifty meters higher than we were.

"What's the matter?" I asked, glad of the rest.

"The mountains are higher," she said matter-of-factly. "Let's turn to the right and see if we can find a pass."

"Higher? What are you talking about?"

"Higher. You know, taller, sticking up more than they did the last time I was around, of slightly greater magnitude in elevation, bigger than—"

"I know the definition of higher," I said. "But why? Are you sure?"

"Of course I'm sure. The air heater for the balloon is going flat-out; we're as high as we can go. The last time I came through here, it was plenty to get me across. But not today."

"Why?"

"Condensation. The topography can vary quite a bit here. Certain metals and rocks are molten on Venus. They boil off on a hot day, and they can condense on the mountain tops where it's cooler. Then they melt when it warms up and flow back to the valleys."

"You mean you brought me here in the middle of winter?"

She threw me a withering glance.

"You're the one who booked passage for winter. Besides, it's night, and it's not even midnight yet. I hadn't thought the mountains would be this high for another week."

"Can't we get around?"

She surveyed the slope critically.

"There's a permanent pass about five hundred kilometers to the east. But that would take us another week. Do you want to?"

"What's the alternative?"

"Parking the cycle here and going on foot. The desert is just over this range. With any luck we'll see our first jewels today."

I was realizing that I knew far too little about Venus to make a good decision. I had finally admitted to myself that I was lucky to have Ember along to keep me out of trouble.

"We'll do what you think best."

"All right. Turn hard left and we'll park."

We tethered the cycle by a long tungsten-alloy rope. The reason for that, I learned, was to prevent it from being buried in case there was more condensation while we were gone. It floated at the end of the cable with its heaters going full blast. And we started up the mountain.

Fifty meters doesn't sound like much. And it's not, on level ground. Try it sometime on a seventy-five-degree slope. Luckily for us, Ember had seen this possibility and come prepared with alpine equipment. She sank pitons here and there and kept us together with ropes and pulleys. I followed her lead, staying slightly behind her tagalong. It was uncanny how that thing followed her up, placing its feet in precisely the spot she had stepped. Behind me, my tagalong was doing the same thing. Then there was Malibu, almost running along, racing back to see how we were doing, going to the top and chattering about what was on the other side.

I don't suppose it would have been much for a mountain climber. Personally I'd have preferred to slide on down the mountainside and call it quits. I would have, but Ember just kept going up. I don't think I've ever been so tired as the moment when we reached the top and stood looking over the desert.

Ember pointed ahead of us.

"There's one of the jewels going off now," she said.

"Where?" I asked, barely interested. I could see nothing.

"You missed it. It's down lower. They don't form up this high. Don't worry, you'll see more by and by."

And down we went. This wasn't too hard. Ember set the example by sitting down in a smooth place and letting go. Malibu was close behind her, squealing happily as he bounced and rolled down the slippery rock face. I saw Ember hit a bump and go flying in the air to come down on her head. Her suit was already stiffened. She continued to bounce her way down, frozen in a sitting position.

I followed them down in the same way. I didn't much care for the idea of bouncing around like that, but I cared even less for a slow, painful descent. It wasn't too bad. You don't feel much after your suit freezes in impact mode. It expands slightly away from your skin and becomes harder than metal, cushioning you from anything but the most severe blows that could bounce your brain against your skull and give you internal injuries. We never got going nearly fast enough for that.

Ember helped me up at the bottom after my suit unfroze. She looked like she had enjoyed the ride. I hadn't. One bounce seemed to have impacted my back slightly. I didn't tell her about it but just started off after her, feeling a pain with each step.

"Where on Mars do you live?" she asked brightly.

"Uh? Oh, at Coprates. That's on the northern slope of the Canyon."

"Yes, I know. Tell me more about it. Where will we live? Do you have a surface apartment, or are you stuck down in the underground? I can hardly wait to see the place."

She was getting on my nerves. Maybe it was just the lower-back pain.

"What makes you think you're going with me?"

"But of course you're taking me back. You said, just—"

"I said nothing of the sort. If I had a recorder I could prove it to you. No, our conversations over the last days have been a series of monologues. You tell me what fun you're going to have when we get to Mars, and I just grunt something. That's because I haven't the heart, or haven't *had* the heart, to tell you what a hare-brained scheme you're talking about."

I think I had finally managed to drive a barb into her. At any rate, she didn't say anything for a while. She was realizing that she had overextended herself and was counting the spoils before the battle was won.

"What's hare-brained about it?" she said at last.

"Just everything."

"No, come on, tell me."

"What makes you think I want a daughter?"

She seemed relieved. "Oh, don't worry about that. I won't be any trouble. As soon as we land, you can file dissolution papers. I won't contest it. In fact, I can sign a binding agreement not to contest anything before you even adopt me. This is strictly a business arrangement, Kiku. You don't have to worry about being a mother to me. I don't need one. I'll—"

"What makes you think it's just a business arrangement to *me?*" I exploded. "Maybe I'm old-fashioned. Maybe I've got funny ideas. But I won't enter into an adoption of convenience. I've already had my one child, and I was a good parent. I won't adopt you just to get you to Mars. That's my final word."

She was studying my face. I think she decided I meant it.

"I can offer you twenty thousand Marks."

I swallowed hard.

"Where did you get that kind of money?"

"I told you I've been soaking the good people of Prosperity. What the hell is there for me to spend it on out here? I've been putting it away for an emergency like this. Up against an unfeeling Neanderthal with funny ideas about right and wrong, who——"

"That's enough of that." I'm ashamed to say that I was tempted. It's unpleasant to find that what you had thought of as moral scruples suddenly seem not quite so important in the face of a stack of money. But I was helped along by my backache and the nasty mood it had given me.

"You think you can buy me. Well, I'm not for sale. I told you, I think it's wrong."

"Well, *damn* you, Kiku, damn you to hell." She stomped her foot hard on the ground, and her tagalong redoubled the gesture. She was going to go on damning me, but we were blasted by an explosion as her foot hit the ground.

It had been quiet before, as I said. There's no wind, no animals, hardly anything to make a sound on Venus. But when a sound gets going, watch out. That thick atmosphere is murder. I thought my head was going to come off. The sound waves battered against our suits, partially stiffening them. The only thing that saved us from deafness was the millimeter of low-pressure air between the suit field and our eardrums. It cushioned the shock enough that we were left with just a ringing in our ears.

"What was that?" I asked.

Ember sat down on the ground. She hung her head, uninterested in anything but her own disappointment.

"Blast jewel," she said. "Over that way." She pointed, and I could see a dull glowing spot about a kilometer off. There were dozens of smaller points of light—infralight—scattered around the spot.

"You mean you set it off just by stomping the ground?"

She shrugged. "They're unstable. They're full of nitroglycerine, as near as anyone can figure."

"Well, let's go pick up the pieces."

"Go ahead." She was going limp on me. And she stayed that way, no matter how I cajoled her. By the time I finally got her on her feet, the glowing spots were gone, cooled off. We'd never find them now. She wouldn't talk to me as we continued down into the valley. All the rest of the day we were accompanied by distant gunshots.

We didn't talk much the next day. She tried several times to reopen the negotiations, but I made it clear that my mind was made up. I pointed out to her that I had rented her cycle and services according to the terms she had set. Absolutely free, she had said, except for consumables, which I had paid for. There had been no mention of adoption. If there had, I assured her, I would have turned her down just as I was doing now. Maybe I even believed it.

That was during the short time the morning after our argument when it seemed like she was having no more to do with the trip. She just sat there in the tent while I made breakfast. When it came time to go, she pouted and said she wasn't going looking for blast jewels, that she'd just as soon stay right there or turn around.

After I pointed out our verbal contract, she reluctantly got up. She didn't like it, but honored her word.

Hunting blast jewels proved to be a big anticlimax. I'd had visions of scouring the countryside for days. Then the exciting moment of finding one. Eureka! I'd have howled. The reality was nothing like that. Here's how you hunt blast jewels: you stomp down hard on the ground, wait a few seconds, then move on and stomp again. When you see and hear an explosion, you simply walk to where it occurred and pick them up. They're scattered all over, lit up in the infrared bands from the heat of the explosion. They might as well have had neon arrows flashing over them. Big adventure.

When we found one, we'd pick it up and pop it into a cooler mounted on our tagalongs. They are formed by the pressure of the explosion, but certain parts of them are volatile at Venus temperatures. These elements will boil out and leave you with a grayish powder in about three hours if you don't cool them down. I don't know why they lasted as long as they did. They were considerably hotter than the air when we picked them up. So I thought they should have melted right off.

Ember said it was the impaction of the crystalline lattice that gave the jewels the temporary strength to outlast the temperature. Things behave differently in the temperature and pressure extremes of Venus. As they cooled off, the lattice was weakened and a progressive decay set in. That's why it was important to get them as soon as possible after the explosion to get unflawed gems.

We spent the whole day at that. Eventually we collected about ten kilos of gems, ranging from pea size to a few the size of an apple.

I sat beside the campfire and examined them that night. Night by my watch, anyway. Another thing I was beginning to miss was the twenty-five-hour cycle of night and day. And while I was at it, moons. It would have cheered me up considerably to spot Diemos or Phobos that night. But the sun just squatted up there in the horizon, moving slowly to the north in preparation for its transition to the morning sky.

The jewels were beautiful, I'll say that much for them. They were a wine-red color, tinged with brown. But when the light caught them right, there was no predicting what I might see. Most of the raw gems were coated with a dull substance that hid their full glory. I experimented with chipping some of them. What was left behind when I flaked off the patina was a slippery surface that sparkled even in candlelight. Ember showed me how to suspend them from a string and strike them. Then they would ring like tiny bells, and every once in a while one would shed all its imperfections and emerge as a perfect eight-sided equilateral.

I was cooking for myself that day. Ember had

cooked from the first, but she no longer seemed interested in buttering me up.

"I hired on as a guide," she pointed out, with considerable venom. "Webster's defines guide as—"

"I know what a guide is."

"—and it says nothing about cooking. Will you marry me?"

"No." I wasn't even surprised.

"Same reasons?"

"Yes. I won't enter into an agreement like that lightly. Besides, you're too young."

"Legal age is twelve. I'll be twelve in one week."

"That's too young. On Mars you must be fourteen."

"What a dogmatist. You're not kidding, are you? Is it really fourteen?"

That's typical of her lack of knowledge of the place she was trying so hard to get to. I don't know where she got her ideas about Mars. I finally concluded that she made them up whole in her daydreams.

We ate the meal I prepared in silence, toying with our collection of jewels. I estimate that I had about a thousand Marks worth of uncut stones. And I was getting tired of the Venusian bush. I figured on spending another day collecting, then heading back for the cycle. It would probably be a relief for both of us. Ember could start laying traps for the next stupid tourist to reach town, or even head for Venusburg and try in earnest.

When I thought of that, I wondered why she was still out here. If she had the money to pay the tremendous bribe she had offered me, why wasn't she in town where the tourists were as thick as flies? I was going to ask her that. But she came up to me and sat down very close.

"Would you like to make love?" she asked.

I'd had about enough inducements. I snorted, got up, and walked through the wall of the tent.

Once outside, I regretted it. My back was hurting something terrible, and I belatedly realized that my inflatable mattress would not go through the wall of the tent. If I got it through somehow, it would only burn up. But I couldn't back out after walking out like that. I felt committed. Maybe I couldn't think straight because of the backache; I don't know. Anyway, I picked out a soft-looking spot of ground and lay down.

I can't say it was all that soft.

I came awake in the haze of pain. I knew, without trying, that if I moved I'd get a knife in my back. Naturally I wasn't anxious to try.

My arm was lying on something soft. I moved my head—confirming my suspicions about the knife—and saw that it was Ember. She was asleep, lying on her back. Malibu was curled up in her arm.

She was a silver-plated doll, with her mouth open and a look of relaxed vulnerability on her face. I felt a smile growing on my lips, just like the ones she had coaxed out of me back in Prosperity. I wondered why I'd been treating her so badly. At least it seemed to me that morning that I'd been treating her badly. Sure, she'd used me and tricked me and seemed to want to use me again. But what had she hurt? Who was suffering for it? I couldn't think of anyone at the moment. I resolved to apologize to her when she woke up and try to start over again. Maybe we could even reach some sort of accommodation on this adoption business.

And while I was at it, maybe I could unbend enough to ask her to take a look at my back. I hadn't even mentioned it to her, probably for fear of getting deeper in her debt. I was sure she wouldn't have taken payment for it in cash. She preferred flesh.

I was about to awaken her, but I happened to glance on my other side. There was something there. I almost didn't recognize it for what it was.

It was three meters away, growing from the cleft of two rocks. It was globular, half a meter across, and glowing a dull-reddish color. It looked like a soft gelatin.

It was a blast jewel, before the blast.

I was afraid to talk, then remembered that talking

would not affect the atmosphere around me and could
not set off the explosion. I had a radio transmitter in
my throat and a receiver in my ear. That's how you
talk on Venus; you subvocalize and people can hear
you.

Moving very carefully, I reached over and gently
touched Ember on the shoulder.

She came awake quietly, stretched, and started to
get up.

"Don't move," I said, in what I hoped was a whisper. It's hard to do when you're subvocalizing, but I
wanted to impress on her that something was wrong.

She came alert, but didn't move.

"Look over to your right. Move very slowly. Don't
scrape against the ground or anything. I don't know
what to do."

She looked, said nothing.

"You're not alone, Kiku," she finally whispered.
"This is one I never heard of."

"How did it happen?"

"It must have formed during the night. No one knows
much about how they form or how long it takes. No
one's ever been closer than about five hundred meters
to one. They always explode before you can get that
close. Even the vibrations from the prop of a cycle will
set them off before you can get close enough to see
them."

"So what do we do?"

She looked at me. It's hard to read expressions on a
reflective face, but I think she was scared. I know I
was.

"I'd say sit tight."

"How dangerous is this?"

"Brother. I don't know. There's going to be quite a
bang when that monster goes off. Our suits will protect
us from most of it. But it's going to lift us and accelerate us *very* fast. That kind of sharp acceleration
can mess up your insides. I'd say a concussion at the
very least."

I gulped. "Then—"

"Just sit tight. I'm thinking."

So was I. I was frozen there with a hot knife some-where in my back. I knew I'd have to squirm sometime. The damn thing was moving.

I blinked, afraid to rub my eyes, and looked again. No, it wasn't. Not on the outside anyway. It was more like the movement you can see inside a living cell be-neath a microscope. Internal flows, exchanges of fluids from here to there. I watched it and was hypnotized.

There were worlds in the jewel. There was ancient Barsoom of my childhood fairy tales; there was Middle Earth with brooding castles and sentient forests. The jewel was a window into something unimaginable, a place where there were no questions and no emotions but a vast awareness. It was dark and wet without menace. It was growing, and yet complete as it came into being. It was bigger than this ball of hot mud called Venus and had its roots down in the core of the planet. There was no corner of the universe that it did not reach.

It was aware of me. I felt it touch me and felt no surprise. It examined me in passing but was totally un-interested. I posed no questions for it, whatever it was. It already knew me and had always known me.

I felt an overpowering attraction. The thing was ex-erting no influence on me; the attraction was a yearn-ing within me. I was reaching for a completion that the jewel possessed and I knew I could never have. Life would always be a series of mysteries for me. For the jewel, there was nothing but awareness. Awareness of everything.

I wrenched my eyes away at the last possible instant. I was covered in sweat, and I knew I'd look back in a moment. It was the most beautiful thing I will ever see.

"Kiku, listen to me."

"What?" I remembered Ember as from a huge dis-tance.

"Listen. Wake up. Don't look at that thing."

"Ember, do you see anything? Do you feel some-thing?"

"I see something. I . . . I don't want to talk about

it. I can't talk about it. Wake up, Kiku, and don't look back."

I felt like I was already a pillar of salt; so why not look back? I knew that my life would never be quite like what it had been. It was like some sort of involuntary religious conversion, as if all of a sudden I knew what the universe was for. The universe was a beautiful silk-lined box for the display of the jewel I had just beheld.

"Kiku, that thing should already have gone off. We shouldn't be here. I moved when I woke up. I tried to sneak up on one before and got five hundred meters away from it. I set my foot down soft enough to walk on water, and it blew. So this thing can't be here."

"That's nice," I said. "How do we cope with the fact that it *is* here?"

"All right, all right, it is here. But it must not be finished. It must not have enough nitro in it yet to blow up. Maybe we can get away."

I looked back at it, then away again. It was like my eyes were welded to it with elastic bands; they'd stretch enough to let me turn away, but they kept pulling me back.

"I'm not sure I want to."

"I know," she whispered. "I . . . hold on, don't look back. We have to get away."

"Listen," I said, looking at her with an act of will. "Maybe one of us can get away. Maybe both. But it's more important that you not be injured. If I'm hurt, you can maybe fix me up. If you're hurt, you'll probably die, and if we're both hurt, we're dead."

"Yeah. So?"

"So, I'm the closest to the jewel. You can start backing away from it first, and I'll follow you. I'll shield you from the worst of the blast, if it goes off. How does that sound?"

"Not too good." But she thought it over and could see no flaws in my reasoning. I think she didn't relish being the protected instead of the heroine. Childish, but natural. She proved her maturity by bowing to the inevitable.

"All right. I'll try to get ten meters from it. I'll let you know when I'm there, and you can move back. I think we can survive it at ten meters."

"Twenty."

"But . . . oh, all right. Twenty. Good luck, Kiku. I think I love you." She paused. "Uh, Kiku?"

"What is it? You should get moving. We don't know how long it'll stay stable."

"All right. But I have to say this. My offer last night, the one that got you so angry?"

"Yeah?"

"Well, it wasn't meant as a bribe. I mean, like the twenty thousand Marks. I just . . . well, I don't know much about that yet. I guess it was the wrong time?"

"Yeah, but don't worry about it. Just get moving."

She did, a centimeter at a time. It was lucky that neither of us had to worry about holding our breath. I think the tension would have been unbearable.

And I looked back. I couldn't help it. I was in the sanctuary of a cosmic church when I heard her calling me. I don't know what sort of power she used to reach me where I was. She was crying.

"Kiku, please listen to me."

"Huh? Oh, what is it?"

She sobbed in relief. "Oh, Christ, I've been calling you for an hour. *Please* come on. Over here. I'm back far enough."

My head was foggy. "Oh, Ember, there's no hurry. I want to look at it just another minute. Hang on."

"*No!* If you don't start moving right this minute, I'm coming back and I'll drag you out."

"You can't do—Oh. All right, I'm coming." I looked over at her sitting on her knees. Malibu was beside her. The little otter was staring in my direction. I looked at her and took a sliding step, scuttling on my back. My back was not something to think about.

I got two meters back, then three. I had to stop to rest. I looked at the jewel, then back at Ember. It was hard to tell which drew me the strongest. I must have reached a balance point. I could have gone either way.

Then a small silver streak came at me, running as fast as it could go. It reached me and dived across. *"Malibu!"* Ember screamed. I turned. The otter seemed happier than I ever saw him, even in the waterslide in town. He leaped, right at the jewel. . . .

Regaining consciousness was a very gradual business. There was no dividing line between different states of awareness for two reasons: I was deaf, and I was blind. So I cannot say when I went from dreams to reality; the blend was too uniform, there wasn't enough change to notice.

I don't remember learning that I was deaf and blind. I don't remember learning the hand-spelling language that Ember talked to me with. The first rational moment that I can recall as such was when Ember was telling me her plans to get back to Prosperity.

I told her to do whatever she felt best, that she was in complete control. I was desolated to realize that I was not where I had thought I was. My dreams had been of Barsoom. I thought I had become a blast jewel and had been waiting in a sort of detached ecstasy for the moment of explosion.

She operated on my left eye and managed to restore some vision. I could see things that were a meter from my face, hazily. Everything else was shadows. At least she was able to write things on sheets of paper and hold them up for me to see. It made things quicker. I learned that she was deaf, too. And Malibu was dead. Or might be. She had put him in the cooler and thought she might be able to patch him up when she got back. If not, she could always make another otter.

I told her about my back. She was shocked to hear that I had hurt it on the slide down the mountain, but she had sense enough not to scold me about it. It was short work to fix it up. Nothing but a bruised disc, she told me.

It would be tedious to describe all of our trip back. It was difficult, because neither of us knew much about blindness. But I was able to adjust pretty quickly.

Being led by the hand was easy enough, and I
stumbled only rarely after the first day. On the second
day we scaled the mountains, and my tagalong mal-
functioned. Ember discarded it and we traded off with
hers. We could only do it when I was sitting still, as
hers was made for a much shorter person. If I tried
to walk with it, it quickly fell behind and jerked me
off balance.

Then it was a matter of being set on the cycle and
pedaling. There was nothing to do but pedal. I missed
the talking we did on the way out. I missed the blast
jewel. I wondered if I'd ever adjust to life without it.

But the memory had faded when we arrived back
at Prosperity. I don't think the human mind can really
contain something of that magnitude. It was slipping
away from me by the hour, like a dream fades away
in the morning. I found it hard to remember what it
was that was so great about the experience. To this
day, I can't really tell about it except in riddles. I'm
left with shadows. I feel like an earthworm who has
been shown a sunset and has no place to store the
memory.

Back in town it was a simple matter for Ember to
restore our hearing. She just didn't happen to be carrying any spare eardrums in her first-aid kit.

"It was an oversight," she told me. "Looking back,
it seems obvious that the most likely injury from a
blast jewel would be burst eardrums. I just didn't
think."

"Don't worry about it. You did beautifully."

She grinned at me. "Yes, I did, didn't I?"

The vision was a larger problem. She didn't have
any spare eyes and no one in town was willing to sell
one of theirs at any price. She gave me one of hers as
as a temporary measure. She kept her infraeye and
took to wearing an eye patch over the other. It made
her look bloodthirsty. She told me to buy another at
Venusburg, as our blood types weren't much of a
match. My body would reject it in about three weeks.

The day came for the weekly departure of the blimp
to Last Chance. We were sitting in her workshop,

facing each other with our legs crossed and the pile of blast jewels between us.

They looked awful. Oh, they hadn't changed. We had even polished them up until they sparkled three times as much as they had back in the firelight of our tent. But now we could see them for the rotten, yellowed, broken fragments of bone that they were. We had told no one what we had seen out in the Fahrenheit Desert. There was no way to check on it, and all our experience had been purely subjective. Nothing that would stand up in a laboratory. We were the only ones who knew their true nature. Probably we would always remain the only ones. What could we tell anyone?

"What do you think will happen?" I asked.

She looked at me keenly. "I think you already know that."

"Yeah." Whatever they were, however they survived and reproduced, the one fact we knew for sure was that they couldn't survive within a hundred kilometers of a city. Once there had been blast jewels in the very spot where we were sitting. And humans do expand. Once again, we would not know what we were destroying.

I couldn't keep the jewels. I felt like a ghoul. I tried to give them to Ember, but she wouldn't have them either.

"Shouldn't we tell someone?" Ember asked.

"Sure. Tell anyone you want. Don't expect people to start tiptoeing until you can prove something to them. Maybe not even then."

"Well, it looks like I'm going to spend a few more years tiptoeing. I find I just can't bring myself to stomp on the ground."

I was puzzled. "Why? You'll be on Mars. I don't think the vibrations will travel that far."

She stared at me. "What's this?"

There was a brief confusion; then I found myself apologizing profusely to her, and she was laughing and telling me what a dirty rat I was, then taking it back

and saying I could play that kind of trick on her any-
time I wanted.

It was a misunderstanding. I honestly thought I had
told her about my change of heart while I was deaf
and blind. It must have been a dream, because she
hadn't gotten it and had assumed the answer was a
permanent no. She had said nothing about adoption
since the explosion.

"I couldn't bring myself to pester you about it anymore, after what you did for me," she said, breathless
with excitement. "I owe you a lot, maybe my life.
And I used you badly when you first got here."

I denied it, and told her I had thought she was not
talking about it because she thought it was in the bag.

"When did you change your mind?" she asked.

I thought back. "At first I thought it was while you
were caring for me when I was so helpless. Now I can
recall when it was. It was shortly after I walked out
of the tent for that last night on the ground."

She couldn't find anything to say about that. She just
beamed at me. I began to wonder what sort of papers
I'd be signing when we got to Venusburg: adoption, or
marriage contract.

I didn't worry about it. It's uncertainties like that
which make life interesting. We got up together, leaving the pile of jewels on the floor. Walking softly, we
hurried out to catch the blimp.

ALGIRDAS JONAS BUDRYS

Science Fiction in the Marketplace

Algirdas Jonas Budrys, professionally known as Algis Budrys, Paul Janvier, John A. Sentry, and other names—but primarily as Algis Budrys—is a remarkable writer who burst like a skyrocket on the skies of science fiction in the early fifties, and has since established a remarkable career not only as a writer but as an editor, translator, speech writer, up to the early 1960's when events restricted his work as a freelance writer. Recently he has returned to auctorial activities, to everyone's pleasure.

He is a most active man. In addition to all his other work, he has written over a hundred and twenty science fiction stories and eight science fiction novels. He has also published a large number of non-science fiction stories in such magazines as THE SATURDAY EVENING POST and PLAYBOY, and over a hundred articles in such publications as THE NEW YORK TIMES, THE CONGRESSIONAL RECORD, ESQUIRE, THE NEW REPUBLIC. He has written biographies. His novels have often been nominated for Best Novel in their respective years of appearance. The magazine version of one of these, "Rogue Moon," was voted into the Hall of Fame by Science Fiction Writers of America; and has had many appearances in the best-of-the-year anthologies. A short story of his, "The Master of the Hounds" in THE SATURDAY EVENING POST, won the Mystery Writers of America Edgar Special Award.

He is renowned as a science fiction critic, with numerous essays, review columns in various science fiction genre magazines, and in the book industry, trade publications. The renown is justified. He is as unique in his dissection of an essay question as he is in construction of his classic novels such as ROGUE MOON, FALLING TORCH, and MICHAELMAS. He is, therefore, the ideal person to explore the topic of the article that follows.

The "science fiction" shelves in the stores are crowded, showing healthy turnover, and proliferating. But there's some question of what it is they sell under that label.

It's not so much the Conan stories or the fantasy which are mixed in with what a strict constructionist would call science fiction. We now have the "SF" carry-all into which we comfortably tuck everything the "science fiction" audience will buy, and "SF" can readily stand for "Speculative Fiction" or "Social Fabulation," or "Somehow It Fits," as you like. (A "Sci-Fi," of course, is a stereo apparatus in a depressed mood.)

And the "Bermuda Triangle" books eventually move out once the store manager gets it through his head that SF buyers have a different set of superstitions.

But there's a major problem in determining what sort of SF is worthy of selling. It is not, of course, a major problem to readers—they know what they want, and buy it. Spending their own money for it tends to absolve their consciences of the need to decide whether they have proper taste or lack of it. But for the rest of us—the writers, the critics, the teachers, and the scholars—this has become a matter of great moment. And to some extent this affects the reader, because it interferes between him and a clear view of the product.

Being something of a reader myself, I find it necessary to ignore the favorable quotations plastered over the cover. Since they are frequently quite clever, and always so sure of themselves, I have from time to time purchased books which read rather borderline when a few pages are sampled, but which do, I am assured, contain sterling qualities in there someplace. What I usually find instead are places where the author knew an instance of sterling quality should occur; critics finding the same place have then been kind enough to give him credit for shipping at least an empty crate to market.

On the other hand, I have from time to time purchased out of sheer desperation books with titles like "Cosmic Head-Breaker" or "The Menace from Shrdlu!" simply because there was nothing else I hadn't read. When one of these turns out to be literate, entertaining, and thoughtful, I then have to explain to my friends what I'm doing recommending a story blurbed as "Two Outcasts and a Joygirl Challenge the Stars!" There is no explaining the cover art, which resembles the posters at the All-Night Underground theater. Well, unlike the art on the critically acclaimed book, it is at least representational, if overwrought.

Actually, I think we readers are accustomed to this game and don't get caught out too often anymore. But what used to be merely an understood way of jollying the customer has now become symptomatic of an intense polarization within the professional SF community. And this—insofar as it confuses apprentice writers, distracts people such as librarians who have taken a "science fiction" course because they would like to know more about the field, and causes bookstore managers to lose faith in any meaningful correlation between rave reviews and sales—does affect readers immediately, and will affect what is offered to them in the future.

There must be thousands of coherent ways in which to view SF—at least as many as there are writers and editors. I think it's entirely likely that there must in fact be as many different ways as there are individual readers, because I have never met two people who read the same story the same way. In all the time I have been keeping my eyes and ears open, I have never heard a believable explanation of how reading works. I haven't heard many explanations of any kind. But let us not bog down on this point. As a practical matter, there are now only two points of view—the "academic," and what I guess might be called the "commercial." If there is middle ground, or ground beyond the pale, no one standing on it has much chance to be heard for the present.

In a way, that's good. Simplifying an incredibly complicated situation has at least made argument possible, and possibly fruitful argument. A better understanding of who we are and what we do may eventually result in our doing something that readers will like even better. But meanwhile, watch out for traps.

As Professor Gunn's essay indicates, it's difficult to discuss academe's position without constructing a straw opponent and stuffing it with pat attitudes. But how about "A storyteller will outsell a writer"? When I surveyed the top SF editors on behalf of this essay, that was not only the best direct quote but an accurate summary of the consensus among the people who do the most to stock the bookstore shelves with a product that makes its publishers happy. On the surface, such a statement is not only oversimplified but full of undefined terms, and paradoxical. But the context of polarization has made its meaning clear, if still oversimplified.

And you are not going to get the answer to "What is Truth?" from me, either—at least, not here—because the subject is simply too complex for definition within a brief piece of informal prose. All I can do is oversimplify for you in a different way, and from then on both of us take our chances. As follows:

Science fiction is overwhelmingly commercial. The

genre we recognize today is founded on Hugo Gernsback's discovery in the 1920's that he could sell
"scientifiction" on the American newsstand in a genre
magazine, namely *Amazing Stories*. It is further condi-
tioned by the mighty and in some sense immortal personality of John W. Campbell, Jr., author of wildly
successful "superscience" stories in the early 1930's,
and then as editor of *Astounding,* the magazine that
made a go of "science fiction" when "scientifiction"
and "superscience" proved to be flops on any long-
term basis. By inspiration and hard-nosed trial and
error, Campbell evolved the first respectable and yet
commercial SF product for the mass market. The
highest percentage of everything—nearly everything—
you see in SF today is either evolved from Campbellian
science fiction or done in deliberate reaction against it.

Campbell was many men, as most geniuses are,
and not all of them were proven right in the end. But
when he sat behind his editorial desk, he was first and
foremost concerned with what the public would buy.
He knew what he personally liked, and he found out
what he could tolerate. He was aware that there were
competing media which—almost always throughout
his career at *ASF*—numbered among them one or
more titles that outsold him. First the Ray Palmer-
edited *Amazing Stories* from Ziff-Davis, and then the
1950's *Startling Stories* from the Thrilling pulp group,
had that distinction. Both were in a sense descended
from Gernsback predecessors. Both were unabashed
pulps with a minimal science content—*Amazing* in
particular at one point outsold *ASF* nearly three-to-one
by verging on lunacy. What Campbell looked for,
among the larger pool of people who would buy magazines with spaceships on their covers, were people
with whom he could relate on a dignified level. He
found them.

Campbell wedded believable technological extrapolation with social speculation. He isolated a literate
audience by creating a stable of competent prose technicians who were also equipped by education and
intelligence to propose believable social situations aris-

ing from advances in technology. Neither the writers nor the readers were, generally speaking, educated in the arts, and few of them saw as an art what Campbell now labelled "science fiction," but what Robert A. Heinlein was soon to propose was "speculative fiction."

When Raymond Healy and J. Francis McComas edited the excellent *Adventures in Time and Space* in 1948 as the definitive SF anthology, it was almost solidly Campbellian. It defined a "Golden Age" in *ASF* over the period of, roughly, 1938 to some time midway in World War II, and it made Campbellian SF synonymous with their coined term "modern science fiction."

The "Golden Age" in hindsight has since been extended into the late 1940's, and tacked on to it is the first flush of *The Magazine of Fantasy and Science Fiction* and *Galaxy Magazine.* Both those new rivals of the earliest 1950's became repositories for stories and writers who, Campbell-trained and indoctrinated, were escaping the older Campbell's net. (In many ways, as Campbell's thinking evolved, these major competitors often house more "modern science fiction" than was to be found in *ASF.*)

"Modern science fiction," immediately became the only worthwhile standard. McComas was one of *F&SF*'s two founding editors. *Galaxy*'s editor was Horace Gold, whose every effort to attract some other audience and promulgate a more generally saleable but still serious SF is perceivable as evidence for a pervasive consciousness of Campbell. No one studied each new issue of *ASF* more attentively, or more fervently.

"Modern science fiction" was "good." Healy and McComas had proven it so, and no one asked whether only it was "good," or whether the bases of this judgment, which was founded on a functional, technical appraisal of a short list of standard ingredients, were the only bases possible.

The major critic of his day, Damon Knight, taught a great many of us specifically what was "bad" about "half-bad" work; more than that, he taught us to be concerned about logic as well as prose craftsmanship. He did it by writing functional analyses, and these by their nature always measured accomplishment against some standard. Although Knight himself was aware of many creative modes, and lobbied for them, he went against Campbell by implication, not direct statement, and his implications emerge only in hindsight now. At the time, he was perceived generally as a Campbellian, so tall did Campbell and "modern science fiction" stand. That fault is ours, not Knight's.

In doing his work, Knight was apt to expose one or another Campbell author less than perfect. These were perceived as piquant, funny instances, not as a general examination. Knight never published an essay directly exploring the limitations of breadth or depth in "modern science fiction" as synonymous with Campbellianism, which they were in most eyes. Except for a tentative theory of symbolic function which Knight founded on James Blish's superficially flawed but peculiarly effective story, "Common Time," his criticism never proposed anything radical. He was copied in this restricted mode by anyone with pretensions to scholarship. The result in the eyes of the SF community was a tacit validation of the Campbellian ideal.

"Modern science fiction" is, at its best, excellent writing of one kind of SF. It was the best of its time, and the direct progenitor of whatever was seen as good in the evolving SF of the 1950's and the early 1960's.

During this period, which saw heavy reprinting of 1940's serials as books, and prominent anthologization of "modern science fiction," there was a spate of unanimity between the fledgling critical establishment and the publishers. In what was then a comparatively small bookstore market, sales efforts were directed at the Campbellian audience and seemingly there was no other which would support sales. Marginal publishers with nonCampbellian titles were scored by the reviewers and the letter-writing members of the audience, and found themselves on the remainder shelves.

Specifically why this happened is a question that

requires further study. Superficially, it appears there were only two nonCampbellian sources of SF. One, the work available to publishers with marginal budgets and frequently idiosyncratic or naive editorial taste, was reprinting from the raggedy-edged heap of pulps which flourished in the decade of newsstand genre fiction preceding the advent of home television in the late 1940's. The longer the stories in those media, the worse they tended to be as examples of either literature or speculation. Two, good work outside the Campbellian universe was apt to be marketed as "suspense" or "allegory," or, when by a writer such as Aldous Huxley or George Orwell, obviously something from the main body of literature, which was seen as excluding SF.

This view of the situation, and restricted sales, continued until Kingsley Amis came to this country in the mid-fifties to present a series of lectures at Princeton. These were later collected as *New Maps of Hell,* the first nonCampbellian (and hence "nonKnightly") body of SF criticism which had to be generally respected. It represented a view so shockingly disruptive of "modern science fiction" standards that many members of the SF community were unable to assimilate it.

For years, most reaction to Amis was less reasonable than it was outraged. In some quarters, it was puzzled; here was a consistent view of SF measured as social satire, embodying Amis's "comic inferno" term, lent weight by ivied halls, and implying an artistic accomplishment at some hands—notably Frederik Pohl's—where Campbellians had simply read competence underlying a kind of frivolity. (*The Space Merchants,* for instance, was a notably successful commercial property of its time, but most SF community members saw it as technically flawed and certainly not a serious social extrapolation.)

Amis in fact endures. Although his view is as narrow as Campbell's, it implies greater depths, and certainly depths which are more susceptible to academic examination than are such concrete matters as whether the author has clearly stated who struck Henry. Or, for that matter, whether he struck him with anything that makes sense in terms of physical laws. What is important to Amis is the author's innate wit, whether presented in jest or not, and to some extent what the author's intellectual intention may have been.

Amis represents an awareness of the thing Campbell ignored; the effect on the author's work of the things covered in a Liberal Arts curriculum. Even when the author himself denies any such bent, criticism from the Amis standpoint is fully entitled to discuss his work as if it were otherwise, and to measure its value relative to what it accomplishes in those terms. In other words, SF is art—conscious or unconscious, but art, and whatever artistic can be found in it is freely assimilable into the growing body of study of SF as an art. Curiously enough, although this school of thought lends weight to the product of intellect, it contains at its core the statement that art is independent of intellect. That is a true statement in my experience, but few scholars who have elaborated the "literary" view of SF appear at all willing to work with or discuss it, and most "literary" critics write as if authors always build their fabulations in every detail on some sort of scrupulous intellectual model.

When Amis appeared, the effect of his views gathered momentum simultaneously with the founding of the Milford Science Fiction Writers' Conference by Damon Knight, James Blish, and Judith Merril.

Milford and its lineal descendant, the famous Clarion SF writing course, have been greatly and cumulatively influential since the mid-1950's. Their alumni are the most critically appreciated new SF authors. Some of the older, Campbellian authors Milford attracted show major subsequent changes in the technique and attitude of their work. At Milford, in the context of a few individuals intensely confined to one room, it became possible to understand that Knight's thinking was complex and eclectic—as we all should have known from his artificially aborted 1951 magazine, *Worlds Beyond,* and as anyone can see now from looking at his *Orbit* series of original anthologies.

Important as that is, it is only one of the American counterparts of what became the English "New Wave" movement represented by Michael Moorcock's *New Worlds* magazine, which surfaced the fierce overseas re-thinking of SF whose first sign here had been the Amis lecture. The "New Wave" was immediately challenged, but the challenge itself, like the reaction to *New Maps of Hell,* began the establishment in the U.S.A. of an active and growing critical and scholarly enterprise. It became possible for such men as Professor Gunn to pioneer college courses in SF—not in SF writing or editing, or similar craftsmanly pursuits, but in SF itself as a subject for study. This establishment formed links with scholarship first in England and then throughout the world, and is great in its numbers today.

It is not a question of who is "right" and who not, or of specifically what intellectual statement precipitated which art. Harlan Ellison, for instance, vehemently denied membership in the "New Wave." But the germ of the idea for his *Dangerous Visions* original anthologies came to him shortly after his first exposure to Milford, and in that beginning Judith Merril was to have been the editor. It is no longer a question of whether it's cloudy or sunny today; it's "What is the climate?"

From these beginnings—in which at one time most SF people were willing to believe that SF is somehow unique, while simultaneously groping to discover general literature standards that could be applied to it— we have come to the present pass.

It's impossible to tell how much of the current boom is the result of many people discussing SF in serious terms. Quite a bit of it, I would imagine. Certainly the people who discuss SF at all, as distinguished from those who just buy it and read it, discuss it in vocabularies derived from academe. And the day of the abashed SF writer—"Oh, I'm an engineer. Well, yes,

I do sometimes write little things for the magazines"—is over. But there is one small problem at the present time. Royalty statements indicate that, by and large, the SF written to academic standards does not sit well with the present readership at large.

There is no reason for the editors to be lying about the facts of the matter. An editor is paid for discovering audiences, the larger the better. Theoretical worth is irrelevant in that context. Editors of every theoretical persuasion have come and gone. The highest-paid, most prestigiously situated, most active editors in the field today—the survivors of years of campaigning—were essentially unanimous when I interviewed them. What sells best is "good story." What sells worst is "gloom and doom," "messages," and "artiness." Not one of them has enjoyed more than spot success with consciously "literary" works. Not one of them is any longer interested in bringing out more than an occasional title of the sort they claim academe favors most. There have been some who tried; none of them was supported by the SF audience.

Now let us go back and define some terms.

Academe in fact appreciates much of the SF that sells well; this is observed data. But a great deal of SF today is being written by people who intensely studied academic standards for SF before becoming writers of it, and who write as if to fit the verbal constructs of critics. This SF is of the kind that editors reject because experience has shown that SF in which the intellectualizing shows in the narrative—as distinguished from the story—is the kind that does not sell.

Pessimistic social concern is intellectually fashionable today, particularly in the academic setting. Again, the readers don't want it.

"Experimental" writing—the rediscovery as claimed innovations of such perennials as second-person or present-tense forms of address; the use of an intellectual resolution for a statement of idea, as distinguished from plot-resolution of a story; eccentric punctuation, sentence structure and paragraphing; multiple moods; direct interjections from author to reader —none of that is selling any better than it ever has since its first flush in the college quarterlies of the 1920's. Its appearance in a manuscript is immediately recognized by the top editors as "literary"—that is, visibly concerned with technique . . . with "writing," if you will, as distinguished from "storytelling."

The question is not whether the editors are "right." Surely anyone with any acquaintance of "academe" knows it is not the monolith some make it out to be. Rather, it more closely resembles a set of alphabet blocks tumbling down a circular staircase, and in there somewhere is a theory and a spokesman for any point of view one favors. So the editors cannot be completely right. And one of them at least, as an academically recognized scholar of the works of James Joyce, can hardly undervalue technical experimentation or claim that it cannot lead to worthwhile results.

Appositely, "academe," as Professor Gunn points out, is concerned at times with such nuts and bolts as "story," "plot," "characterization," and so forth. If it were not, it could not teach because it could not fully analyze.

The situation is complex, confused, and ironic. But while there may be an audience out there somewhere which gives a damn about all that, no one has found it.

Certainly, there are individual readers in quite respectable numbers who read, and discuss their reading, as if they appreciated the fine points of theory and the relative perfection of technique. But they do not exist in numbers that account for the sales figures of some SF work, and when that latter work is approximated in similar additional examples, it sells above average well. So there is a trend toward the maximum audience.

What does that maximum audience want? What is the essential ingredient that it finds attractive, and will search for? What makes it ignore the work of the conscious and acclaimed intellectualizer, in favor of writers who may appreciate academe and be appreciated by it, but who make no obvious bow to it in their writing?

If the endurance of *Star Trek* as a phenomenon is any indicator, the key ingredients occur most thickly in "modern science fiction." The basic premise of the voyages of the starship *Enterprise* is solidly Campbellian, and most of the individual episodes of that TV series would, with a little fleshing-up, fit very nicely in a 1940 *ASF*. There is something to be learned, however, from the fact that the "science" in *Star Trek* is pure set-decoration, and there is room to wonder just how essential "science"—i.e., consumer technology —is to "science fiction." It's also interesting to note that *Star Trek* has always been perceived as somehow different from the standard pulp-like TV adventure series—and more satisfying to those who like it at all.

This observation to my mind opens a door into an enormous room which ought to fill up with critics and scholars. *Star Trek* has undoubtedly created a major percentage of the SF reading audience today. There is no question but that "modern science fiction" is limited not only intellectually but artistically. It cannot illuminate as much of life as there obviously is. Yet Campbellianism may be stronger than ever today. Still, it cannot be true that the evolution of SF can go no further without leaving its audience behind, or else the readers are not in fact interested in going where no man has gone before on the ultimate frontier. That limitless frontier is the capacity of Man to be interested in himself.

I find it difficult to accept the proposition that SF is a somehow special form of literature, with its own rules, if those rules are assumed to be restrictive. I am much more ready to assert that there is evidence SF contains *more* of whatever essential it is that causes people to read fiction of any kind, and bit by bit over the years to come we are going to find it, by playing off "academe" and "commerce" against the private thing that happens within the mind of the artist, and which then communicates to the audience.

I think a place to start is in exploring how reading works. One common tie between the "academic" and the "editor" is that we are concerned with how fiction is made. We speak of components, functions, standards, and frequently these days we do things to encourage writers to display this concern publicly, in the manuscript itself. But readers are concerned with how stories are received. Those of us who have devoted our conscious lives to nuts, bolts, undercarriages, and tire pressures may have forgotten something about transportation.

JAMES GUNN

The Academic Viewpoint

James Gunn, author and professor of English at the University of Kansas, who began his writing of science fiction in 1948 and has since done some seventy stories and sixteen books while editing three more, is a master of two difficult disciplines. One is writing and the other is teaching. For over twenty years he has successfully accomplished what many a writing teacher and many a teaching writer has found impossible, the harnessing of these two highly creative occupations in one working tandem.

With all this, he has found time to serve as regional chairman of the American College Public Relations Association, and on the Information Committee of the National Association of State Universities and Land Grant Colleges. He has also won national awards for his work as an editor and a director of public relations. He has been awarded the Byron Caldwell Smith prize in recognition of literary achievement and has also been president of the Science Fiction Writers of America.

He has been a member of the Executive Committee of the Science Fiction Research Association, and was presented with the Pilgrim Award of SFRA in 1976. Also, he has been given a special award by the 1976 World Science Fiction Convention for his book ALTERNATE WORLDS.

He has written articles, verse, and criticism. He has done radio scripts, screen plays, and television plays. A number of his stories have been dramatized in both mediums. One, "The Immortal," was an ABC-TV "Movie of the Week" in 1969 and became an hour-long series, also titled THE IMMORTAL, in 1970. Meanwhile, his written work has been reprinted worldwide.

Consequently, if there is one writer in science fiction who is fully qualified in both areas, that of the writer and that of the academic scholar of science fiction, it is James Gunn. He is a professional behind the typewriter and equally a professional in the academic area, and as such, no one is quite as qualified as he to deal with the subject of the article that follows. . . .

When the dean of basketball coaches, the late Forrest C. "Phog" Allen, was asked by James Naismith, the inventor of basketball, what he intended to do with his life, Allen replied, "Coach basketball." Naismith responded, "You don't coach basketball; you just play it."

For many years a similar opinion existed about science fiction: you don't teach science fiction; you just read it.

As later events demonstrated, both opinions were incorrect. The first regular course in science fiction was taught at Colgate University in 1962 by Prof. Mark Hillegas, now at Southern Illinois, and Sam Moskowitz organized evening courses in science fiction at City College of New York in 1953 and 1954.

Since then science fiction has spread into thousands of college classrooms and tens of thousands of high schools, and even into junior high schools and primary schools.

This surprising interest of academia in science fiction has aroused suspicion and alarm among science fiction readers, writers, and editors. Their attitudes have been summed up by Ben Bova's editorial "Teaching Science Fiction" in *Analog* (June 1974) and Lester del Rey's "The Siren Song of Academe" in *Galaxy* (March 1975), and symbolized by *Locus* co-editor and co-publisher Dena Brown's comment at the 1970 organizing meeting of the Science Fiction Research Association, "Let's take science fiction out of the classroom and put it back in the gutter where it belongs."

Part of what frightens science fiction people about academia is the danger that it will be taught poorly, dustily, inadequately, or drably. But even if taught with knowledge, skill, and enthusiasm, science fiction may be perverted by the academic viewpoint, some of them believe.

Teachers, they suspect, look at books differently from ordinary readers, and, like Medusa, their look turns things to stone. Science fiction readers point at their own high school experiences of hating Shakespeare or Dickens because they were forced to read them.

Even at the college level, professors encounter the frequent student attitude: "Why do we have to analyze fiction or poetry? It ruins them."

These are the concerns of the science fiction world. How does academia respond?

First, the notion that all science fiction teachers are alike is simply lack of knowledge about what is done in the classroom. Science fiction is taught for a variety of reasons, at all levels. In colleges, for instance, it often is taught for its content to help teach political science or psychology, anthropology, religion, future studies, or even the hard sciences. Anthologies for these specific purposes multiply in publishers' catalogs. Most objections to the teaching of science fiction, however, do not concern themselves with this use, although a bit of feeling adheres to the exploitation of science fiction for some other purpose than the one God intended.

Even within English departments, teaching approaches vary. Some professors teach the ideas; some, the themes; some, the history and the genre; and some, the great books. In general, all of these may be dismissed from the concerns of the science fiction vested interests; if any of the subjects are taught knowledgeably and capably, the judgments of their teachers about ideas, themes, definitions, history, and great books need not coincide with those of any held within the science fiction world, where there is, after all, almost as great a diversity of opinion as may be found outside it.

In addition to the approaches listed above, some teachers may include one or more science fiction books in a course in contemporary literature, popular literature, or the literature of women, or of children, or of some other area of experience. And some professors teach science fiction as if it were any other kind of literature, and apply to it the same critical concerns they apply to other books.

Here, perhaps, lies the greatest possibility for a break with science fiction tradition. What values do teachers of literature search out when they teach science fiction—or, for that matter, fiction of any kind?

Surprising as it may be to critics of the teaching of literature, the first consideration is story. Story is as appealing to professors as it is to lay readers. "Pleasure in fiction is rooted in our response to narrative movement—to story itself," Professor Robert Scholes wrote in his essay, "As the Wall Crumbles," in *Nebula Ten.*

But story is relatively unambiguous, at least in a work of fiction in which story predominates, and teaching at all levels tends to gravitate toward those works whose qualities teaching can enhance. This is not to say that these works are necessarily best in some abstract sense, but that they are teachable. Many persons outside academia suggest that at this point science fiction is in danger: qualities in a piece of fiction may be overvalued simply because they are less accessible.

The danger is real. In some academic circles, as among a certain group of avant-garde writers, story has been discarded as too obvious or too easy. Susceptible students and readers have been persuaded that story is a lesser art, if it is an art at all, and difficulty, ambiguity, and obscurity are essential to good fiction. The critics of academia suggest that if these aspects of fiction are highly valued in classes, authors will be seduced into such corrupt practices.

The danger is real, but it is not as great as the doomsayers fear. Authors are not as susceptible as all that (if they're not doing their own thing they aren't worth much as authors), and the teaching of literature is not as pernicious as all that. Story still counts for much in a literature class.

Witness the fact that the books most frequently taught by academics (as reported by Jack Williamson in 1972) were Heinlein's *Stranger in a Strange Land*, Miller's *A Canticle for Leibowitz*, Wells's *The War of the Worlds*, Pohl and Kornbluth's *The Space Merchants*, Herbert's *Dune*, Huxley's *Brave New World*, Le Guin's *The Left Hand of Darkness*, Bradbury's *The Martian Chronicles*, Silverberg's *Science Fiction Hall of Fame*, Wells's *The Time Machine*, and Asimov's *I, Robot*. Other books among those a bit less frequently taught would reveal none unfamiliar to the average science fiction reader; the total list represents, with a few arguments, a reasonable "best" list for any knowledgeable fan, and even the arguable titles have been honored by science fiction critics and readers.

Admittedly, the list may reveal some bias toward what passes for excellence in writing, skill in characterization, or verisimilitude in description. Few teachers include "Doc" Smith or Edgar Rice Burroughs, from whose science fiction adventures a generation of readers were weaned (though I, for one, always include *A Princess of Mars*, and I would be surprised if some teacher somewhere does not teach *The Skylark of Space* or *Grey Lensman*).

What then do science fiction teachers look for in a work of science fiction?

They are concerned, of course, with teaching the art of reading and the skills of criticism (along with the ability to communicate) rather than merely the specific work at hand. They apply principles to texts, both to make the piece of prose, poetry, or drama more accessible but also to enable students to apply similar principles to reading they may do in other classes or outside of classes. They want students to get more out of their reading, to read more alertly, more knowledgeably, more enjoyably.

Critics who complain that this kind of approach to literature kills enjoyment are restricting the enjoyment of literature only to those natural readers who understand intuitively what is not immediately observable, or to those works that have no depths.

What is not immediately observable to a casual reader of science fiction? The best way to answer that question might be to list the aspects of fiction that a good teacher looks for.

1. CONSISTENCY OF STORY
2. STORY PREMISES
3. APPLICATION OF THE PREMISES
4. CREDIBILITY OF THE CHARACTERS
5. CONSISTENCY OF THEME
6. IMAGERY
7. STYLE
8. TOTAL ARTFULNESS
9. CHALLENGE TO THE IMAGINATION
10. OVERALL IMPRESSION

1. CONSISTENCY OF STORY. A good reader continually adjusts his expectations of a piece of fiction as the author gradually reveals the directions in which his characters are moving, or are being forced to move. A well-written work handles the reader's expectations skillfully, confidently, neither changing directions nor disappointing expectations previously aroused. A careless reader may never notice inconsistencies in various parts of a work, and a casual reader may forgive them. An author should be held to the highest standards of accountability, both for the improvement of reading and the improvement of writing; an author is not at

liberty to do what he wishes without accepting the consequences.

2. STORY PREMISES. A good reader picks up the clues an author plants about the foundations on which his world and his story rest. In a science fiction work, this includes the science and the sociology—the answers to the question: how did we get there from here? In a skillfully written work, if the reader grants the author's premises, he must grant the conclusions, but part of the tension of the work always exists between the conclusions and the premises. The casual reader misses an important part of the dialogue in which the good writer hopes to engage him, and allows the less-able writer to pass unchallenged.

3. APPLICATION OF THE PREMISES. A good reader challenges the writer at every point, debating the working out of the author's thesis, his arrival at the conclusions, checking back continually against what he already knows, theorizing that any discrepancy must be significant. This is not a tedious process but one that, once recognized, becomes automatic with the alert reader.

4. CREDIBILITY OF THE CHARACTERS. Are the characters real people? Should we take them seriously? Are they meant to be realistic? Do they react consistently? It is my thesis (see my chapter in Reginald Bretnor's symposium *The Craft of Science Fiction,* Harper & Row, 1976) that characters in a science fiction work should be judged differently from those in mainstream fiction (often they are more important as representatives than as individuals), but characters should be understandably motivated. They should not act arbitrarily or inconsistently; they should act for their own reasons and not for the author's convenience. This is not because of any abstract literary morality but because the fiction is better if they do.

5. CONSISTENCY OF THEME. Does the story have a message? Not all fiction has anything to say other than to reinforce the assumptions basic to the culture from which the fiction springs, such as: good will prevail, or good will prevail only if men and

women of intelligence and character work at it hard enough. But some fiction attempts to say something more—about the nature or goal of life, the nature or difficulties of society, or the nature or problems of people. The good reader asks what the work means besides its obvious story line. Ursula Le Guin's *The Left Hand of Darkness,* for instance, is about not only whether the world of Winter joins the Ekumen, not only whether Genly Ai is successful or even survives, but about the ways in which sex shapes our society and its institutions. Another question is how well the theme is woven into the fabric of the story, not appended to it like a sermon.

6. IMAGERY. One way in which meaning emerges from fiction is through the imagery implicit in the work, often without the conscious knowledge of author or reader—the literal images, the symbols, the similes, and the metaphors. Once teachers begin talking about images, symbols, and metaphors, the ordinary reader turns his mind off, and authors have been known to object to teachers reading something into their writing that they did not intend, often accusing teachers of falsifying what they were trying to do. As in most criticisms of teaching, there is some truth to the charge; some teachers and some critics build a mountain of interpretation out of a molehill of evidence, and many ignore the author's intention—indeed, it was a tenet of the so-called "new criticism" (now almost fifty years old) that considering the author's intention is a trap, called "the intentional fallacy." Nevertheless, images do occur in works of fiction, and they do influence the reactions of readers to the work. Examples abound, even in science fiction, from the power imagery of technology to the guilt imagery of the mad scientist in whatever his contemporary guise.

7. STYLE. Style is the manner in which words are chosen and put together. Complexity or uniqueness is not necessarily good. Sometimes simplicity or transparency are superior. What we term style is often mistakenly reserved for "high style," for individual mannerisms, for that which calls attention to itself,

but what a careful reader notices is the suitability of style to subject and the appropriateness of language and sentence structure—whether what is said is enhanced by the way it is said. Innumerable would-be writers have been misled by teachers who told them, "Before you can be a successful writer, you must find your own style." Fred Pohl is fond of quoting a French saying, "Style is the problem solved."

8. TOTAL ARTFULNESS. The different parts of a piece of fiction do not exist in isolation, though they often must be discussed in this fashion if they are to be understood. Few skills—from the golfer's swing to the dancer's routine—can be understood by watching them in their entirety. The separate acts must be broken down into understandable units that can be learned and then reassembled into the whole. All the considerations about fiction that have been discussed up to this point may in themselves be well done but they may not together form a coherent work, and then the good teacher points out why the whole is larger than the sum of its parts.

8. CHALLENGE TO THE IMAGINATION. A piece of fiction might have every virtue the teacher can describe and still be dull; and a piece of fiction can lack almost every virtue and still rise above its circumstances by the way in which it challenges the imagination. The teacher and the reader may wish that great ideas were matched by great execution, but it is not always so, and the good teacher recognizes the appeal of works that are otherwise deficient. This is not to say that the public is always right, but to recognize, as Professor Leslie Fiedler pointed out to an audience of science fiction writers a few years ago, "For too long critics have tried to tell readers why they should like what they don't like; they should be trying to discover why people like what they like."

10. OVERALL IMPRESSION. After a work has been analyzed—which means, literally, separated into its constituent parts—it must be put back together. Students object to having what they like dissected as if it were something dead, almost as much as they

object to being forced to study something they consider dead. After the good teacher has helped his students analyze any work of fiction, then, the teacher should help them regain their vision of the work in its entirety—its overall impression of readability, of narrative excitement, of fictional pleasure. The teacher should bring it back to life. It is a difficult task but not an impossible one.

Properly done, the study of literature does not diminish the enjoyment of reading; it enhances that enjoyment, just as a good critical article about a short story or a novel illuminates the work for the reader, who goes to it with new appreciation and understanding. To believe otherwise is to uphold the blessings of ignorance, to maintain that the individual's enjoyment of any complex art—and fiction is a complex art—depends upon how little he knows about it.

Science fiction has not achieved as much as it might because it has enjoyed few good critics. A critic is more than a reviewer; a reviewer discusses his personal evaluation of a work, while a critic relates his evaluation to larger principles and theories, to standards he or others have established for the greater body of work to which the piece at hand is related. Critics raise standards for writers as well as readers; we can be thankful for the work of Damon Knight, James Blish, D. Schuyler Miller, and a few others in its past, and the current work of Alexei and Cory Panshin, Lester del Rey, Joanna Russ, Barry Malzberg, the writers for *Delap's F&SF Review*, and A. J. Budrys.

Their judgments have not always coincided—there is no reason they should—but science fiction is better because they have judged and made their criteria plain. The judgments of academia may not be the same as those of science fiction critics or its readers, but, without having read Budrys's contribution to this volume, I would hazard the guess that his criteria for judging a work of science fiction are not much different from those I have set down here.

ISAAC ASIMOV

The Bicentennial Man

In the introduction to this Nebula Awards volume it was mentioned that science fiction writers—successful science fiction writers—are unique. No one, however, is quite as unusual as Isaac Asimov. He is unique in almost any direction you look. He has written more on more subjects, and better on more subjects, and more unexpectedly on most subjects, and in more ways on more subjects, than anyone else in the field. He writes poetry, limericks, short stories, novels, essays, articles, nonfiction books, trilogies, jokes, and so on—more of them than anyone else could imagine. He has written the first successful science fiction detective story, after being told by the revered John Campbell, long-time editor of ASTOUNDING and later ANALOG SCIENCE FICTION, that it couldn't be done. He has written curious articles about chemicals that have not yet been invented, such as a chemical that travels in time.

However did this remarkable man come to create this enormous body of work?

He was born January 2, 1920, apparently with an incredible appetite for reading and an equally incredible ability to recall almost everything he has ever read. A third talent, which did not surface until some little time after he had already made his name as a science fiction writer, was the talent of taking the turgid prose in which a great many other people write about matters in the field of science, history, and just about everything else, and turning it into a clear and readable language so effective that other people came very close to remembering the facts so presented as well as Isaac Asimov did himself. But it is as a writer of science fiction that we know and treasure him best. From his early classics in the field, novels such as I, ROBOT, The Foundation series, and PEBBLE IN THE SKY are some of his early science fiction that come to mind. His magnificent story NIGHTFALL and a host of others down the years lead us now to the award-winning novelette which follows, THE BICENTENNIAL MAN. In it we are back again with Isaac Asimov's three laws of robotics which have stood the test of time, and once again back up a novelette to be remembered.

I

Andrew Martin said, "Thank you," and took the seat offered him. He didn't look driven to the last resort, but he had been.

He didn't, actually, look anything, for there was a smooth blankness to his face, except for the sadness one imagined one saw in his eyes. His hair was smooth, light brown, rather fine; and he had no facial hair. He looked freshly and cleanly shaved. His clothes were distinctly old-fashioned, but neat, and predominantly a velvety red-purple in color.

Facing him from behind the desk was the surgeon. The nameplate on the desk included a fully identifying series of letters and numbers which Andrew didn't bother with. To call him Doctor would be quite enough.

"When can the operation be carried through, Doctor?" he asked.

Softly, with that certain inalienable note of respect that a robot always used to a human being, the surgeon said, "I am not certain, sir, that I understand how or upon whom such an operation could be performed."

There might have been a look of respectful intransigence on the surgeon's face, if a robot of his sort, in lightly bronzed stainless steel, could have such an expression—or any expression.

Andrew Martin studied the robot's right hand, his cutting hand, as it lay motionless on the desk. The fingers were long and were shaped into artistically metallic, looping curves so graceful and appropriate that one could imagine a scalpel fitting them and becoming, temporarily, one piece with them. There would be no hesitation in his work, no stumbling, no quivering, no mistakes. That confidence came with specialization, of course, a specialization so fiercely desired by humanity that few robots were, any longer, independently brained. A surgeon, of course, would have to be. But this one, though brained, was so limited in his capacity that he did not recognize Andrew, had probably never heard of him .

"Have you ever thought you would like to be a man?" Andrew asked.

The surgeon hesitated a moment, as though the question fitted nowhere in his allotted positronic pathways. "But I am a robot, sir."

"Would it be better to be a man?"

"If would be better, sir, to be a better surgeon. I could not be so if I were a man, but only if I were a more advanced robot. I would be pleased to be a more advanced robot."

"It does not offend you that I can order you about? That I can make you stand up, sit down, move right or left, by merely telling you to do so?"

"It is my pleasure to please you, sir. If your orders were to interfere with my functioning with respect to you or to any other human being, I would not obey you. The First Law, concerning my duty to human safety, would take precedence over the Second Law relating to obedience. Otherwise, obedience is my pleasure. Now, upon whom am I to perform this operation?"

"Upon me," Andrew said.

"But that is impossible. It is patently a damaging operation."

"That does not matter," said Andrew, calmly.

"I must not inflict damage," said the surgeon.

"On a human being, you must not," said Andrew, "but I, too, am a robot."

2

Andrew had appeared much more a robot when he had first been manufactured. He had then been as much a robot in appearance as any that had ever existed—smoothly designed and functional.

He had done well in the home to which he had been brought in those days when robots in households, or on the planet altogether, had been a rarity. There had been four in the home: Sir and Ma'am and Miss and Little Miss. He knew their names, of course, but he never used them. Sir was Gerald Martin.

His own serial number was NDR-. . . . He eventually forgot the numbers. It had been a long time, of course; but if he had wanted to remember, he could not have forgotten. He had not wanted to remember.

Little Miss had been the first to call him Andrew, because she could not use the letters, and all the rest followed her in doing so.

Little Miss . . . She had lived for ninety years and was long since dead. He had tried to call her Ma'am once, but she would not allow it. Little Miss she had been to her last day.

Andrew had been intended to perform the duties of a valet, a butler, even a lady's maid. Those were the experimental days for him and, indeed, for all robots anywhere save in the industrial and exploratory factories and stations off Earth.

The Martins enjoyed him, and half the time he was prevented from doing his work because Miss and Little Miss wanted to play with him. It was Miss who first understood how this might be arranged. "We order you to play with us and you must follow orders."

"I am sorry, Miss, but a prior order from Sir must surely take precedence."

But she said, "Daddy just said he *hoped* you would take care of the cleaning. That's not much of an order. I *order* you."

Sir did not mind. Sir was fond of Miss and of Little Miss, even more than Ma'am was; and Andrew was fond of them, too. At least, the effect they had upon his actions were those which in a human being would have been called the result of fondness. Andrew thought of it as fondness for he did not know any other word for it.

It was for Little Miss that Andrew had carved a pendant out of wood. She had ordered him to. Miss, it seemed, had received an ivorite pendant with scroll-work for her birthday and Little Miss was unhappy over it. She had only a piece of wood, which she gave Andrew together with a small kitchen knife.

He had done it quickly and Little Miss had said, "That's *nice,* Andrew. I'll show it to Daddy."

Sir would not believe it. "Where did you really get this, Mandy?" Mandy was what he called Little Miss. When Little Miss assured him she was really telling the truth, he turned to Andrew. "Did you do this, Andrew?"

"Yes, Sir."

"The design, too?"

"Yes, Sir."

"From what did you copy the design?"

"It is a geometric representation, Sir, that fits the grain of the wood."

The next day, Sir brought him another piece of wood—a larger one—and an electric vibro-knife. "Make something out of this, Andrew. Anything you want to," he said.

Andrew did so as Sir watched, then looked at the product a long time. After that, Andrew no longer waited on tables. He was ordered to read books on furniture design instead, and he learned to make cabinets and desks.

"These are amazing productions, Andrew," Sir soon told him.

"I enjoy doing them, Sir," Andrew admitted.

"Enjoy?"

"It makes the circuits of my brain somehow flow more easily. I have heard you use the word 'enjoy' and the way you use it fits the way I feel. I enjoy doing them, Sir."

3

Gerald Martin took Andrew to the regional offices of the United States Robots and Mechanical Men Corporation. As a member of the Regional Legislature he had no trouble at all in gaining an interview with the chief robopsychologist. In fact, it was only as a member of the Regional Legislature that he qualified as a robot owner in the first place—in those early days when robots were rare.

Andrew did not understand any of this at the time. But in later years, with greater learning, he could review that early scene and understand it in its proper light.

The robopsychologist, Merton Mansky, listened with a growing frown and more than once managed to stop his fingers at the point beyond which they would have irrevocably drummed on the table. He had drawn features and a lined forehead, but he might actually have been younger than he looked.

"Robotics is not an exact art, Mr. Martin," Mansky explained. "I cannot explain it to you in detail, but the mathematics governing the plotting of the positronic pathways is far too complicated to permit of any but approximate solutions. Naturally, since we build everything around the Three Laws, those are incontrovertible. We will, of course, replace your robot—"

"Not at all," said Sir. "There is no question of failure on his part. He performs his assigned duties perfectly. The point is he also carves wood in exquisite fashion and never the same twice. He produces works of art."

Mansky looked confused. "Strange. Of course, we're attempting generalized pathways these days. Really creative, you think?"

"See for yourself." Sir handed over a little sphere

of wood on which there was a playground scene in which the boys and girls were almost too small to make out, yet they were in perfect proportion and they blended so naturally with the grain that it, too, seemed to have been carved.

Mansky was incredulous. "*He* did that?" He handed it back with a shake of his head. "The luck of the draw. Something in the pathways."

"Can you do it again?"

"Probably not. Nothing like this has ever been reported."

"Good! I don't in the least mind Andrew's being the only one."

"I suspect that the company would like to have your robot back for study," Mansky said.

"Not a chance!" Sir said with sudden grimness. "Forget it." He turned to Andrew, "Let's go home, now."

4

Miss was dating boys and wasn't about the house much. It was Little Miss, not as little as she once was, who filled Andrew's horizon now. She never forgot that the very first piece of wood carving he had done had been for her. She kept it on a silver chain about her neck.

It was she who first objected to Sir's habit of giving away Andrew's work. "Come on, Dad, if anyone wants one of them, let him pay for it. It's worth it."

"It isn't like you to be greedy, Mandy."

"Not for us, Dad. For the artist."

Andrew had never heard the word before, and when he had a moment to himself he looked it up in the dictionary.

Then there was another trip, this time to Sir's lawyer.

"What do you think of this, John?" Sir asked.

The lawyer was John Finegold. He had white hair and a pudgy belly, and the rims of his contact lenses were tinted a bright green. He looked at the small plaque Sir had given him. "This is beautiful. But I've already heard the news. Isn't this a carving made by your robot? The one you've brought with you."

"Yes, Andrew does them. Don't you, Andrew?"

"Yes, Sir," said Andrew.

"How much would you pay for that, John?" Sir asked.

"I can't say. I'm not a collector of such things."

"Would you believe I have been offered two hundred and fifty dollars for that small thing. Andrew has made chairs that have sold for five hundred dollars. There's two hundred thousand dollars in the bank from Andrew's products."

"Good heavens, he's making you rich, Gerald."

"Half rich," said Sir. "Half of it is in an account in the name of Andrew Martin."

"The robot?"

"That's right, and I want to know if it's legal."

"Legal . . . ?" Feingold's chair creaked as he leaned back in it. "There are no precedents, Gerald. How did your robot sign the necessary papers?"

"He can sign his name. Now, is there anything further that ought to be done?"

"Um." Feingold's eyes seemed to turn inward for a moment. Then he said, "Well, we can set up a trust to handle all finances in his name and that will place a layer of insulation between him and the hostile world. Beyond that, my advice is you do nothing. No one has stopped you so far. If anyone objects, let *him* bring suit."

"And will you take the case if the suit is brought?"

"For a retainer, certainly."

"How much?"

"Something like that," Feingold said, and pointed to the wooden plaque.

"Fair enough," said Sir.

Feingold chuckled as he turned to the robot. "Andrew, are you pleased that you have money?"

"Yes, sir."

"What do you plan to do with it?"

"Pay for things, sir, which otherwise Sir would have to pay for. It would save him expense, sir."

5

Such occasions arose. Repairs were expensive, and revisions were even more so. With the years, new models of robots were produced and Sir saw to it that Andrew had the advantage of every new device, until he was a model of metallic excellence. It was all done at Andrew's expense. Andrew insisted on that.

Only his positronic pathways were untouched. Sir insisted on that.

"The new models aren't as good as you are, Andrew," he said. "The new robots are worthless. The company has learned to make the pathways more precise, more closely on the nose, more deeply on the track. The new robots don't shift. They do what they're designed for and never stray. I like you better."

"Thank you, Sir."

"And it's your doing, Andrew, don't you forget that. I am certain Mansky put an end to generalized pathways as soon as he had a good look at you. He didn't like the unpredictability. Do you know how many times he asked for you back so he could place you under study? Nine times! I never let him have you, though; and now that he's retired, we may have some peace."

So Sir's hair thinned and grayed and his face grew pouchy, while Andrew looked even better than he had when he first joined the family. Ma'am had joined an art colony somewhere in Europe, and Miss was a poet in New York. They wrote sometimes, but not often. Little Miss was married and lived not far away. She said she did not want to leave Andrew. When her child, Little Sir, was born, she let Andrew hold the bottle and feed him.

With the birth of a grandson, Andrew felt that Sir finally had someone to replace those who had gone. Therefore, it would not be so unfair now to come to him with the request.

"Sir, it is kind of you to have allowed me to spend my money as I wished."

"It was your money, Andrew."

"Only by your voluntary act, Sir. I do not believe the law would have stopped you from keeping it all."

"The law won't persuade me to do wrong, Andrew."

"Despite all expenses, and despite taxes, too, Sir, I have nearly six hundred thousand dollars."

"I know that, Andrew."

"I want to give it to you, Sir."

"I won't take it, Andrew."

"In exchange for something you can give me, Sir."

"Oh? What is that, Andrew?"

"My freedom, Sir."

"Your—"

"I wish to buy my freedom, Sir."

6

It wasn't that easy. Sir had flushed, had said, "For God's sake!" Then he had turned on his heel and stalked away.

It was Little Miss who finally brought him round, defiantly and harshly—and in front of Andrew. For thirty years no one had ever hesitated to talk in front of Andrew, whether or not the matter involved Andrew. He was only a robot.

"Dad, why are you taking this as a personal affront? He'll still be here. He'll still be loyal. He can't help that; it's built in. All he wants is a form of words. He wants to be called free. Is that so terrible? Hasn't he earned this chance? Heavens, he and I have been talking about it for years!"

"Talking about it for years, have you?"

"Yes, and over and over again he postponed it for fear he would hurt you. I *made* him put the matter up to you."

"He doesn't know what freedom is. He's a robot."

"Dad, you don't know him. He's read everything in the library. I don't know what he feels inside, but I don't know what *you* feel inside either. When you talk to him you'll find he reacts to the various abstractions as you and I do, and what else counts? If someone else's reactions are like your own, what more can you ask for?"

"The law won't take that attitude," Sir said, angrily. "See here, you!" He turned to Andrew with a deliberate grate in his voice. "I can't free you except by doing it legally. If this gets into the courts, you not only won't get your freedom but the law will take official cognizance of your money. They'll tell you that a robot has no right to earn money. Is this rigmarole worth losing your money?"

"Freedom is without price, Sir," said Andrew. "Even the chance of freedom is worth the money."

7

It seemed the court might also take the attitude that freedom was without price, and might decide that for no price, however great, could a robot buy its freedom.

The simple statement of the regional attorney who represented those who had brought a class action to oppose the freedom was this: "The word 'freedom' has no meaning when applied to a robot. Only a human being can be free." He said it several times, when it seemed appropriate; slowly, with his hand coming down rhythmically on the desk before him to mark the words.

Little Miss asked permission to speak on behalf of Andrew.

She was recognized by her full name, something Andrew had never heard pronounced before: "Amanda Laura Martin Charney may approach the bench."

"Thank you, Your Honor. I am not a lawyer and I don't know the proper way of phrasing things, but I hope you will listen to my meaning and ignore the words.

"Let's understand what it means to be free in Andrew's case. In some ways, he *is* free. I think it's at least twenty years since anyone in the Martin family gave him an order to do something that we felt he might not do of his own accord. But we can, if we wish, give him an order to do anything, couching it as harshly as we wish, because he is a machine that belongs to us. Why should we be in a position to do so, when he has served us so long, so faithfully, and has earned so much money for us? He owes us nothing more. The debit is entirely on the other side.

"Even if we were legally forbidden to place Andrew in involuntary servitude, he would still serve us voluntarily. Making him free would be a trick of words only, but it would mean much to him. It would give him everything and cost us nothing."

For a moment the judge seemed to be suppressing a smile. "I see your point, Mrs. Charney. The fact is that there is no binding law in this respect and no precedent. There is, however, the unspoken assumption that only a man may enjoy freedom. I can make new law here, subject to reversal in a higher court; but I cannot lightly run counter to that assumption. Let me address the robot. Andrew!"

"Yes, Your Honor."

It was the first time Andrew had spoken in court, and the judge seemed astonished for a moment at the human timbre of his voice.

"Why do you want to be free, Andrew? In what way will this matter to you?"

"Would *you* wish to be a slave, Your Honor," Andrew asked.

"But you are not a slave. You are a perfectly good robot—a genius of a robot, I am given to understand, capable of an artistic expression that can be matched nowhere. What more could you do if you were free?"

"Perhaps no more than I do now, Your Honor, but with greater joy. It has been said in this courtroom that only a human being can be free. It seems to me that only someone who *wishes* for freedom can be free. I wish for freedom."

And it was that statement that cued the judge. The crucial sentence in his decision was "There is no right to deny freedom to any object with a mind advanced enough to grasp the concept and desire the state."

It was eventually upheld by the World Court.

8

Sir remained displeased, and his harsh voice made Andrew feel as if he were being short-circuited. "I don't want your damned money, Andrew. I'll take it only because you won't feel free otherwise. From now on, you can select your own jobs and do them as you please. I will give you no orders, except this one: Do as you please. But I am still responsible for you. That's part of the court order. I hope you understand that."

Little Miss interrupted. "Don't be irascible, Dad. The responsibilty is no great chore. You know you won't have to do a thing. The Three Laws still hold."

"Then how is he free?"

"Are not human beings bound by their laws, Sir?" Andrew replied.

"I'm not going to argue." Sir left the room, and Andrew saw him only infrequently after that.

Little Miss came to see him frequently in the small house that had been built and made over for him. It had no kitchen, of course, nor bathroom facilities. It had just two rooms; one was a library and one was a combination storeroom and workroom. Andrew accepted many commissions and worked harder as a free robot than he ever had before, till the cost of the house was paid for and the structure was signed over to him.

One day Little Sir—no, "George!"—came. Little Sir had insisted on that after the court decision. "A free robot doesn't call anyone Little Sir," George had said. "I call you Andrew. You must call me George."

His preference was phrased as an order, so Andrew called him George—but Little Miss remained Little Miss.

One day when George came alone, it was to say that Sir was dying. Little Miss was at the bedside, but Sir wanted Andrew as well.

Sir's voice was still quite strong, though he seemed unable to move much. He struggled to raise his hand.

"Andrew," he said, "Andrew—Don't help me, George. I'm only dying; I'm not crippled. Andrew, I'm glad you're free. I just wanted to tell you that."

Andrew did not know what to say. He had never been at the side of someone dying before, but he knew it was the human way of ceasing to function. It was an involuntary and irreversible dismantling, and Andrew did not know what to say that might be appropriate. He could only remain standing, absolutely silent, absolutely motionless.

When it was over, Little Miss said to him, "He may not have seemed friendly to you toward the end, Andrew, but he was old, you know; and it hurt him that you should want to be free."

Then Andrew found the words. "I would never have been free without him, Little Miss."

9

Only after Sir's death did Andrew begin to wear clothes. He began with an old pair of trousers at first, a pair that George had given him.

George was married now, and a lawyer. He had joined Feingold's firm. Old Feingold was long since dead, but his daughter had carried on. Eventually the firm's name became Feingold and Martin. It remained so even when the daughter retired and no Feingold took her place. At the time Andrew first put on clothes, the Martin name had just been added to the firm.

George had tried not to smile the first time he saw Andrew attempting to put on trousers, but to Andrew's eyes the smile was clearly there. George showed Andrew how to manipulate the static charge to allow the trousers to open, wrap about his lower body, and move shut. George demonstrated on his own trousers, but Andrew was quite aware it would take him a while to duplicate that one flowing motion.

"But why do you want trousers, Andrew? Your body is so beautifully functional it's a shame to cover it—

especially when you needn't worry about either temperature control or modesty. And the material doesn't cling properly—not on metal."

Andrew held his ground. "Are not human bodies beautifully functional, George? Yet you cover yourselves."

"For warmth, for cleanliness, for protection, for decorativeness. None of that applies to you."

"I feel bare without clothes. I feel different, George," Andrew responded.

"Different! Andrew, there are millions of robots on Earth now. In this region, according to the last census, there are almost as many robots as there are men."

"I know, George. There are robots doing every conceivable type of work."

"And none of them wear clothes."

"But none of them are free, George."

Little by little, Andrew added to his wardrobe. He was inhibited by George's smile and by the stares of the people who commissioned work.

He might be free, but there was built into Andrew a carefully detailed program concerning his behavior to people, and it was only by the tiniest steps that he dared advance; open disapproval would set him back months. Not everyone accepted Andrew as free. He was incapable of resenting that, and yet there was a difficulty about his thinking process when he thought of it. Most of all, he tended to avoid putting on clothes —or too many of them—when he thought Little Miss might come to visit him. She was older now and was often away in some warmer climate, but when she returned the first thing she did was visit him.

On one of her visits, George said, ruefully, "She's got me, Andrew. I'll be running for the legislature next year. 'Like grandfather,' she says, 'like grandson.' "

"Like grandfather . . ." Andrew stopped, uncertain.

"I mean that I, George, the grandson, will be like Sir, the grandfather, who was in the legislature once."

"It would be pleasant, George, if Sir were still—" He paused, for he did not want to say, "in working order." That seemed inappropriate.

"Alive," George said. "Yes, I think of the old monster now and then, too."

Andrew often thought about this conversation. He had noticed his own incapacity in speech when talking with Goerge. Somehow the language had changed since Andrew had come into being with a built-in vocabulary. Then, too, George used a colloquial speech, as Sir and Little Miss had not. Why should he have called Sir a monster when surely that word was not appropriate. Andrew could not even turn to his own books for guidance. They were old, and most dealt with woodworking, with art, with furniture design. There were none on language, none on the ways of human beings.

Finally, it seemed to him that he must seek the proper books; and as a free robot, he felt he must not ask George. He would go to town and use the library. It was a triumphant decision and he felt his electro-potential grow distinctly higher until he had to throw in an impedance coil.

He put on a full costume, including even a shoulder chain of wood. He would have preferred the glitter plastic, but George had said that wood was much more appropriate and that polished cedar was considerably more valuable as well.

He had placed a hundred feet between himself and the house before gathering resistance brought him to a halt. He shifted the impendance coil out of circuit, and when that did not seem to help enough he returned to his home and on a piece of notepaper wrote neatly, "I have gone to the library," and placed it in clear view on his worktable.

10

Andrew never quite got to the library.

He had studied the map. He knew the route, but not the appearance of it. The actual landmarks did not resemble the symbols on the map and he would hesitate. Eventually, he thought he must have somehow gone wrong, for everything looked strange.

He passed an occasional field-robot, but by the time he decided he should ask his way none were in sight. A vehicle passed and did not stop.

Andrew stood irresolute, which meant calmly motionless, for coming across the field toward him were two human beings.

He turned to face them, and they altered their course to meet him. A moment before, they had been talking loudly. He had heard their voices. But now they were silent. They had the look that Andrew associated with human uncertainty; and they were young, but not very young. Twenty, perhaps? Andrew could never judge human age.

"Would you describe to me the route to the town library, sirs?"

One of them, the taller of the two, whose tall hat lengthened him still farther, almost grotesquely, said, not to Andrew, but to the other, "It's a robot."

The other had a bulbous nose and heavy eyelids. He said, not to Andrew but to the first, "It's wearing clothes."

The tall one snapped his fingers. "It's the free robot. They have a robot at the old Martin place who isn't owned by anybody. Why else would it be wearing clothes?"

"Ask it," said the one with the nose.

"Are you the Martin robot?" asked the tall one.

"I am Andrew Martin, sir," Andrew said.

"Good. Take off your clothes. Robots don't wear clothes." He said to the other, "That's disgusting. Look at him!"

Andrew hesitated. He hadn't heard an order in that tone of voice in so long that his Second Law circuits had momentarily jammed.

The tall one repeated, "Take off your clothes. I order you."

Slowly, Andrew began to remove them.

"Just drop them," said the tall one.

The nose said, "If it doesn't belong to anyone, it could be ours as much as someone else's."

"Anyway," said the tall one, "who's to object to

anything we do. We're not damaging property." He turned to Andrew. "Stand on your head."

"The head is not meant—" Andrew began.

"That's an order. If you don't know how, try anyway."

Andrew hesitated again, then bent to put his head on the ground. He tried to lift his legs but fell, heavily.

The tall one said, "Just lie there." He said to the other, "We can take him apart. Ever take a robot apart?"

"Will he let us?"

"How can he stop us?"

There was no way Andrew could stop them, if they ordered him in a forceful enough manner not to resist. The Second Law of obedience took precedence over the Third Law of self-preservation. In any case, he could not defend himself without possibly hurting them, and that would mean breaking the First Law. At that thought, he felt every motile unit contract slightly and he quivered as he lay there.

The tall one walked over and pushed at him with his foot. "He's heavy. I think we'll need tools to do the job."

The nose said, "We could order him to take himself apart. It would be fun to watch him try."

"Yes," said the tall one, thoughtfully, "but let's get him off the road. If someone comes along—"

It was too late. Someone had, indeed, come along and it was George. From where he lay, Andrew had seen him topping a small rise in the middle distance. He would have liked to signal him in some way, but the last order had been "Just lie there!"

George was running now, and he arrived on the scene somewhat winded. The two young men stepped back a little and then waited thoughtfully.

"Andrew, has something gone wrong?" George asked, anxiously.

Andrew replied, "I am well, George."

"Then stand up. What happened to your clothes?"

"That your robot, Mac?" the tall young man asked.

George turned sharply. "He's no one's robot. What's been going on here."

"We politely asked him to take his clothes off. What's that to you, if you don't own him."

George turned to Andrew. "What were they doing, Andrew?"

"It was their intention in some way to dismember me. They were about to move me to a quiet spot and order me to dismember myself."

George looked at the two young men, and his chin trembled.

The young men retreated no farther. They were smiling.

The tall one said, lightly, "What are you going to do, pudgy? Attack us?"

George said, "No. I don't have to. This robot has been with my family for over seventy-five years. He knows us and he values us more than he values anyone else. I am going to tell him that you two are threatening my life and that you plan to kill me. I will ask him to defend me. In choosing between me and you two, he will choose me. Do you know what will happen to you when he attacks you?"

The two were backing away slightly, looking uneasy.

George said, sharply, "Andrew, I am in danger and about to come to harm from these young men. Move toward them!"

Andrew did so, and the young men did not wait. They ran.

"All right, Andrew, relax," George said. He looked unstrung. He was far past the age where he could face the possibility of a dustup with one young man, let alone two.

"I couldn't have hurt them, George. I could see they were not attacking you."

"I didn't order you to attack them. I only told you to move toward them. Their own fears did the rest."

"How can they fear robots?"

"It's a disease of mankind, one which has not yet been cured. But never mind that. What the devil are you doing here, Andrew? Good thing I found your note. I was just on the point of turning back and hiring a helicopter when I found you. How did you get it into your head to go to the library? I would have brought you any books you needed."

"I am a——" Andrew began.

"Free robot. Yes, yes. All right, what did you want in the library?"

"I want to know more about human beings, about the world, about everything. And about robots, George. I want to write a history about robots."

George put his arm on the other's shoulder. "Well, let's walk home. But pick up your clothes first. Andrew, there are a million books on robotics and all of them include histories of the science. The world is growing saturated not only with robots but with information about robots."

Andrew shook his head, a human gesture he had lately begun to adopt. "Not a history of robotics, George. A history of *robots*, by a robot. I want to explain how robots feel about what has happened since the first ones were allowed to work and live on Earth."

George's eyebrows lifted, but he said nothing in direct response.

II

Little Miss was just past her eighty-third birthday, but there was nothing about her that was lacking in either energy or determination. She gestured with her cane oftener than she propped herself up with it.

She listened to the story in a fury of indignation. "George, that's horrible. Who were those young ruffians?"

"I don't know. What difference does it make? In the end they did not do any damage."

"They might have. You're a lawyer, George; and if you're well off, it's entirely due to the talents of Andrew. It was the money *he* earned that is the foundation of everything we have. He provides the continuity for this family, and I will *not* have him treated as a wind-up toy."

"What would you have me do, Mother?" George asked.

"I said you're a lawyer. Don't you listen? You set up a test case somehow, and you force the regional courts to declare for robot rights and get the legislature to pass the necessary bills. Carry the whole thing to the World Court, if you have to. I'll be watching, George, and I'll tolerate no shirking."

She was serious, so what began as a way of soothing the fearsome old lady became an involved matter with enough legal entanglement to make it interesting. As senior partner of Feingold and Martin, George plotted strategy. But he left the actual work to his junior partners, with much of it a matter for his son, Paul, who was also a member of the firm and who reported dutifully nearly every day to his grandmother. She, in turn, discussed the case every day with Andrew.

Andrew was deeply involved. His work on his book on robots was delayed again, as he pored over the legal arguments and even, at times, made very diffident suggestions. "George told me that day I was attacked that human beings have always been afraid of robots," he said one day. "As long as they are, the courts and the legislatures are not likely to work hard on behalf of robots. Should not something be done about public opinion?"

So while Paul stayed in court, George took to the public platform. It gave him the advantage of being informal, and he even went so far sometimes as to wear the new, loose style of clothing which he called drapery.

Paul chided him, "Just don't trip over it on stage, Dad."

George replied, despondently, "I'll try not to."

He addressed the annual convention of holo-news editors on one occasion and said, in part: "If, by virtue of the Second Law, we can demand of any robot unlimited obedience in all respects not involving harm to a human being, then any human being, *any* human being, has a fearsome power over any robot, *any* robot. In particular, since Second Law supersedes

Third Law, *any* human being can use the law of obedience to overcome the law of self-protection. He can order any robot to damage itself or even to destroy itself for any reason, or for no reason.

"Is this just? Would we treat an animal so? Even an inanimate object which had given us good service has a claim on our consideration. And a robot is not insensitive; it is not an animal. It can think well enough so that it can talk to us, reason with us, joke with us. Can we treat them as friends, can we work together with them, and not give them some of the fruits of that friendship, some of the benefits of co-working?

"If a man has the right to give a robot any order that does not involve harm to a human being, he should have the decency never to give a robot any order that involves harm to a robot, unless human safety absolutely requires it. With great power goes great responsibility, and if the robots have Three Laws to protect men, is it too much to ask that men have a law or two to protect robots?"

Andrew was right. It was the battle over public opinion that held the key to courts and legislature. In the end, a law was passed that set up conditions under which robot-harming orders were forbidden. It was endlessly qualified and the punishments for violating the law were totally inadequate, but the principle was established. The final passage by the World Legislature came through on the day of Little Miss' death.

That was no coincidence. Little Miss held on to life desperately during the last debate and let go only when word of victory arrived. Her last smile was for Andrew. Her last words were, "You have been good to us, Andrew." She died with her hand holding his, while her son and his wife and children remained at a respectful distance from both.

12

Andrew waited patiently when the receptionist-robot disappeared into the inner office. The receptionist might have used the holographic chatterbox, but unquestionably it was perturbed by having to deal with another robot rather than with a human being.

Andrew passed the time revolving the matter in his mind: Could "unroboted" be used as an analog of "unmanned," or had unmanned become a metaphoric term sufficiently divorced from its original literal meaning to be applied to robots—or to women for that matter? Such problems frequently arose as he worked on his book on robots. The trick of thinking out sentences to express all complexities had undoubtedly increased his vocabulary.

Occasionally, someone came into the room to stare at him and he did not try to avoid the glance. He looked at each calmly, and each in turn looked away.

Paul Martin finally emerged. He looked surprised, or he would have if Andrew could have made out his expression with certainty. Paul had taken to wearing the heavy makeup that fashion was dictating for both sexes. Though it made sharper and firmer the somewhat bland lines of Paul's face, Andrew disapproved. He found that disapproving of human beings, as long as he did not express it verbally, did not make him very uneasy. He could even write the disapproval. He was sure it had not always been so.

"Come in, Andrew. I'm sorry I made you wait, but there was something I *had* to finish. Come in, you had said you wanted to talk to me, but I didn't know you meant here in town."

"If you are busy, Paul, I am prepared to continue to wait."

Paul glanced at the interplay of shifting shadows on the dial on the wall that served as timepieces and said, "I can make some time. Did you come alone?"

"I hired an automatobile."

"Any trouble?" Paul asked, with more than a trace of anxiety.

"I wasn't expecting any. My rights are protected."

Paul looked all the more anxious for that. "Andrew, I've explained that the law is unenforceable, at least under most conditions. And if you insist on wearing clothes, you'll run into trouble eventually; just like that first time."

"And *only* time, Paul. I'm sorry you are displeased."

"Well, look at it this way: you are virtually a living legend, Andrew, and you are too valuable in many different ways for you to have any right to take chances with yourself. By the way, how's the book coming?"

"I am approaching the end, Paul. The publisher is quite pleased."

"Good!"

"I don't know that he's necessarily pleased with the book as a book. I think he expects to sell many copies because it's written by a robot and that's what pleases him."

"Only human, I'm afraid."

"I am not displeased. Let it sell for whatever reason, since it will mean money and I can use some."

"Grandmother left you—"

"Little Miss was generous, and I'm sure I can count on the family to help me out further. But it is the royalties from the book on which I am counting to help me through the next step."

"What next step is that?"

"I wish to see the head of U.S. Robots and Mechanical Men Corporation. I have tried to make an appointment; but so far I have not been able to reach him. The Corporation did not cooperate with me in the writing of the book, so I am not surprised, you understand."

Paul was clearly amused. "Cooperation is the last thing you can expect. They didn't cooperate with us in our great fight for robot rights. Quite the reverse, and you can see why. Give a robot rights and people may not want to buy them."

"Nevertheless," said Andrew, "if *you* call them, you may be able to obtain an interview for me."

"I'm no more popular with them than you are, Andrew."

"But perhaps you can hint that by seeing me they

may head off a campaign by Feingold and Martin to strengthen the rights of robots further."

"Wouldn't that be a lie, Andrew?"

"Yes, Paul, and I can't tell one. That is why you must call."

"Ah, you can't lie, but you can urge me to tell a lie, is that it? You're getting more human all the time, Andrew."

13

The meeting was not easy to arrange, even with Paul's supposedly weighted name. But it finally came about. When it did, Harley Smythe-Robertson, who, on his mother's side, was descended from the original founder of the corporation and who had adopted the hyphen-ation to indicate it, looked remarkably unhappy. He was approaching retirement age and his entire tenure as president had been devoted to the matter of robot rights. His gray hair was plastered thinly over the top of his scalp; his face was not made up, and he eyed Andrew with brief hostility from time to time.

Andrew began the conversation. "Sir, nearly a cen-tury ago, I was told by a Merton Manskyk of this corporation that the mathematics governing the plot-ting of the positronic pathways was far too complicated to permit of any but approximate solutions and that, therefore, my own capacities were not fully predict-able."

"That was a century ago." Smythe-Robertson hesi-tated, then said icily, "*Sir*. It is true no longer. Our robots are made with precision now and are trained precisely to their jobs."

"Yes," said Paul, who had come along, as he said, to make sure that the corporation played fair, "with the result that my receptionist must be guided at every point once events depart from the conventional, how-ever slightly."

"You would be much more displeased if it were to improvise," Smythe-Robertson said.

"Then you no longer manufacture robots like myself which are flexible and adaptable."

"No longer."

"The research I have done in connection with my book," said Andrew, "indicates that I am the oldest robot presently in active operation."

"The oldest presently," said Smythe-Robertson, "and the oldest ever. The oldest that will ever be. No robot is useful after the twenty-fifth year. They are called in and replaced with newer models."

"No robot as presently manufactured is useful after the *twentieth* year," said Paul, with a note of sarcasm creeping into his voice. "Andrew is quite exceptional in this respect."

Andrew, adhering to the path he had marked out for himself, continued, "As the oldest robot in the world and the most flexible, am I not unusual enough to merit special treatment from the company?"

"Not at all," Smythe-Robertson said, freezing up. "Your unusualness is an embarrassment to the company. If you were on lease, instead of having been an outright sale through some mischance, you would long since have been replaced."

"But that is exactly the point," said Andrew. "I am a free robot and I own myself. Therefore I come to you and ask you to replace me. You cannot do this without the owner's consent. Nowadays, that consent is extorted as a condition of the lease, but in my time this did not happen."

Smythe-Robertson was looking both startled and puzzled, and for a moment there was silence. Andrew found himself staring at the hologram on the wall. It was a death mask of Susan Calvin, patron saint of all roboticists. She had been dead for nearly two centuries now, but as a result of writing his book Andrew knew her so well he could half persuade himself that he had met her in life.

Finally Smythe-Robertson asked, "How can I replace you for you? If I replace you, as robot, how can I donate the new robot to you as owner since in the very act of replacement you cease to exist." He smiled grimly.

"Not at all difficult," Paul interposed. "The seat of Andrew's personality is his positronic brain and it is the one part that cannot be replaced without creating a new robot. The positronic brain, therefore, is Andrew the owner. Every other part of the robotic body can be replaced without affecting the robot's personality, and those other parts are the brain's possessions. Andrew, I should say, wants to supply his brain with a new robotic body."

"That's right," said Andrew, calmly. He turned to Smythe-Robertson. "You have manufactured androids, haven't you? Robots that have the outward appearance of humans, complete to the texture of the skin?"

"Yes, we have. They worked perfectly well, with their synthetic fibrous skins and tendrons. There was virtually no metal anywhere except for the brain, yet they were nearly as tough as metal robots. They were tougher, weight for weight."

Paul looked interested. "I didn't know that. How many are on the market?"

"None," said Smythe-Robertson. "They were much more expensive than metal models and a market survey showed they would not be accepted. They looked too human."

Andrew was impressed. "But the corporation retains its expertise, I assume. Since it does, I wish to request that I be replaced by an organic robot, an android."

Paul looked surprised. "Good Lord!" he said.

Smythe-Robertson stiffened. "Quite impossible!"

"Why is it impossible?" Andrew asked. "I will pay any reasonable fee, of course."

"We do not manufacture androids."

"You do not *choose* to manufacture androids," Paul interjected quickly. "That is not the same as being unable to manufacture them."

"Nevertheless," Smythe-Robertson responded, "the manufacture of androids is against public policy."

"There is no law against it," said Paul.

"Nevertheless, we do not manufacture them—and we will not."

Paul cleared his throat. "Mr. Smythe-Robertson," he said, "Andrew is a free robot who comes under the purview of the law guaranteeing robot rights. You are aware of this, I take it?"

"Only too well."

"This robot, as a free robot, chooses to wear clothes. This results in his being frequently humiliated by thoughtless human beings despite the law against the humiliation of robots. It is difficult to prosecute vague offenses that don't meet with the general disapproval of those who must decide on guilt and innocence."

"U.S. Robots understood that from the start. Your father's firm unfortunately did not."

"My father is dead now, but what I see is that we have here a clear offense with a clear target."

"What are you talking about?" said Smythe-Robertson.

"My client, Andrew Martin—he has just become my client—is a free robot who is entitled to ask U.S. Robots and Mechanical Men Corporation for the rights of replacement, which the corporation supplies to anyone who owns a robot for more than twenty-five years. In fact, the corporation insists on such replacement."

Paul was smiling and thoroughly at ease. "The positronic brain of my client," he went on, "is the owner of the body of my client—which is certainly more than twenty-five years old. The positronic brain demands the replacement of the body and offers to pay any reasonable fee for an android body as that replacement. If you refuse the request, my client undergoes humiliation and we will sue.

"While public opinion would not ordinarily support the claim of a robot in such a case, may I remind you that U.S. Robots is not popular with the public generally. Even those who most use and profit from robots are suspicious of the corporation. This may be a hangover from the days when robots were widely feared.

It may be resentment against the power and wealth of U.S. Robots, which has a worldwide monopoly. Whatever the cause may be, the resentment exists. I think you will find that you would prefer not to be faced with a lawsuit, particularly since my client is wealthy and will live for many more centuries and will have no reason to refrain from fighting the battle forever."

Smythe-Robertson had slowly reddened. "You are trying to force—"

"I force you to do nothing," said Paul. "If you wish to refuse to accede to my client's reasonable request, you may by all means do so and we will leave without another word. But we will sue, as is certainly our right, and you will find that you will eventually lose."

"Well . . ."

"I see that you are going to accede," said Paul. "You may hesitate but you will come to it in the end. Let me assure you, then, of one further point: If, in the process of transferring my client's positronic brain from his present body to an organic one, there is any damage, however slight, then I will never rest until I've nailed the corporation to the ground. I will, if necessary, take every possible step to mobilize public opinion against the corporation if one brainpath of my client's platinum-iridium essence is scrambled." He turned to Andrew and asked, "Do you agree to all this, Andrew?"

Andrew hesitated a full minute. It amounted to the approval of lying, of blackmail, of the badgering and humiliation of a human being. But not physical harm, he told himself, not physical harm.

He managed at last to come out with a rather faint "Yes."

14

He felt as though he were being constructed again. For days, then for weeks, finally for months, Andrew found himself not himself somehow, and the simplest actions kept giving rise to hesitation.

Paul was frantic. "They've damaged you, Andrew. We'll have to institute suit!"

Andrew spoke very slowly. "You . . . mustn't. You'll never be able to prove . . . something . . . like m-m-m-m—"

"Malice?"

"Malice. Besides, I grow . . . stronger, better. It's the tr-tr-tr—"

"Tremble?"

"Trauma. After all, there's never been such an op-op-op- . . . before."

Andrew could feel his brain from the inside. No one else could. He knew he was well, and during the months that it took him to learn full coordination and full positronic interplay he spent hours before the mirror.

Not quite human! The face was stiff—too stiff—and the motions were too deliberate. They lacked the careless, free flow of the human being, but perhaps that might come with time. At least now he could wear clothes without the ridiculous anomaly of a metal face going along with it.

Eventually, he said, "I will be going back to work."

Paul laughed. "That means you are well. What will you be doing? Another book?"

"No," said Andrew, seriously. "I live too long for any one career to seize me by the throat and never let me go. There was a time when I was primarily an artist, and I can still turn to that. And there was a time when I was a historian, and I can still turn to that. But now I wish to be a robobiologist."

"A robopsychologist, you mean."

"No. That would imply the study of positronic brains, and at the moment I lack the desire to do that. A robobiologist, it seems to me, would be concerned with the working of the body attached to that brain."

"Wouldn't that be a roboticist?"

"A roboticist works with a metal body. I would be

studying an organic humanoid body, of which I have
the only one, as far as I know."

"You narrow your field," said Paul, thoughtfully.
"As an artist, all conception is yours; as a historian
you deal chiefly with robots; as a robobiologist, you
will deal with yourself."

Andrew nodded. "It would seem so."

Andrew had to start from the very beginning, for
he knew nothing of ordinary biology and almost nothing of science. He became a familiar sight in the
libraries, where he sat at the electronic indices for
hours at a time, looking perfectly normal in clothes.
Those few who knew he was a robot in no way
interfered with him.

He built a laboratory in a room which he added to
his house; and his library grew, too.

Years passed, and Paul came to him one day and
said, "It's a pity you're no longer working on the
history of robots. I understand U.S. Robots is adopting
a radically new policy."

Paul had aged, and his deteriorating eyes had been
replaced with photoptic cells. In that respect, he had
drawn closer to Andrew.

"What have they done?" Andrew asked.

"They are manufacturing central computers, gigantic
positronic brains, really, which communicate with anywhere from a dozen to a thousand robots by microwave. The robots themselves have no brains at all.
They are the limbs of the gigantic brain, and the two
are physically separate."

"Is that more efficient?"

"U.S. Robots claims it is. Smythe-Robertson established the new direction before he died, however, and
it's my notion that it's a backlash at you. U.S. Robots
is determined that they will make no robots that will
give them the type of trouble you have, and for that
reason they separate brain and body. The brain will
have no body to wish changed; the body will have no
brain to wish anything.

"It's amazing, Andrew," Paul went on, "the influence you have had on the history of robots. It was your artistry that encouraged U.S. Robots to make robots more precise and specialized; it was your freedom that resulted in the establishment of the principle of robotic rights; it was your insistence on an android body that made U.S. Robots switch to brain-body separation."

Andrew grew thoughtful. "I suppose in the end the corporation will produce one vast brain controlling several billion robotic bodies. All the eggs will be in one basket. Dangerous. Not proper at all."

"I think you're right," said Paul, "but I don't suspect it will come to pass for a century at least and I won't live to see it. In fact, I may not live to see next year."

"Paul!" cried Andrew, in concern.

Paul shrugged. "Men are mortal, Andrew. We're not like you. It doesn't matter too much, but it does make it important to assure you on one point. I'm the last of the human Martins. The money I control personally will be left to the trust in your name, and as far as anyone can foresee the future, you will be economically secure."

"Unnecessary," Andrew said, with difficulty. In all this time, he could not get used to the deaths of the Martins.

"Let's not argue. That's the way it's going to be. Now, what are you working on?"

"I am designing a system for allowing androids—myself—to gain energy from the combustion of hydrocarbons, rather than from atomic cells."

Paul raised his eyebrows. "So that they will breathe and eat?"

"Yes."

"How long have you been pushing in that direction?"

"For a long time now, but I think I have finally designed an adequate combustion chamber for catalyzed controlled breakdown."

"But why, Andrew? The atomic cell is surely infinitely better."

"In some ways, perhaps. But the atomic cell is inhuman."

15

It took time, but Andrew had time. In the first place, he did not wish to do anything till Paul had died in peace. With the death of the great-grandson of Sir, Andrew felt more nearly exposed to a hostile world and for that reason was all the more determined along the path he had chosen.

Yet he was not really alone. If a man had died, the firm of Feingold and Martin lived, for a corporation does not die any more than a robot does.

The firm had its directions and it followed them soullessly. By way of the trust and through the law firm, Andrew continued to be wealthy. In return for their own large annual retainer, Feingold and Martin involved themselves in the legal aspects of the new combustion chamber. But when the time came for Andrew to visit U.S. Robots and Mechanical Men Corporation, he did it alone. Once he had gone with Sir and once with Paul. This time, the third time, he was alone and manlike.

U.S. Robots had changed. The actual production plant had been shifted to a large space station, as had grown to be the case with more and more industries. With them had gone many robots. The Earth itself was becoming parklike, with its one-billion-person population stabilized and perhaps not more than thirty percent of its at-least-equally-large robot population independently brained.

The Director of Research was Alvin Magdescu, dark of complexion and hair, with a little pointed beard and wearing nothing above the waist but the breastband that fashion dictated. Andrew himself was well covered in the older fashion of several decades back.

Magdescu offered his hand to his visitor. "I know you, of course, and I'm rather pleased to see you.

You're our most notorious product and it's a pity old Smythe-Robertson was so set against you. We could have done a great deal with you."

"You still can," said Andrew.

"No, I don't think so. We're past the time. We've had robots on Earth for over a century, but that's changing. It will be back to space with them, and those that stay here won't be brained."

"But there remains myself, and I stay on Earth."

"True, but there doesn't seem to be much of the robot about you. What new request have you?"

"To be still less a robot. Since I am so far organic, I wish an organic source of energy. I have here the plans . . ."

Magdescu did not hasten through them. He might have intended to at first, but he stiffened and grew intent. At one point, he said, "This is remarkably ingenious. Who thought of all this?"

"I did," Andrew replied.

Magdescu looked up at him sharply, then said, "It would amount to a major overhaul of your body, and an experimental one, since such a thing has never been attempted before. I advise against it. Remain as you are."

Andrew's face had limited means of expression, but impatience showed plainly in his voice. "Dr. Magdescu, you miss the entire point. You have no choice but to accede to my request. If such devices can be built into my body, they can be built into human bodies as well. The tendency to lengthen human life by prosthetic devices has already been remarked on. There are no devices better than the ones I have designed or am designing.

"As it happens, I control the patents by way of the firm of Feingold and Martin. We are quite capable of going into business for ourselves and of developing the kind of prosthetic devices that may end by producing human beings with many of the properties of robots. Your own business will then suffer.

"If, however, you operate on me now and agree to do so under similar circumstances in the future, you will receive permission to make use of the patents and control the technology of both robots and of the prosthetization of human beings. The initial leasing will not be granted, of course, until after the first operation is completed successfully, and after enough time has passed to demonstrate that it is indeed successful."

Andrew felt scarcely any First Law inhibition to the stern conditions he was setting a human being. He was learning to reason that what seemed like cruelty might, in the long run, be kindness.

Magdescu was stunned. "I'm not the one to decide something like this. That's a corporate decision that would take time."

"I can wait a reasonable time," said Andrew, "but only a reasonable time." And he thought with satisfaction that Paul himself could not have done it better.

16

It took only a reasonable time, and the operation was a success.

"I was very much against the operation, Andrew," Magdescu said, "but not for the reasons you might think. I was not in the least against the experiment, if it had been on someone else. I hated risking *your* positronic brain. Now that you have the positronic pathways interacting with simulated nerve pathways, it might have been difficult to rescue the brain intact if the body had gone bad."

"I had every faith in the skill of the staff at U.S. Robots," said Andrew. "And I can eat now."

"Well, you can sip olive oil. It will mean occasional cleanings of the combustion chamber, as we have explained to you. Rather an uncomfortable touch, I should think."

"Perhaps, if I did not expect to go further. Self-cleaning is not impossible. In fact, I am working on a device that will deal with solid food that may be expected to contain incombustible fractions—indigestible matter, so to speak, that will have to be discarded."

"You would then have to develop an anus."

"Or the equivalent."

"What else, Andrew . . . ?"

"Everything else."

"Genitalia, too?"

"Insofar as they will fit my plans. My body is a canvas on which I intend to draw . . ."

Magdescu waited for the sentence to be completed, and when it seemed that it would not be, he completed it himself. "A man?"

"We shall see," Andrew said.

"That's a puny ambition, Andrew. You're better than a man. You've gone downhill from the moment you opted to become organic."

"My brain has not suffered."

"No, it hasn't. I'll grant you that. But, Andrew, the whole new breakthrough in prosthetic devices made possible by your patents is being marketed under your name. You're recognized as the inventor and you're being honored for it—as you should be. Why play further games with your body?"

Andrew did not answer.

The honors came. He accepted membership in several learned societies, including one that was devoted to the new science he had established—the one he had called robobiology but which had come to be termed prosthetology. On the one hundred and fiftieth anniversary of his construction, a testimonial dinner was given in his honor at U.S. Robots. If Andrew saw an irony in this, he kept it to himself.

Alvin Magdescu came out of retirement to chair the dinner. He was himself ninety-four years old and was alive because he, too, had prosthetized devices that, among other things, fulfilled the function of liver and kidneys. The dinner reached its climax when Magdescu, after a short and emotional talk, raised his glass to toast The Sesquicentennial Robot.

Andrew had had the sinews of his face redesigned

to the point where he could show a human range of emotions, but he sat through all the ceremonies solemnly passive. He did not like to be a Sesquicentennial Robot.

17

It was prosthetology that finally took Andrew off the Earth.

In the decades that followed the celebration of his sesquicentennial, the Moon had come to be a world more Earthlike than Earth in every respect but its gravitational pull; and in its underground cities there was a fairly dense population. Prosthetized devices there had to take the lesser gravity into account. Andrew spent five years on the Moon working with local prosthetologists to make the necessary adaptations. When not at his work, he wandered among the robot population, every one of which treated him with the robotic obsequiousness due a man.

He came back to an Earth that was humdrum and quiet in comparison, and visited the offices of Feingold and Martin to announce his return.

The current head of the firm, Simon DeLong, was surprised. "We had been told you were returning, Andrew"—he had almost said Mr. Martin—"but we were not expecting you till next week."

"I grew impatient," said Andrew briskly. He was anxious to get to the point. "On the Moon, Simon, I was in charge of a research team of twenty human scientists. I gave orders that no one questioned. The Lunar robots deferred to me as they would to a human being. Why, then, am I not a human being?"

A wary look entered DeLong's eyes. "My dear Andrew, as you have just explained, you are treated as a human being by both robots *and* human beings. You are, therefore, a human being *de facto*."

"To be a human being *de facto* is not enough. I want not only to be treated as one, but to be legally identified as one. I want to be a human being *de jure*."

"Now, that is another matter," DeLong said. "There

we would run into human prejudice and into the un-
doubted fact that, however much you may be *like*
a human being, you are *not* a human being."

"In what way not?" Andrew asked. "I have the
shape of a human being and organs equivalent to those
of a human being. My organs, in fact, are identical
to some of those in a prosthetized human being. I
have contributed artistically, literally, and scientifically
to human culture as much as any human being now
alive. What more can one ask?"

"I myself would ask nothing more. The trouble is
that it would take an act of the World Legislature to
define you as a human being. Frankly, I wouldn't
expect that to happen."

"To whom on the Legislature could I speak?"

"To the Chairman of the Science and Technology
Committee, perhaps."

"Can you arrange a meeting?"

"But you scarcely need an intermediary. In your
position, you can——"

"No. *You* arrange it." It didn't even occur to Andrew that he was giving a flat order to a human being.
He had grown so accustomed to that on the Moon. "I
want him to know that the firm of Feingold and Martin
is backing me in this to the hilt."

"Well, now——"

"To the hilt, Simon. In one hundred and seventy-
three years I have in one fashion or another contributed
greatly to this firm. I have been under obligation to
individual members of the firm in times past. I am
not, now. It is rather the other way around now and
I am calling in my debts."

"I will do what I can," DeLong said.

18

The Chairman of the Science and Technology Committee was from the East Asian region and was a
woman. Her name was Chee Li-hsing and her transparent garments—obscuring what she wanted obscured
only by their dazzle—made her look plastic-wrapped.

"I sympathize with your wish for full human rights," she said. "There have been times in history when segments of the human population fought for full human rights. What rights, however, can you possibly want that you do not have?"

"As simple a thing as my right to life," Andrew stated. "A robot can be dismantled at any time."

"A human being can be executed at any time."

"Execution can only follow due process of law. There is no trial needed for my dismantling. Only the word of a human being in authority is needed to end me. Besides . . . besides . . ." Andrew tried desperately to allow no sign of pleading, but his carefully designed tricks of human expression and tone of voice betrayed him here. "The truth is I want to be a man. I have wanted it through six generations of human beings."

Li-hsing looked up at him out of darkly sympathetic eyes. "The Legislature can pass a law declaring you one. They could pass a law declaring that a stone statue be defined as a man. Whether they will actually do so is, however, as likely in the first case as the second. Congresspeople are as human as the rest of the population and there is always that element of suspicion against robots."

"Even now?"

"Even now. We would all allow the fact that you have earned the prize of humanity, and yet there would remain the fear of setting an undesirable precedent."

"What precedent? I am the only free robot, the only one of my type, and there will never be another. You may consult U.S. Robots."

" 'Never' is a long word, Andrew—or, if you prefer, Mr. Martin—since I will gladly give you my personal accolade as man. You will find that most congresspeople will not be so willing to set the precedent, no matter how meaningless such a precedent might be. Mr. Martin, you have my sympathy, but I cannot tell you to hope. Indeed . . ."

She sat back and her forehead wrinkled. "Indeed, if the issue grows too heated, there might well arise a certain sentiment, both inside the Legislature and outside, for that dismantling you mentioned. Doing away with you could turn out to be the easiest way of resolving the dilemma. Consider that before deciding to push matters."

Andrew stood firm. "Will no one remember the technique of prosthetology, something that is almost entirely mine?"

"It may seem cruel, but they won't. Or if they do, it will be remembered against you. People will say you did it only for yourself. It will be said it was part of a campaign to roboticize human beings, or to humanify robots; and in either case evil and vicious. You have never been part of a political hate campaign, Mr. Martin; but I tell you that you would be the object of vilification of a kind neither you nor I would credit, and there would be people to believe it all. Mr. Martin, let your life be."

She rose, and next to Andrew's seated figure she seemed small and almost childlike.

"If I decide to fight for my humanity, will you be on my side?"

She thought, then replied, "I will be—insofar as I can be. If at any time such a stand would appear to threaten my political future, I might have to abandon you, since it is not an issue I feel to be at the very root of my beliefs. I am trying to be honest with you."

"Thank you, and I will ask no more. I intend to fight this through, whatever the consequences, and I will ask you for your help only for as long as you can give it."

19

It was not a direct fight. Feingold and Martin counseled patience and Andrew muttered, grimly, that he had an endless supply of that. Feingold and Martin then entered on a campaign to narrow and restrict the area of combat.

They instituted a lawsuit denying the obligation to

pay debts to an individual with a prosthetic heart on the grounds that the possession of a robotic organ removed humanity, and with it the constitutional rights of human beings. They fought the matter skillfully and tenaciously, losing at every step but always in such a way that the decision was forced to be as broad as possible, and then carrying it by way of appeals to the World Court.

It took years, and millions of dollars.

When the final decision was handed down, DeLong held what amounted to a victory celebration over the legal loss. Andrew was, of course, present in the company offices on the occasion.

"We've done two things, Andrew," said DeLong, "both of which are good. First of all, we have established the fact that no number of artificial parts in the human body causes it to cease being a human body. Secondly, we have engaged public opinion in the question in such a way as to put it fiercely on the side of a broad interpretation of humanity, since there is not a human being in existence who does not hope for prosthetics if they will keep him alive."

"And do you think the Legislature will now grant me my humanity?" Andrew asked.

DeLong looked faintly uncomfortable. "As to that, I cannot be optimistic. There remains the one organ which the World Court has used as the criterion of humanity. Human beings have an organic cellular brain and robots have a platinum-iridium positronic brain if they have one at all—and you certainly have a positronic brain. No, Andrew, don't get that look in your eye. We lack the knowledge to duplicate the work of a cellular brain in artificial structures close enough to the organic type as to allow it to fall within the court's decision. Not even you could do it."

"What should we do, then?"

"Make the attempt, of course. Congresswoman Li-hsing will be on our side and a growing number of other congresspeople. The President will undoubtedly go along with a majority of the Legislature in this matter."

"Do we have a majority?"

"No. Far from it. But we might get one if the public will allow its desire for a broad interpretation of humanity to extend to you. A small chance, I admit; but if you do not wish to give up, we must gamble for it."

"I do not wish to give up."

20

Congresswoman Li-hsing was considerably older than she had been when Andrew had first met her. Her transparent garments were long gone. Her hair was now close-cropped and her coverings were tubular. Yet still Andrew clung, as closely as he could within the limits of reasonable taste, to the style of clothing that had prevailed when he had first adopted clothing more than a century before.

"We've gone as far as we can, Andrew," Li-hsing admitted. "We'll try once more after recess, but, to be honest, defeat is certain and then the whole thing will have to be given up. All my most recent efforts have only earned me certain defeat in the coming congressional campaign."

"I know," said Andrew, "and it distressed me. You said once you would abandon me if it came to that. Why have you not done so?"

"One can change one's mind, you know. Somehow, abandoning you became a higher price than I cared to pay for just one more term. As it is, I've been in the Legislature for over a quarter of a century. It's enough."

"Is there no way we can change minds, Chee?"

"We've changed all that are amenable to reason. The rest—the majority—cannot be moved from their emotional antipathies."

"Emotional antipathy is not a valid reason for voting one way or the other."

"I know that, Andrew, but they don't advance emotional antipathy as their reason."

"It all comes down to the brain, then," Andrew said cautiously. "But must we leave it at the level of cells versus positrons? Is there no way of forcing a functional definition? Must we say that a brain is made of this or that? May we not say that a brain is something —anything—capable of a certain level of thought?"

"Won't work," said Li-hsing. "Your brain is manmade, the human brain is not. Your brain is constructed, theirs developed. To any human being who is intent on keeping up the barrier between himself and a robot, those differences are a steel wall a mile high and a mile thick."

"If we could get at the source of their antipathy, the very source—"

"After all your years," Li-hsing said, sadly, "you are still trying to reason out the human being. Poor Andrew, don't be angry, but it's the robot in you that drives you in that direction."

"I don't know," said Andrew. "If I could bring myself . . ."

1 [Reprise]

If he could bring himself . . .

He had known for a long time it might come to that, and in the end he was at the surgeon's. He had found one, skillful enough for the job at hand—which meant a surgeon-robot, for no human surgeon could be trusted in this connection, either in ability or in intention.

The surgeon could not have performed the operation on a human being, so Andrew, after putting off the moment of decision with a sad line of questioning that reflected the turmoil within himself, had put First Law to one side by saying "I, too, am a robot."

He then said, as firmly as he had learned to form the words even at human beings over these past decades, "I *order* you to carry through the operation on me."

In the absence of the First Law, an order so firmly given from one who looked so much like a man activated the Second Law sufficiently to carry the day.

21

Andrew's feeling of weakness was, he was sure, quite imaginary. He had recovered from the operation. Nevertheless, he leaned, as unobtrusively as he could manage, against the wall. It would be entirely too revealing to sit.

Li-hsing said, "The final vote will come this week, Andrew. I've been able to delay it no longer, and we must lose. And that will be it, Andrew."

"I am grateful for your skill at delay. It gave me the time I needed, and I took the gamble I had to."

"What gamble is this?" Li-hsing asked with open concern.

"I couldn't tell you, or even the people at Feingold and Martin. I was sure I would be stopped. See here, if it is the brain that is at issue, isn't the greatest difference of all the matter of immortality. Who really cares what a brain looks like or is built of or how it was formed. What matters is that human brain cells die, *must* die. Even if every other organ in the body is maintained or replaced, the brain cells, which cannot be replaced without changing and therefore killing the personality, must eventually die.

"My own positronic pathways have lasted nearly two centuries without perceptible change, and can last for centuries more. Isn't *that* the fundamental barrier: human beings can tolerate an immortal robot, for it doesn't matter how long a machine lasts, but they cannot tolerate an immortal human being since their own mortality is endurable only so long as it is universal. And for that reason they won't make me a human being."

"What is it you're leading up to, Andrew?" Li-hsing asked.

"I have removed that problem. Decades ago, my positronic brain was connected to organic nerves. Now, one last operation has arranged that connection in such a way that slowly—quite slowly—the potential is being drained from my pathways."

Li-hsing's finely wrinkled face showed no expression for a moment. Then her lips tightened. "Do you mean you've arranged to die, Andrew? You can't have. That violates the Third Law."

"No," said Andrew, "I have chosen between the death of my body and the death of my aspirations and desires. To have let my body live at the cost of the greater death is what would have violated the Third Law."

Li-hsing seized his arm as though she were about to shake him. She stopped herself. "Andrew, it won't work! Change it back."

"It can't be done. Too much damage was done. I have a year to live—more or less. I will last through the two-hundredth anniversary of my construction. I was weak enough to arrange that."

"How can it be worth it? Andrew, you're a fool."

"If it brings me humanity, that will be worth it. If it doesn't, it will bring an end to striving and that will be worth it, too."

Then Li-hsing did something that astonished herself. Quietly, she began to weep.

22

It was odd how that last deed caught the imagination of the world. All that Andrew had done before had not swayed them. But he had finally accepted even death to be human, and the sacrifice was too great to be rejected.

The final ceremony was timed, quite deliberately, for the two-hundredth anniversary. The World President was to sign the act and make the people's will law. The ceremony would be visible on a global network and would be beamed to the Lunar state and even to the Martian colony.

Andrew was in a wheelchair. He could still walk, but only shakily.

With mankind watching, the World President said, "Fifty years ago, you were declared The Sesquicentennial Robot, Andrew." After a pause, and in a more solemn tone, he continued, "Today we declare you The Bicentennial Man, Mr. Martin."

And Andrew, smiling, held out his hand to shake that of the President.

23

Andrew's thoughts were slowly fading as he lay in bed. Desperately he seized at them. *Man! He was a man!* He wanted that to be his last thought. He wanted to dissolve—die—with that.

He opened his eyes one more time and for one last time recognized Li-hsing, waiting solemnly. Others were there, but they were only shadows, unrecognizable shadows. Only Li-hsing stood out against the deepening gray.

Slowly, inchingly, he held out his hand to her and very dimly and faintly felt her take it.

She was fading in his eyes as the last of his thoughts trickled away. But before she faded completely, one final fugitive thought came to him and rested for a moment on his mind before everything stopped.

"Little Miss," he whispered, too low to be heard.

JAMES TIPTREE, JR.

Houston, Houston,
Do You Read?

James Tiptree, Jr., aside from the award-winning story that follows this introduction, has been justly lauded as one of the excellent writers to appear in science fiction in recent years. Precise biographical data, however, have been difficult to come by. However, with the author's assistance, the following facts have at last been collected and are hereby presented to the reader.

James Tiptree, Jr., was born in September 1967, in the import section of the McLean Giant Food Store. His birth occurred in front of a display of Tiptree's English Marmalade, which appeared to him to be a nice inconspicuous name that editors would not recall having rejected. The subsequent acceptance of his next thirty or forty stories shocked and nonplussed him, but gave him the opportunity to form many genuine epistolary friendships, since he had the bad habit of writing fan letters to writers he admired. In the course of a correspondence with Jeffrey D. Smith, a fanzine editor in Baltimore, he gave a biographical interview, in which he mentioned having been brought up by a pair of explorer-adventurers who alternated life in the Congo and the Midwest. He also reported that he had enlisted in the Army Air Force in World War II, becoming a photo-intelligence officer, and subsequent to what was then hoped to be the outbreak of World Peace, he went in for a little business, a little government work, and finally settled upon a doctorate and a short research and teaching career in one of the "soft" sciences. (A "soft" science is one where you bounce back when you trip.) He refrained from mentioning to his friends that he had started life as a serious painter, because a companion personality, Racoona Sheldon, then being slowly born, seemed to need that as a biographical touch. Tiptree's writing career took a parabolic form, the downside of the curve being accounted for by a depression which caused his stories to grow blacker and more few. The coup de grace was given him in October 1977, when it was revealed that he did not exist. He feels that it was, though brief, a wondrous existence. He is survived by a short story or two in press and a novel to be published by Berkley—as well as one Hugo, for THE GIRL WHO WAS PLUGGED IN, and two Nebula Awards for LOVE IS THE PLAN, THE PLAN IS DEATH, in 1973, and for HOUSTON, HOUSTON, DO YOU READ?, in 1976.

Lorimer gazes around the big crowded cabin, trying to listen to the voices, trying also to ignore the twitch in his insides that means he is about to remember something bad. No help; he lives it again, that long-ago moment. Himself running blindly—or was he pushed?—into the strange toilet at Evanston Junior High. His fly open, his dick in his hand, he can still see the grey zipper edge of his jeans around his pale exposed pecker. The hush. The sickening wrongness of shapes, faces turning. The first blaring giggle. *Girls.* He was in the *girls' can.*

He flinches wryly now, so many years later, not looking at the women's faces. The cabin curves around over his head surrounding him with their alien things: the beading rack, the twins' loom, Andy's leather work, the damned kudzu vine wriggling everywhere, the chickens. So cosy. . . . Trapped, he is. Irretrievably trapped for life in everything he does not enjoy. Structurelessness. Personal trivia, unmeaning intimacies. The claims he can somehow never meet. Ginny: *You never talk to me* . . . Ginny, love, he thinks involuntarily. The hurt doesn't come.

Bud Geirr's loud chuckle breaks in on him. Bud is joking with some of them, out of sight around a bulk-head. Dave is visible, though. Major Norman Davis on the far side of the cabin, his bearded profile bent to-ward a small dark woman Lorimer can't quite focus on. But Dave's head seems oddly tiny and sharp, in fact the whole cabin looks unreal. A cackle bursts out from the "ceiling"—the bantam hen in her basket.

At this moment Lorimer becomes sure he has been drugged.

Curiously, the idea does not anger him. He leans or rather tips back, perching cross-legged in the zero gee, letting his gaze go to the face of the woman he has been talking with. Connie. Constantia Morelos. A tall moonfaced woman in capacious green pajamas. He has never really cared for talking to women. Ironic.

"I suppose," he says aloud, "it's possible that in some sense we are not here."

That doesn't sound too clear, but she nods in-terestedly. She's watching my reactions, Lorimer tells himself. Women are natural poisoners. Has he said that aloud too? Her expression doesn't change. His vision is taking on a pleasing local clarity. Connie's skin strikes him as quite fine, healthy-looking. Olive tan even after two years in space. She was a farmer, he recalls. Big pores, but without the caked look he as-sociates with women her age.

"You probably never wore make-up," he says. She looks puzzled. "Face paint, powder. None of you have."

"Oh!" Her smile shows a chipped front tooth. "Oh yes, I think Andy has."

"Andy?"

"For plays. Historical plays, Andy's good at that."

"Of course. Historical plays."

Lorimer's brain seems to be expanding, letting in light. He is understanding actively now, the myriad bits and pieces linking into pattern. Deadly patterns, he perceives; but the drug is shielding him in some way. Like an amphetamine high without the pressure. Maybe it's something they use socially? No, they're watching, too.

"Space bunnies, I still don't dig it," Bud Geirr laughs infectiously. He has a friendly buoyant voice people like; Lorimer still likes it after two years.

"You chicks have kids back home, what do your folks think about you flying around out here with old Andy, h'mm?" Bud floats into view, his arm draped around a twin's shoulders. The one called Judy Paris, Lorimer decides; the twins are hard to tell. She drifts passively at an angle to Bud's big body: a jut-breasted plain girl in flowing yellow pajamas, her black hair raying out. Andy's read head swims up to them. He is holding a big green spaceball, looking about sixteen.

"Old Andy." Bud shakes his head, his grin flashing under his thick dark mustache. "When I was your age folks didn't let their women fly around with me."

Connie's lips quirk faintly. In Lorimer's head the pieces slide toward pattern. I know, he thinks. Do you know I know? His head is vast and crystalline, very nice really. Easier to think. Women. . . . No compact generalization forms in his mind, only a few speaking faces on a matrix of pervasive irrelevance. Human, of course. Biological necessity. Only so, so . . . diffuse? Pointless? . . . His sister Amy, soprano con tremulo: "Of course women could contribute as much as men if you'd treat us as equals. You'll see!" And then marrying that idiot the second time. Well, now he can see.

"Kudzu vines," he says aloud. Connie smiles. How they all smile.

"How 'boot that?" Bud says happily. "Ever think we'd see chicks in zero gee, hey, Dave? Artits-stico. Woo-ee!" Across the cabin Dave's bearded head turns to him, not smiling.

"And ol' Andy's had it all to his self. Stunt your growth, lad." He punches Andy genially on the arm, Andy catches himself on the bulkhead. But can't be drunk, Lorimer thinks; not on that fruit cider. But he doesn't usually sound so much like a stage Texan either. A drug.

"Hey, no offense," Bud is saying earnestly to the boy, "I mean that. You have to forgive one underprilly, underprivileged, brother. These chicks are good people. Know what?" he tells the girl, "You could look stupendous if you fix yourself up a speck. Hey, I can show you, old Buddy's a expert. I hope you don't mind my saying that. As a matter of fact you look real stupendous to me right now."

He hugs her shoulders, flings out his arm and hugs Andy too. They float upward in his grasp, Judy grinning excitedly, almost pretty.

"Let's get some more of that good stuff." Bud propels them both toward the serving rack which is decorated for the occasion with sprays of greens and small real daisies.

"Happy New Year! Hey, Happy New Year, y'all!"

Faces turn, more smiles. Genuine smiles, Lorimer thinks, maybe they really like their new years. He feels he has infinite time to examine every event, the implications evolving in crystal facets. I'm an echo chamber. Enjoyable, to be the observer. But others are observing too. They've started something here. Do they realize? So vulnerable, three of us, five of them in this fragile ship. They don't know. A dread unconnected to action lurks behind his mind.

"By god we made it," Bud laughs. "You space chickies, I have to give it to you. I commend you, by god I say it. We wouldn't be here, wherever we are. Know what, I jus' might decide to stay in the service after all. Think they have room for old Bud in your space program, sweetie?"

"Knock that off, Bud," Dave says quietly from the far wall. "I don't want to hear us use the name of the Creator like that." The full chestnut beard gives him a patriarchal gravity. Dave is forty-six, a decade older than Bud and Lorimer. Veteran of six successful missions.

"Oh my apologies, Major Dave old buddy." Bud chuckles intimately to the girl. "Our commanding ossifer. Stupendous guy. Hey, Doc!" he calls. "How's your attitude? You making out dinko?"

"Cheers," Lorimer hears his voice reply, the complex stratum of his feelings about Bud rising like a kraken in the moonlight of his mind. The submerged silent thing he has about them all, all the Buds and Daves and big, indomitable, cheerful, able, disciplined, slow-minded mesomorphs he has cast his life with. Meso-ectos, he corrected himself; astronauts aren't muscleheads. They like him, he has been careful about that. Liked him well enough to get him on *Sunbird,* to make him the official scientist on the first circumsolar mission. That little Doc Lorimer, he's cool, he's on the team. No shit from Lorimer, not like those other scientific assholes. He does the bit well with his small neat build and his deadpan remarks. And the years of turning out for the bowling, the volleyball, the tennis, the skeet, the skiing that broke his ankle, the touch football that broke his collarbone. Watch that Doc, he's a sneaky one. And the big men banging him on the back, accepting him. Their token scientist . . . The trouble is, he isn't any kind of scientist any more. Living off his postdoctoral plasma work, a lucky hit. He hasn't really been into the math for years, he isn't up to it now. Too many other interests, too much time spent explaining elementary stuff. I'm a half-jock, he thinks. A foot taller and a hundred pounds heavier and I'd be just like them. One of them. An alpha. They probably sense it underneath, the beta bile. Had the jokes worn a shade thin in *Sunbird,* all that year going out? A year of Bud and Dave playing gin. That damn exercycle, gearing it up too tough for me. They didn't mean it, though. We were a team.

The memory of gaping jeans flicks at him, the painful end part—the grinning faces waiting for him when he stumbled out. The howls, the dribble down his leg. Being cool, pretending to laugh too. You shitheads, I'll show you. *I am not a girl.*

Bud's voice rings out, chanting "And a hap-pee New Year to you-all down there!" Parody of the oily NASA

tone. "Hey, why don't we shoot 'em a signal? Greet-
ings to all you Earthlings, I mean, all you little Lunies.
Hap-py New Year in the good year whatsis." He
snuffles comically. "There is a Santy Claus, Houston,
ye-ew nevah saw nothin' like this! Houston, wherever
you are," he sings out. "Hey, Houston! Do you read?"

In the silence Lorimer sees Dave's face set into
Major Norman Davis, commanding.

And without warning he is suddenly back there,
back a year ago in the cramped, shook-up command
module of *Sunbird,* coming out from behind the sun.
It's the drug doing this, he thinks as memory closes
around him, it's so real. Stop. He tries to hang onto
reality, to the sense of trouble building underneath.

—But he can't, he is *there,* hovering behind Dave
and Bud in the triple couches, as usual avoiding his
official station in the middle, seeing beside them their
reflections against blackness in the useless port window. The outer layer has been annealed, he can just
make out a bright smear that has to be Spica floating
through the image of Dave's head, making the bandage
look like a kid's crown.

"Houston, Houston, Sunbird," Dave repeats; "Sunbird calling Houston. Houston, do you read? Come in,
Houston."

The minutes start by. They are giving it seven out,
seven back; seventy-eight million miles, ample margin.

"The high gain's shot, that's what it is," Bud says
cheerfully. He says it almost every day.

"No way." Dave's voice is patient, also as usual.
"It checks out. Still too much crap from the sun, isn't
that right, Doc?"

"The residual radiation from the flare is just about
in line with us," Lorimer says. "They could have a
hard time sorting us out." For the thousandth time he
registers his own faint, ridiculous gratification at being consulted.

"Shit, we're outside Mercury." Bud shakes his head.
"How we gonna find out who won the Series?"

He often says that too. A ritual, out here in

eternal night. Lorimer watches the sparkle of Spica drift by the reflection of Bud's curly face-bush. His own whiskers are scant and scraggly, like a blond Fu Manchu. In the aft corner of the window is a striped glare that must be the remains of their port energy accumulators, fried off in the solar explosion that hit them a month ago and fused the outer layers of their windows. That was when Dave cut his head open on the sexlogic panel. Lorimer had been banged in among the gravity wave experiment, he still doesn't trust the readings. Luckily the particle stream has missed one piece of the front window; they still have about twenty degrees of clear vision straight ahead. The brilliant web of the Pleiades shows there, running off into a blur of light.

Twelve minutes . . . thirteen. The speaker sighs and clicks emptily. Fourteen. Nothing.

"Sunbird to Houston, Sunbird to Houston. Come in, Houston. Sunbird out." Dave puts the mike back in its holder. "Give it another twenty-four."

They wait ritually. Tomorrow Packard will reply. Maybe.

"Be good to see old Earth again," Bud remarks.

"We're not using any more fuel on attitude," Dave reminds him. "I trust Doc's figures."

It's not my figures, it's the elementary facts of celestial mechanics, Lorimer thinks; in October there's only one place for Earth to be. He never says it. Not to a man who can fly two-body solutions by intuition once he knows where the bodies are. Bud is a good pilot and a better engineer; Dave is the best there is. He takes no pride in it. "The Lord helps us, Doc, if we let Him."

"Going to be a bitch docking if the radar's screwed up," Bud says idly. They all think about that for the hundredth time. It will be a bitch. Dave will do it. That was why he is hoarding fuel.

The minutes tick off.

"That's it," Dave says—and a voice fills the cabin, shockingly.

"Judy?" It is high and clear. A girl's voice.

"Judy, I'm so glad we got you. What are you doing on this band?"

Bud blows out his breath; there is a frozen instant before Dave snatches up the mike.

"Sunbird, we read you. This is Mission Sunbird calling Houston, ah, Sunbird One calling Houston Ground Control. Identify, who are you? Can you relay our signal? Over."

"Some skip," Bud says. "Some incredible ham."

"Are you in trouble, Judy?" the girl's voice asks. "I can't hear, you sound terrible. Wait a minute."

"This is United States Space Mission Sunbird One," Dave repeats. "Mission Sunbird calling Houston Space Center. You are dee-exxing our channel. Identify, repeat identify yourself and say if you can relay to Houston. Over."

"Dinko, Judy, try it again," the girl says .

Lorimer abruptly pushes himself up to the Lurp, the Long-Range Particle Density Cumulator experiment, and activates its shaft motor. The shaft whines, jars; lucky it was retracted during the flare, lucky it hasn't fused shut. He sets the probe pulse on max and begins a rough manual scan.

"You are intercepting official traffic from the United States space mission to Houston Control," Dave is saying forcefully. "If you cannot relay to Houston get off the air, you are committing a federal offense. Say again, can you relay our signal to Houston Space Center? Over."

"You still sound terrible," the girl says. "What's Houston? Who's talking, anyway? You know we don't have much time." Her voice is sweet but very nasal.

"Jesus, that's close," Bud says. "That is close."

"Hold it." Dave twists around to Lorimer's improvised radarscope.

"There." Lorimer points out a tiny stable peak at the extreme edge of the read-out slot, in the transcoronal scatter. Bud cranes too.

"A bogey!"

"Somebody else out here."

"Hello, hello? We have you now," the girl says.

"Why are you so far out? Are you dinko, did you catch the flare?"

"Hold it," warns Dave. "What's the status, Doc?"

"Over three hundred thousand kilometers, guesstimated. Possibly headed away from us, going around the sun. Could be cosmonauts, a Soviet mission?"

"Out to beat us. They missed."

"With a *girl?*" Bud objects.

"They've done that. You taping this, Bud?"

"Roger-r-r." He grins. "That sure didn't sound like a Russky chic. Who the hell's Judy?"

Dave thinks for a second, clicks on the mike. "This is Major Norman Davis commanding United States spacecraft Sunbird One. We have you on scope. Request you identify yourself. Repeat, who are you? Over."

"Judy, stop joking," the voice complains. "We'll lose you in a minute, don't you realize we worried about you?"

"Sunbird to unidentified craft. This is not Judy. I say again, this is not Judy. Who are you? Over."

"What—" the girl says, and is cut off by someone else saying, "Wait a minute, Ann." The speaker squeals. Then a different woman says, "This is Lorna Bethune in Escondita. What is going on here?"

"This is Major Davis commanding United States Mission Sunbird on course for Earth. We do not recognize any spacecraft Escondita. Will you identify yourself? Over."

"I just did." She sounds older, with the same nasal drawl. "There is no spaceship Sunbird and you're not on course for Earth. If this is an andy joke it isn't any good."

"This is no joke, madam!" Dave explodes. "This is the American circumsolar mission and we are American astronauts. We do not appreciate your interference. Out."

The woman starts to speak and is drowned in a jibber of static. Two voices come through briefly. Lorimer thinks he hears the words "Sunbird program" and something else. Bud works the squelcher; the interference subsides to a drone.

"Ah, Major Davis?" the voice is fainter. "Did I hear you say you are on course for Earth?"

Dave frowns at the speaker and then says curtly, "Affirmative."

"Well, we don't understand your orbit. You must have very unusual flight characteristics, our readings show you won't node with anything on your present course. We'll lose the signal in a minute or two. Ah, would you tell us where you see Earth now? Never mind the coordinates, just tell us the constellation."

Dave hesitates and then holds up the mike. "Doc."

"Earth's apparent position is in Pisces," Lorimer says to the voice. "Approximately three degrees from P. Gamma."

"It is not," the woman says. "Can't you see it's in Virgo? Can't you see out at all?"

Lorimer's eyes go to the bright smear in the port window. "We sustained some damage—"

"Hold it," snaps Dave.

"—to one window during a disturbance we ran into at perihelion. Naturally we know the relative direction of Earth on this date, October nineteen."

"October? It's March, March fifteen. You must—" Her voice is lost in a shriek.

"E-M front," Bud says, tuning. They are all leaning at the speaker from different angles, Lorimer is head-down. Space-noise wails and crashes like surf, the strange ship is too close to the coronal horizon. "—Behind you," they hear. More howls. "Band, try . . . ship . . . if you can, you signal—" Nothing more comes through.

Lorimer pushes back, staring at the spark in the window. It has to be Spica. But is it elongated, as if a second point-source is beside it? Impossible. An excitement is trying to flare out inside him, the women's voices resonate in his head.

"Playback," Dave says. "Houston will really like to hear this."

They listen again to the girl calling Judy, the woman

saying she is Lorna Bethune. Bud holds up a finger. "Man's voice in there." Lorimer listens hard for the words he thought he heard. The tape ends.

"Wait till Packard gets this one." Dave rubs his arms. "Remember what they pulled on Howie? Claiming they rescued him."

"Seems like they want us on their frequency." Bud grins. "They must think we're fa-a-ar gone. Hey, looks like this other capsule's going to show up, getting crowded out here."

"If it shows up," Dave says. "Leave it on voice alert, Bud. The batteries will do that."

Lorimer watches the spark of Spica, or Spica-plus-something, wondering if he will ever understand. The casual acceptance of some trick or ploy out here in this incredible loneliness. Well, if these strangers are from the same mold, maybe that is it. Aloud he says, "Escondita is an odd name for a Soviet mission. I believe it means 'hidden' in Spanish."

"Yeah," says Bud. "Hey, I know what that accent is, it's Australian. We had some Aussie bunnies at Hickan. Or-style-ya, woo-ee! You s'pose Woomara is sending up some kind of com-bined do?"

Dave shakes his head. "They have no capability whatsoever."

"We ran into some fairly strange phenomena back there, Dave," Lorimer says thoughtfully. "I'm beginning to wish we could take a visual check."

"Did you goof, Doc?"

"No. Earth is where I said, if it's October. Virgo is where it would appear in March."

"Then that's it," Dave grins, pushing out of the couch. "You been asleep five months, Rip van Winkle? Time for a hand before we do the roadwork."

"What I'd like to know is what that chick looks like," says Bud, closing down the transceiver. "Can I help you into your space-suit, Miss? Hey, Miss, pull that in, psst-psst-psst! You going to listen, Doc?"

"Right." Lorimer is getting out his charts. The others go aft through the tunnel to the small day-room, making no further comment on the presence of the strange ship or ships out here. Lorimer himself is more shaken than he likes; it was that damn phrase.

The tedious exercise period comes and goes. Lunch-time: They give the containers a minimum warm to conserve the batteries. Chicken à la king again; Bud puts ketchup on his and breaks their usual silence with a funny anecdote about an Australian girl, laboriously censoring himself to conform to *Sunbird's* unwritten code on talk. After lunch Dave goes forward to the command module. Bud and Lorimer continue their current task checking out the suits and packs for a damage-assessment EVA to take place as soon as the radiation count drops.

They are just clearing away when Dave calls them. Lorimer comes through the tunnel to hear a girl's voice blare, "—dinko trip. What did Lorna say? Gloria over!"

He starts up the Lurp and begins scanning. No results this time. "They're either in line behind us or in the sunward quadrant," he reports finally. "I can't isolate them."

Presently the speaker holds another thin thread of sound.

"That could be their ground control," says Dave. "How's the horizon, Doc?"

"Five hours; Northwest Siberia, Japan, Australia."

"I told you the high gain is fucked up." Bud gingerly feeds power to his antenna motor. "Easy, eas-ee. The frame is twisted, that's what it is."

"Don't snap it," Dave says, knowing Bud will not.

The squeaking fades, pulses back. "Hey, we can really use this," Bud says. "We can calibrate on them."

A hard soprano says suddenly "—should be outside your orbit. Try around Beta Aries."

"Another chick. We have a fix," Bud says happily. "We have a fix now. I do believe our troubles are over. That monkey was torqued one hundred forty-nine degrees. Woo-ee!"

The first girl comes back. "We seen them, Margo! But they're so small, how can they live in there? Maybe they're tiny aliens! Over."

"That's Judy." Bud chuckles. "Dave, this is screwy, it's all in English. It has to be some U.N. thingie."

Dave massages his elbows, flexes his fists; thinking. They wait. Lorimer considers a hundred and forty-nine degrees from Gamma Piscium.

In thirteen minutes the voice from Earth says, "Judy, call the others, will you? We're going to play you the conversation, we think you should all hear. Two minutes. Oh, while we're waiting, Zebra wants to tell Connie the baby is fine. And we have a new cow."

"Code," says Dave.

The recording comes on. The three men listen once more to Dave calling Houston in a rattle of solar noise. The transmission clears up rapidly and cuts off with the woman saying that another ship, the *Gloria*, is behind them, closer to the sun.

"We looked up history," the Earth voice resumes. "There was a Major Norman Davis on the first Sunbird flight. Major was a military title. Did you hear them say 'Doc'? There was a scientific doctor on board, Doctor Orren Lorimer. The third member was Captain—that's another title—Bernhard Geirr. Just the three of them, all males of course. We think they had an early reaction engine and not too much fuel. The point is, the first Sunbird mission was lost in space. They never came out from behind the sun. That was about when the big flares started. Jan thinks they must have been close to one, you heard them say they were damaged."

Dave grunts. Lorimer is fighting excitement like a brush discharge sparking in his gut.

"Either they are who they say they are or they're ghosts; or they're aliens pretending to be people. Jan says maybe the disruption in those super-flares could collapse the local time dimension. Pluggo. What did you observe there, I mean the highlights?"

Time dimension . . . never came back . . . Lorimer's mind narrows onto the reality of the two unmoving bearded heads before him, refuses to admit the words he thought he heard: *Before the year two thousand.*

The language, he thinks. The language would have to have changed. He feels better.

A deep baritone voice says, "Margo?" In *Sunbird* eyes come alert.

"—like the big one fifty years ago." The man has the accent too. "We were really lucky being right there when it popped. The most interesting part is that we confirmed the gravity turbulence. Periodic but not waves. It's violent, we got pushed around some. Space is under monster stress in those things. We think France's theory that our system is passing through a micro-black-hole cluster looks right. So long as one doesn't plonk us."

"France?" Bud mutters. Dave looks at him speculatively.

"It's hard to imagine anything being kicked out in time. But they're here, whatever they are, they're over eight hundred kays outside us scooting out toward Aldebaran. As Lorna said, if they're trying to reach Earth they're in trouble unless they have a lot of spare gees. Should we try to talk to them? Over. Oh, great about the cow. Over again."

"Black holes." Bud whistles softly. "That's one for you, Doc. Was we in a black hole?"

"Not in one or we wouldn't be here." If we are here, Lorimer adds to himself. A micro-black-hole cluster . . . what happens when fragments of totally collapsed matter approach each other, or collide, say in the photosphere of a star? Time disruption? Stop it. Aloud he says, "They could be telling us something, Dave."

Dave says nothing. The minutes pass.

Finally the Earth voice comes back, saying that it will try to contact the strangers on their original frequency. Bud glances at Dave, tunes the selector.

"Calling Sunbird One?" the girl says slowly through her nose. "This is Luna Central calling Major Norman Davis of Sunbird One. We have picked up your conversation with our ship Escondita. We are very puzzled as to who you are and how you got there. If you really are Sunbird One we think you must have been jumped forward in time when you passed the solar flare." She pronounces it Cockney-style, "toime."

"Our ship Gloria is near you, they see you on their radar. We think you may have a serious course problem because you told Lorna you were headed for Earth and you think it is now October with Earth in Pisces. It is not October, it is March fifteen. I repeat, the Earth date"—she says "dyte"—"is March fifteen, time twenty hundred hours. You should be able to see Earth very close to Spica in Virgo. You said your window is damaged. Can't you go out and look? We think you have to make a big course correction. Do you have enough fuel? Do you have a computer? Do you have enough air and water and food? Can we help you? We're listening on this frequency. Luna to Sunbird One, come in."

On *Sunbird* nobody stirs. Lorimer struggles against internal eruptions. *Never came back. Jumped forward in time.* The cyst of memories he has schooled himself to suppress bulges up in the lengthening silence. "Aren't you going to answer?"

"Don't be stupid," Dave says.

"Dave. A hundred and forty-nine degrees is the difference between Gamma Piscium and Spica. That transmission is coming from where they say Earth is."

"You goofed."

"I did not goof. It has to be March."

Dave blinks as if a fly is bothering him.

In fifteen minutes the Luna voice runs through the whole thing again, ending "Please, come in."

"Not a tape." Bud unwraps a stick of gum, adding the plastic to the neat wad back of the gyro leads. Lorimer's skin crawls, watching the ambiguous dazzle of Spica. Spica-plus-Earth? Unbelief grips him, rocks him with a complex pang compounded of faces, voices, the sizzle of bacon frying, the creak of his father's wheelchair, chalk on a sunlit blackboard, Ginny's bare legs on the flowered couch, Jenny and Penny running dangerously close to the lawnmower. The girls will be taller now, Jenny is already as tall as her mother. His father is living with Amy in Denver, determined to last till his son gets home. *When I get home.* This has to be insanity, Dave's right; it's a trick, some crazy trick. The language.

Fifteen minutes more; the flat, earnest female voice comes back and repeats it all, putting in more stresses. Dave wears a remote frown, like a man listening to a lousy sports program. Lorimer has the notion he might switch off and propose a hand of gin; wills him to do so. The voice says it will now change frequencies.

Bud tunes back, chewing calmly. This time the voice stumbles on a couple of phrases. It sounds tired.

Another wait; an hour, now. Lorimer's mind holds only the bright point of Spica digging at him. Bud hums a bar of "Yellow Ribbons," falls silent again.

"Dave," Lorimer says finally, "our antenna is pointed straight at Spica. I don't care if you think I goofed, if Earth is over there we have to change course soon. Look, you can see it could be a double light source. We have to check this out."

Dave says nothing. Bud says nothing but his eyes rove to the port window, back to his instrument panel, to the window again. In the corner of the panel is a polaroid snap of his wife. Patty: a tall, giggling, rump-switching red-head; Lorimer has occasional fantasies about her. Little-girl voice, though. And so tall. . . . Some short men chase tall women; it strikes Lorimer as undignified. Ginny is an inch shorter than he. Their girls will be taller. And Ginny insisted on starting a pregnancy before he left, even though he'll be out of commo. Maybe, maybe a boy, a son—*stop it.* Think about anything. Bud. . . . Does Bud love Patty? Who knows? He loves Ginny. At seventy million miles. . . .

"Judy?" Luna Central or whoever it is says. "They don't answer. You want to try? But listen, we've been thinking. If these people really are from the past this must be very traumatic for them. They could be just realizing they'll never see their world again. Myda says these males had children and women they stayed with, they'll miss them terribly. This is exciting for us but it may seem awful to them. They could be too shocked to answer. They could be frightened, maybe they think we're aliens or hallucinations even. See?"

Five seconds later the nearby girl says, "Da, Margo, we were into that too. Dinko. Ah, Sunbird? Major Davis of Sunbird, are you there? This is Judy Paris in the ship Gloria, we're only about a million kay from you, we see you on our screen." She sounds young and excited. "Luna Central has been trying to reach you, we think you're in trouble and we want to help. Please don't be frightened, we're people just like you. We think you're way off course if you want to reach Earth. Are you in trouble? Can we help? If your radio is out can you make any sort of signal? Do you know Old Morse? You'll be off our screen soon, we're truly worried about you. Please reply somehow if you possibly can, Sunbird, come in!"

Dave sits impassive. Bud glances at him, at the port window, gazes stolidly at the speaker, his face blank. Lorimer has exhausted surprise, he wants only to reply to the voices. He can manage a rough signal by heterodyning the probe beam. But what then, with them both against him?

The girl's voice tries again determinedly. Finally she says, "Margo, they won't peep. Maybe they're dead? I think they're aliens."

Are we not? Lorimer thinks. The Luna station comes back with a different, older voice.

"Judy, Myda here, I've had another thought. These people had a very rigid authority code. You remember your history, they peck-ordered everything. You notice Major Davis repeated about being commanding. That's called dominance-submission structure, one of them gave orders and the others did whatever they were told, we don't know quite why. Perhaps they were frightened. The point is that if the dominant one is in shock or panicked maybe the others can't reply unless this Davis lets them."

Jesus Christ, Lorimer thinks. Jesus H. Christ in colors. It is his father's expression for the inexpressible. Dave and Bud sit unstirring.

"How weird," the Judy voice says. "But don't they

know they're on a bad course? I mean, could the dominant one make the others fly right out of the system? Truly?"

It's happened, Lorimer thinks; it has happened. I have to stop this. I have to act now, before they lose us. Desperate visions of himself defying Dave and Bud loom before him. Try persuasion first.

Just as he opens his mouth he sees Bud stir slightly, and with immeasurable gratitude hears him say, "Dave-o, what say we take an eyeball look? One little old burp won't hurt us."

Dave's head turns a degree or two.

"Or should I go out and see, like the chick said?" Bud's voice is mild.

After a long minute Dave says neutrally, "All right. . . . Attitude change." His arm moves up as though heavy; he stars methodically setting in the values for the vector that will bring Spica in line with their functional window.

Now why couldn't I have done that, Lorimer asks himself for the thousandth time, following the familiar check sequence. Don't answer. . . . And for the thousandth time he is obscurely moved by the rightness of them. The authentic ones, the alphas. Their bond. The awe he had felt first for the absurd jocks of his school ball team.

"That's go, Dave, assuming nothing got creamed."

Dave throws the ignition safety, puts the computer on real time. The hull shudders. Everything in the cabin drifts sidewise while the bright point of Spica swims the other way, appears on the front window as the retros cut in. When the star creeps out onto clear glass Lorimer can clearly see its companion. The double light steadies there; a beautiful job. He hands Bud the telescope.

"The one on the left."

Bud looks. "There she is, all right. Hey, Dave, look at that!"

He puts the scope in Dave's hand. Slowly, Dave raises it and looks. Lorimer can hear him breathe. Suddenly Dave pulls up the mike.

"Houston!" he shouts harshly. "Sunbird to Houston, Sunbird calling Houston! Houston, come in!"

Into the silence the speaker squeals, "They fired their engines—wait, she's calling!" And shuts up.

In *Sunbird*'s cabin nobody speaks. Lorimer stares at the twin stars ahead, impossible realities shifting around him as the minutes congeal. Bud's reflected face looks downwards, grin gone. Dave's beard moves silently; praying, Lorimer realizes. Alone of the crew Dave is deeply religious. At Sunday meals he gives a short, dignified grace. A shocking pity for Dave rises in Lorimer; Dave is so deeply involved with his family, his four sons, always thinking about their training, taking them hunting, fishing, camping. And Doris his wife so incredibly active and sweet, going on their trips, cooking and doing things for the community. Driving Penny and Jenny to classes while Ginny was sick that time. Good people, the backbone . . . This can't be, he thinks; Packard's voice is going to come through in a minute, the antenna's beamed right now. Six minutes now. This will all go away . . . *Before the year two thousand*—stop it, the language would have changed. Think of Doris. . . . She has that glow, feeding her five men; women with sons are different. But Ginny, but his dear woman, his *wife,* his *daughters* —grandmothers now? All dead and dust? *Quit that.* Dave is still praying. . . . Who knows what goes on inside those heads? Dave's cry. . . . Twelve minutes, it has to be all right. The second sweep is stuck, no, it's moving. Thirteen. It's all insane, a dream. Thirteen plus . . . fourteen. The speaker hissing and clicking vacantly. Fifteen now. A dream. . . . Or are those women staying off, letting us see? Sixteen. . . .

At twenty Dave's hand moves, stops again. The seconds jitter by, space crackles. Thirty minutes coming up.

"Calling Major Davis in Sunbird?" It is the older woman, a gentle voice. "This is Luna Central. We are the service and communication facility for space flight now. We're sorry to have to tell you that there is no space center at Houston any more. Houston itself was abandoned when the shuttle base moved to White Sands, over two centuries ago."

A cool dust-colored light enfolds Lorimer's brain, isolating it. It will remain so a long time.

The woman is explaining it all again, offering help, asking if they were hurt. A nice dignified speech. Dave still sits immobile, gazing at Earth. Bud puts the mike in his hand.

"Tell them, Dave-o."

Dave looks at it, takes a deep breath, presses the send button.

"Sunbird to Luna Control," he says quite normally. (It's "Central," Lorimer thinks.) "We copy. Ah, negative on life support, we have no problems. We copy the course change suggestion and are proceeding to recompute. Your offer of computer assistance is appreciated. We suggest you transmit position data so we can get squared away. Ah, we are economizing on transmission until we see how our accumulators have held up. Sunbird out."

And so it had begun.

Lorimer's mind floats back to himself now floating in *Gloria,* nearly a year, or three hundred years, later; watching and being watched by them. He still feels light, contented; the dread underneath has come no nearer. But it is so silent. He seems to have heard no voices for a long time. Or was it a long time? Maybe the drug is working on his time sense, maybe it was only a minute or two.

"I've been remembering," he says to the woman Connie, wanting her to speak.

She nods. "You have so much to remember. Oh, I'm sorry—that wasn't good to say." Her eyes speak sympathy.

"Never mind." It is all dreamlike now, his lost world and this other which he is just now seeing plain. "We must seem like very strange beasts to you."

"We're trying to understand," she says. "It's history, you learn the events but you don't really feel what people were like, how it was for them. We hope you'll tell us."

The drug, Lorimer thinks, that's what they're trying. Tell them . . . how can he? Could a dinosaur tell how it was? A montage flows through his mind, dominated by random shots of Operations' north parking lot and Ginny's yellow kitchen telephone with the sickly ivy vines. . . . Women and vines. . . .

A burst of laughter distracts him. It's coming from the chamber they call the gym, Bud and the others must be playing ball in there. Bright idea, really, he muses: Using muscle power, sustained mild exercise. That's why they are all so fit. The gym is a glorified squirrel-wheel, when you climb or pedal up the walls it revolves and winds a gear train, which among other things rotates the sleeping drum. A real Woolagong. . . . Bud and Dave usually take their shifts together, scrambling the spinning gym like big pale apes. Lorimer prefers the easy rhythm of the women, and the cycle here fits him nicely. He usually puts in his shift with Connie, who doesn't talk much, and one of the Judys, who do.

No one is talking now, though. Remotely uneasy he looks around the big cylinder of the cabin, sees Dave and Lady Blue by the forward window. Judy Dakar is behind them, silent for once. They must be looking at Earth; it has been a beautiful expanding disk for some weeks now. Dave's beard is moving, he is praying again. He has taken to doing that, not ostentatiously, but so obviously sincere that Lorimer, a life atheist, can only sympathize.

The Judys have asked Dave what he whispers, of course. When Dave understood that they had no concept of prayer and had never seen a Christian Bible there had been a heavy silence.

"So you have lost all faith," he said finally.

"We have faith," Judy Paris protested.

"May I ask in what?"

"We have faith in ourselves, of course," she told him.

"Young lady, if you were my daughter I'd tan your

britches," Dave said, not joking. The subject was not raised again.

But he came back so well after that first dreadful shock, Lorimer thinks. A personal god, a father-model, man needs that. Dave draws strength from it and we lean on him. Maybe leaders have to believe. Dave was so great; cheerful, unflappable, patiently working out alternatives, making his decisions on the inevitable discrepancies in the position readings in a way Lorimer couldn't do. A bitch. . . .

Memory takes him again; he is once again back in *Sunbird,* gritty-eyed, listening to the women's chatter, Dave's terse replies. God, how they chattered. But their computer work checks out. Lorimer is suffering also from a quirk of Dave's, his reluctance to transmit their exact thrust and fuel reserve. He keeps holding out a margin and making Lorimer compute it back in.

But the margins don't help; it is soon clear that they are in big trouble. Earth will pass too far ahead of them on her next orbit, they don't have the acceleration to catch up with her before they cross her path. They can carry out an ullage maneuver, they can kill enough velocity to let Earth catch them on the second go-by; but that would take an extra year and their life-support would be long gone. The grim question of whether they have enough to enable a single man to wait it out pushes into Lorimer's mind. He pushes it back; that one is for Dave.

There is a final possibility: Venus will approach their trajectory three months hence and they may be able to gain velocity by swinging by it. They go to work on that.

Meanwhile Earth is steadily drawing away from them and so is *Gloria,* closer toward the sun. They pick her out of the solar interference and then lose her again. They know her crew now: the man is Andy Kay, the senior woman is Lady Blue Parks; they appear to do the navigating. Then there is a Connie Morelos and the two twins, Judy Paris and Judy Dakar, who run the communications. The chief Luna voices are women too, Margo and Azella. The men can hear them talking to the *Escondita* which is now swinging in toward the far side of the sun. Dave insists on monitoring and taping everything that comes through. It proves to be largely replays of their exchanges with Luna and *Gloria,* mixed with a variety of highly personal messages. As references to cows, chickens, and other livestock multiply Dave reluctantly gives up his idea that they are code. Bud counts a total of five male voices.

"Big deal," he says. "There were more chick drivers on the road when we left. Means space is safe now, the girlies have taken over. Let them sweat their little asses off." He chuckles. "When we get this bird down, the stars ain't gonna study old Buddy no more, no ma'm. A nice beach and about a zillion steaks and ale and all those sweet things. Hey, we'll be living history, we can charge admission."

Dave's face takes on the expression that means an inappropriate topic has been breached. Much to Lorimer's impatience, Dave discourages all speculation as to what may await them on this future Earth. He confines their transmissions strictly to the problem in hand; when Lorimer tries to get him at least to mention the unchanged-language puzzle Dave only says firmly, "Later." Lorimer fumes; inconceivable that he is three centuries in the future, unable to learn a thing.

They do glean a few facts from the women's talk. There have been nine successful *Sunbird* missions after theirs and one other casualty. And the *Gloria* and her sister ship are on a long-planned fly-by of the two inner planets.

"We always go along in pairs," Judy says. "But those planets are no good. Still, it was worth seeing."

"For Pete's sake, Dave, ask them how many planets have been visited," Lorimer pleads.

"Later."

But about the fifth meal-break Luna suddenly volunteers.

"Earth is making up a history for you, Sunbird," the Margo voice says. "We know you don't want to waste power asking so we thought we'd send you a few main points right now." She laughs. "It's much harder than we thought, nobody here does history."

Lorimer nods to himself; he has been wondering what he could tell a man from 1690 who would want to know what happened to Cromwell—was Cromwell then?—and who had never heard of electricity, atoms, or the U.S.A.

"Let's see, probably the most important is that there aren't as many people as you had, we're just over two million. There was a world epidemic not long after your time. It didn't kill people but it reduced the population. I mean there weren't any babies in most of the world. Ah, sterility. The country called Australia was affected least." Bud holds up a finger.

"And North Canada wasn't too bad. So the survivors all got together in the south part of the American states where they could grow food and the best communications and factories were. Nobody lives in the rest of the world but we travel there sometimes. Ah, we have five main activities, was 'industries' the word? Food, that's farming and fishing. Communications, transport, and space—that's us. And the factories they need. We live a lot simpler than you did, I think. We see your things all over, we're very grateful to you. Oh, you'll be interested to know we use zeppelins just like you did, we have six big ones. And our fifth thing is the children. Babies. Does that help? I'm using a children's book we have here."

The men have frozen during this recital; Lorimer is holding a cooling bag of hash. Bud starts chewing again and chokes.

"Two million people and a space capability?" He coughs. "That's incredible."

Dave gazes reflectively at the speaker. "There's a lot they're not telling us."

"I gotta ask them," Bud says. "Okay?"

Dave nods. "Watch it."

"Thanks for the history, Luna," Bud says. "We really appreciate it. But we can't figure out how you maintain a space program with only a couple of million people. Can you tell us a little more on that?"

In the pause Lorimer tries to grasp the staggering figures. From eight billion to two million . . . Europe, Asia, Africa, South America, America itself—wiped out. *There weren't any more babies.* World sterility, from what? The Black Death, the famines of Asia—those had been decimations. This is magnitudes worse. No, it is all the same: beyond comprehension. An empty world, littered with junk.

"Sunbird?" says Margo. "Da, I should have thought you'd want to know about space. Well, we have only the four real spaceships and one building. You know the two here. Then there's *Indira* and *Pech,* they're on the Mars run now. Maybe the Mars dome was since your day. You had the satellite stations though, didn't you? And the old Luna dome, of course—I remember now, it was during the epidemic. They tried to set up colonies to, ah, breed children, but the epidemic got there too. They struggled terribly hard. We owe a lot to you really, you men I mean. The history has it all, how you worked out a minimal viable program and trained everybody and saved it from the crazies. It was a glorious achievement. Oh, the marker here has one of your names on it. Lorimer. We love to keep it all going and growing, we all love traveling. Man is a rover, that's one of our mottoes."

"Are you hearing what I'm hearing?" Bud asks, blinking comically.

Dave is still staring at the speaker. "Not one word about their government," he says slowly. "Not a word about economic conditions. We're talking to a bunch of monkeys."

"Should I ask them?"

"Wait a minute . . . Roger, ask the name of their chief of state and the head of the space program. And —no, that's all."

"President?" Margo echoes Bud's query. "You mean like queens and kings? Wait, here's Myda. She's been talking about you with Earth."

The older woman they hear occasionally says, "Sunbird? Da, we realize you had a very complex activity, your governments. With so few people we don't have that type of formal structure at all. People from the different activities meet periodically and our communications are good, everyone is kept informed. The people in each activity are in charge of doing it while they're there. We rotate, you see. Mostly in five-year hitches; for example, Margo here was on the zeppelins and I've been on several factories and farms and of course the, well, the education, we all do that. I believe that's one big difference from you. And of course we all work. And things are basically far more stable now, I gather. We change slowly. Does that answer you? Of course you can always ask Registry, they keep track of us all. But we can't, ah, take you to our leader, if that's what you mean." She laughs, a genuine, jolly sound. "That's one of our old jokes. I must say," she goes on seriously, "it's been a joy to us that we can understand you so well. We make a big effort not to let the language drift, it would be tragic to lose touch with the past."

Dave takes the mike. "Thank you, Luna. You've given us something to think about. Sunbird out."

"How much of that is for real, Doc?" Bud rubs his curly head. "They're giving us one of your science fiction stories."

"The real story will come later," says Dave. "Our job is to get there."

"That's a point that doesn't look too good."

By the end of the session it looks worse. No Venus trajectory is any good. Lorimer reruns all the computations; same result.

"There doesn't seem to be any solution to this one, Dave," he says at last. "The parameters are just too tough. I think we've had it."

Dave massages his knuckles thoughtfully. Then he nods: "Roger. We'll fire the optimum sequence on the Earth heading."

"Tell them to wave if they see us go by," says Bud.

They are silent, contemplating the prospect of a slow death in space eighteen months hence. Lorimer wonders if he can raise the other question, the bad one. He is pretty sure what Dave will say. What will he himself decide, what will he have the guts to do?

"Hello, Sunbird?" the voice of *Gloria* breaks in. "Listen, we've been figuring. We think if you use all your fuel you could come back in close enough to our orbit so we could swing out and pick you up. You'd be using solar gravity that way. We have plenty of maneuver but much less acceleration than you do. You have suits and some kind of propellants, don't you? I mean, you could fly across a few kays?"

The three men look at each other; Lorimer guesses he had not been the only one to speculate on that.

"That's a good thought, Gloria," Dave says. "Let's hear what Luna says."

"Why?" asks Judy. "It's our business, we wouldn't endanger the ship. We'd only miss another look at Venus, who cares. We have plenty of water and food and if the air gets a little smelly we can stand it."

"Hey, the chicks are all right," Bud says. They wait.

The voice of Luna comes on. "We've been looking at that too, Judy. We're not sure you understand the risk. Ah, Sunbird, excuse me. Judy, if you manage to pick them up you'll have to spend nearly a year in the ship with these three male persons from a *very different culture*. Myda says you should remember history and it's a risk no matter what Connie says. Sunbird, I hate to be so rude. Over."

Bud is grinning broadly, they all are. "Cave men," he chuckles. "All the chicks land preggers."

"Margo, they're human beings," the Judy voice protests. "This isn't just Connie, we're all agreed. Andy and Lady Blue say it would be very interesting. If it works, that is. We can't let them go without trying."

"We feel that way too, of course," Luna replies. "But there's another problem. They could be carrying diseases. Sunbird, I know you've been isolated for fourteen months, but Murti says people in your day were immune to organisms that aren't around now. Maybe some of ours could harm you, too. You could all get mortally sick and lose the ship."

"We thought of that, Margo," Judy says impatiently.

"Look, if you have contact with them at all somebody has to test, true? So we're ideal. By the time we get home you'll know. And how could we all get sick so fast we couldn't put Gloria in a stable orbit where you could get her later on?"

They wait. "Hey, what about that epidemic?" Bud pats his hair elaborately. "I don't know if I want a career in gay lib."

"You rather stay out here?" Dave asks.

"Crazies," says a different voice from Luna. "Sunbird, I'm Murti, the health person here. I think what we have to fear most is the meningitis-influenza complex, they mutate so readily. Does your Doctor Lorimer have any suggestions?"

"Roger, I'll put him on," says Dave. "But as to your first point, madam, I want to inform you that at time of takeoff the incidence of rape in the United States space cadre was zero point zero. I guarantee the conduct of my crew provided you can control yours. Here is Doctor Lorimer."

But Lorimer cannot of course tell them anything useful. They discuss the men's polio shots, which luckily have used killed virus, and various childhood diseases which still seem to be around. He does not mention their epidemic.

"Luna, we're going to try it," Judy declares. "We couldn't live with ourselves. Now let's get the course figured before they get any farther away."

From there on there is no rest on *Sunbird* while they set up and refigure and rerun the computations for the envelope of possible intersection trajectories. The *Gloria*'s drive, they learn, is indeed low-thrust, although capable of sustained operation. *Sunbird* will have to get most of the way to the rendezvous on her own if they can cancel their outward velocity.

The tension breaks once during the long session, when Luna calls *Gloria* to warn Connie to be sure the female crew members wear concealing garments at all times if the men came aboard.

"Not suit-liners, Connie, they're much too tight." It is the older woman, Myda. Bud chuckles.

"Your light sleepers, I think. And when the men unsuit, your Andy is the only one who should help them. You others stay away. The same for all body functions and sleeping. This is very important, Connie; you'll have to watch it the whole way home. There are a great many complicated taboos. I'm putting an instruction list on the bleeper, is your receiver working?"

"Da, we used it for France's black-hole paper."

"Good. Tell Judy to stand by. Now listen, Connie, listen carefully. Tell Andy he has to read it all. I repeat, *he* has to read every word. Did you hear that?"

"Ah, dinko," Connie answers. "I understand, Myda. He will."

"I think we just lost the ball game, fellas," Bud laments. "Old mother Myda took it all away."

Even Dave laughs. But later when the modulated squeal that is a whole text comes through the speaker, he frowns again. "There goes the good stuff."

The last factors are cranked in; the revised program spins, and Luna confirms them. "We have a pay-out, Dave," Lorimer reports. "It's tight but there are at least two viable options. Provided the main jets are fully functional."

"We're going EVA to check."

That is exhausting; they find a warp in the deflector housing of the port engines and spend four sweating hours trying to wrestle it back. It is only Lorimer's third sight of open space but he is soon too tired to care.

"Best we can do," Dave pants finally. "We'll have to compensate in the psychic mode."

"You can do it, Dave-o," says Bud. "Hey, I gotta change those suit radios, don't let me forget."

In the psychic mode . . . Lorimer surfaces back to his real self, cocooned in *Gloria*'s big cluttered cabin, seeing Connie's living face. It must be hours, how long has he been dreaming?

"About two minutes," Connie smiles.

"I was thinking of the first time I saw you."

"Oh yes. We'll never forget that, ever."

Nor will he . . . He lets it unroll again in his head. The interminable hours after the first long burn, which has sent *Sunbird* yawing so they all have to gulp nausea pills. Judy's breathless voice reading down their approach: "Oh, very good, four hundred thousand . . . Oh great, Sunbird, you're almost three, you're going to break a hundred for sure——" Dave has done it, the big one.

Lorimer's probe is useless in the yaw, it isn't until they stabilize enough for the final burst that they can see the strange blip bloom and vanish in the slot. Converging, hopefully, on a theoretical near-intersection point.

"Here goes everything."

The final burn changes the yaw into a sickening tumble with the starfield looping past the glass. The pills are no more use and the fuel feed to the attitude jets goes sour. They are all vomiting before they manage to hand-pump the last of the fuel and slow the tumble.

"That's it, Gloria. Come and get us. Lights on, Bud. Let's get those suits up."

Fighting nausea they go through the laborious routine in the fouled cabin. Suddenly Judy's voice sings out, "We see you, Sunbird! We see your light! Can't you see us?"

"No time," Dave says. But Bud, half-suited, points at the window. "Fellas, oh, hey, look at that."

"Father, we thank you," says Dave quietly. "All right, move it on, Doc. Packs."

The effort of getting themselves plus the propulsion units and a couple of cargo nets out of the rolling ship drives everything else out of mind. It isn't until they are floating linked together and stabilized by Dave's hand jet that Lorimer has time to look.

The sun blanks out their left. A few meters below them *Sunbird* tumbles empty, looking absurdly small. Ahead of them, infinitely far away, is a point too blurred and yellow to be a star. It creeps: *Gloria,* on her approach tangent.

"Can you start, Sunbird?" says Judy in their helmets. "We don't want to brake any more on account of our exhaust. We estimate fifty kay in an hour, we're coming out on a line."

"Roger. Give me your jet, Doc."

"Goodbye, Sunbird," says Bud. "Plenty of lead, Dave-o."

Lorimer finds it restful in a childish way, being towed across the abyss tied to the two big men. He has total confidence in Dave, he never considers the possibility that they will miss, sail by and be lost. Does Dave feel contempt? Lorimer wonders; that banked-up silence, is it partly contempt for those who can manipulate only symbols, who have no mastery of matter?
. . . He concentrates on mastering his stomach.

It is a long, dark trip. *Sunbird* shrinks to a twinkling light, slowly accelerating on the spiral course that will end her ultimately in the sun with their precious records that are three hundred years obsolete. With, also, the packet of photos and letters that Lorimer has twice put in his suit-pouch and twice taken out. Now and then he catches sight of *Gloria,* growing from a blur to an incomprehensible tangle of lighted crescents.

"Woo-ee, see there," Bud says. "No wonder they can't accelerate, that thing is a flying trailer park. It'd break up."

"It's a space ship. Got those nets tight, Doc?"

Judy's voice suddenly fills their helmets. "I see your lights! Can you see me? Will you have enough left to brake at all?"

"Affirmative to both, Gloria," says Dave.

At that moment Lorimer is turned slowly forward again and he sees—will see it forever: the alien ship in the starfield and on its dark side the tiny lights that are women in the stars, waiting for them. Three—no, four; one suit-light is way out, moving. If that is a tether is must be over a kilometer.

"Hello, I'm Judy Dakar!" The voice is close. "Oh, mother, you're big! Are you all right? How's your air?"

"No problem."

They are in fact stale and steaming wet; too much

adrenalin. Dave uses the jets again and suddenly she is growing, is coming right at them, a silvery spider on a trailing thread. Her suit looks trim and flexible; it is mirror-bright, and the pack is quite small. Marvels of the future, Lorimer thinks; Paragraph One.

"You made it, you made it! Here, tie in. Brake!"

"There ought to be some historic words," Bud murmurs. "If she gives us a chance."

"Hello, Judy," says Dave calmly. "Thanks for coming."

"Contact!" She blasts their ears. "Haul us in, Andy! Brake, brake—the exhaust is back there!"

And they are grabbed hard, deflected into a great arc toward the ship. Dave uses up the last jet. The line loops.

"Don't jerk it," Judy cries. "Oh, I'm *sorry*." She is clinging on them like a gibbon, Lorimer can see her eyes, her excited mouth. Incredible. "Watch out, it's slack."

"Teach me, honey," says Andy's baritone. Lorimer twists and sees him far back at the end of a heavy tether, hauling them smoothly in. Bud offers to help, is refused. "Just hang loose, please," a matronly voice tells them. It is obvious Andy has done this before. They come in spinning slowly, like space fish. Lorimer finds he can no longer pick out the twinkle that is *Sunbird*. When he is swung back, *Gloria* has changed to a disorderly cluster of bulbs and spokes around a big central cylinder. He can see pods and miscellaneous equipment stowed all over her. Not like science fiction.

Andy is paying the line into a floating coil. Another figure floats beside him. They are both quite short, Lorimer realizes as they near.

"Catch the cable," Andy tells them. There is a busy moment of shifting inertial drag.

"Welcome to Gloria, Major Davis, Captain Geirr, Doctor Lorimer. I'm Lady Blue Parks. I think you'll like to get inside as soon as possible. If you feel like climbing go right ahead, we'll pull all this in later."

"We appreciate it, Ma'm."

They start hand-over-hand along the catenary of the

main tether. It has a good rough grip. Judy coasts up to peer at them, smiling broadly, towing the coil. A taller figure waits by the ship's open airlock.

"Hello, I'm Connie. I think we can cycle in two at a time. Will you come with me, Major Davis?"

It's like an emergency on a plane, Lorimer thinks as Dave follows her in. Being ordered about by supernaturally polite little girls.

"Space-going stews," Bud nudges him. "How 'bout that?" His face is sprouting sweat. Lorimer tells him to go next, his own LSP has less load.

Bud goes in with Andy. The woman named Lady Blue waits beside Lorimer while Judy scrambles on the hull securing their cargo nets. She doesn't seem to have magnetic soles; perhaps ferrous metals aren't used in space now. When Judy begins hauling in the main tether on a simple hand winch, Lady Blue looks at it critically.

"I used to make those," she says to Lorimer. What he can see of her features looks compressed, her dark eyes twinkle. He has the impression she is part Black.

"I ought to get over and clean that aft antenna." Judy floats up. "Later," says Lady Blue. They both smile at Lorimer. Then the hatch opens and he and Lady Blue go in. When the toggles seat there comes a rising scream of air and Lorimer's suit collapses.

"Can I help you?" She has opened her faceplate, the voice is rich and live. Eagerly Lorimer catches the latches in his clumsy gloves and lets her lift the helmet off. His first breath surprises him, it takes an instant to identify the gas as fresh air. Then the inner hatch opens, letting in greenish light. She waves him through. He swims into a short tunnel. Voices are coming from around the corner ahead. His hand finds a grip and he stops, feeling his heart shudder in his chest.

When he turns that corner the world he knows will be dead. Gone, rolled up, blown away forever with *Sunbird*. He will be irrevocably in the future. A man from the past, a time traveler. In the future. . . .

He pulls himself around the bend.

The future is a vast bright cylinder, its whole inner surface festooned with unidentifiable objects, fronds of green. In front of him floats an odd tableau: Bud and Dave, helmets off, looking enormous in their bulky white suits and packs. A few meters away hang two bare-headed figures in shiny suits and a dark-haired girl in flowing pink pajamas.

They are all simply staring at the two men, their eyes and mouths open in identical expressions of pleased wonder. The face that has to be Andy's is grinning open-mouthed like a kid at the zoo. He is a surprisingly young boy, Lorimer sees, in spite of his deep voice; blond, downy-cheeked, compactly muscular. Lorimer finds he can scarcely bear to look at the pink woman, can't tell if she really is surpassingly beautiful or plain. The taller suited woman has a shiny, ordinary face.

From overhead bursts an extraordinary sound which he finally recognizes as a chicken cackling. Lady Blue pushes past him.

"All right, Andy, Connie, stop staring and help them get their suits off. Judy, Luna is just as eager to hear about this as we are."

The tableau jumps to life. Afterwards Lorimer can recall mostly eyes, bright curious eyes tugging his boots, smiling eyes upside down over his pack—and always that light, ready laughter. Andy is left alone to help them peel down, blinking at the fittings which Lorimer still finds embarrassing. He seems easy and nimble in his own half-open suit. Lorimer struggles out of the last lacings, thinking, a boy! A boy and four women orbiting the sun, flying their big junky ships to Mars. Should he feel humiliated? He only feels grateful, accepting a short robe and a bulb of tea somebody—Connie?—gives him.

The suited Judy comes in with their nets. The men follow Andy along another passage, Bud and Dave clutching at the small robes. Andy stops by a hatch.

"This greenhouse is for you, it's your toilet. Three's a lot but you have full sun."

Inside is a brilliant jungle, foliage everywhere, glittering water droplets, rustling leaves. Something whirs away—a grasshopper.

"You crank that handle." Andy points to a seat on a large crossduct. "The piston rams the gravel and waste into a compost process and it ends up in the soil core. That vetch is a heavy nitrogen user and a great oxidator. We pump CO_2 in and oxy out. It's a real Woolagong."

He watches critically while Bud tries out the facility.

"What's a Woolagong?" asks Lorimer dazedly.

"Oh, she's one of our inventors. Some of her stuff is weird. When we have a pluggy-looking thing that works we call it a Woolagong." He grins. "The chickens eat the seeds and the hoppers, see, and the hoppers and iguanas eat the leaves. When a greenhouse is going darkside we turn them in to harvest. With this much light I think we could keep a goat, don't you? You didn't have any life at all on your ship, true?"

"No," Lorimer says, "not a single iguana."

"They promised us a Shetland pony for Christmas," says Bud, rattling gravel. Andy joins perplexedly in the laugh.

Lorimer's head is foggy; it isn't only fatigue, the year in *Sunbird* has atrophied his ability to take in novelty. Numbly he uses the Woolagong and they go back out and forward to *Gloria*'s big control room, where Dave makes a neat short speech to Luna and is answered graciously.

"We have to finish changing course now," Lady Blue says. Lorimer's impression has been right, she is a small light part-Negro in late middle age. Connie is part something exotic too, he sees; the others are European types.

"I'll get you something to eat." Connie smiles warmly. "Then you probably want to rest. We saved all the cubbies for you." She says "syved"; their accents are all identical.

As they leave the control room Lorimer sees the withdrawn look in Dave's eyes and knows he must be feeling the reality of being a passenger in an alien ship;

not in command, not deciding the course, the communications going on unheard.

That is Lorimer's last coherent observation, that and the taste of the strange, good food. And then being led aft through what he now knows as the gym, to the shaft of the sleeping drum. There are six irised ports like dog-doors; he pushes through his assigned port and finds himself facing a roomy mattress. Shelves and a desk are in the wall.

"For your excretions." Connie's arm comes through the iris, pointing at bags. "If you have a problem stick your head out and call. There's water."

Lorimer simply drifts toward the mattress, too sweated out to reply. His drifting ends in a curious heavy settling and his final astonishment: The drum is smoothly, silently starting to revolve. He sinks gratefully onto the pad, growing "heavier" as the minutes pass. About a tenth gee, maybe more, he thinks, it's still accelerating. And falls into the most restful sleep he has known in the long weary year.

It isn't till next day that he understands that Connie and two others have been on the rungs of the gym chamber, sending it around hour after hour without pause or effort and chatting as they went.

How they talk, he thinks again floating back to real present time. The bubbling irritant pours through his memory, the voices of Ginny and Jenny and Penny on the kitchen telephone, before that his mother's voice, his sister Amy's. Interminable. What do they always have to talk, talk, talk of?

"Why, everything," says the real voice of Connie beside him now. "It's natural to share."

"Natural. . . ." Like ants, he thinks. They twiddle their antennae together every time they meet. Where did you go, what did you do? Twiddle-twiddle. How do you *feel?* Oh, I feel this, I feel that, blah blah twiddle-twiddle. Total coordination of the hive. Women have no self-respect. Say anything, no sense of the strategy of words, the dark danger of naming. Can't hold in.

"Ants, beehives." Connie laughs, showing the bad

tooth. "You truly see us as insects, don't you? Because they're females?"

"Was I talking aloud? I'm sorry." He blinks away dreams.

"Oh, please don't be. It's so sad to hear about your sister and your children and your, your wife. They must have been wonderful people. We think you're very brave."

But he has only thought of Ginny and them all for an instant—what has he been babbling? What is the drug doing to him?

"What are you doing to us?" he demands, lanced by real alarm now, almost angry.

"It's all right, truly." Her hand touches his, warm and somehow shy. "We all use it when we need to explore something. Usually it's pleasant. It's a laevonoramine compound, a disinhibitor, it doesn't dull you like alcohol. We'll be home so soon, you see. We have the responsibility to understand and you're so locked in." Her eyes melt at him. "You don't feel sick, do you? We have the antidote."

"No . . ." His alarm has already flowed away somewhere. Her explanation strikes him as reasonable enough. "We're not locked in," he says or tries to say. "We talk . . ." He gropes for a word to convey the judiciousness, the adult restraint. Objectivity, maybe? "We talk when we have something to say." Irrelevantly he thinks of a mission coordinator named Forrest, famous for his blue jokes. "Otherwise it would all break down," he tells her. "You'd fly right out of the system." That isn't quite what he means; let it pass.

The voices of Dave and Bud ring out suddenly from opposite ends of the cabin, awakening the foreboding of evil in his mind. They don't know us, he thinks. They should look out, stop this. But he is feeling too serene, he wants to think about his own new understanding, the pattern of them all he is seeing at last.

"I feel lucid," he manages to say. "I want to think."

She looks pleased. "We call that the ataraxia effect. It's so nice when it goes that way."

Ataraxia, philosophical calm. Yes. But there are

monsters in the deep, he thinks or says. The night side. The night side of Orren Lorimer, a self hotly dark and complex, waiting in leash. They're so vulnerable. They don't know we can take them. Images rush up: A Judy spreadeagled on the gym rungs, pink pajamas gone, open to him. Flash sequence of the three of them taking over the ship, the women tied up, helpless, shrieking, raped and used. The team—get the satellite station, get a shuttle down to Earth. Hostages. Make them do anything, no defense whatever . . . Has Bud actually said that? But Bud doesn't know, he remembers. Dave knows they're hiding something, but he thinks it's socialism or sin. When they find out. . . .

How has he himself found out? Simply listening, really, all these months. He listens to their talk much more than the others; "fraternizing," Dave calls it. . . . They all listened at first, of course. Listened and looked and reacted helplessly to the female bodies, the tender bulges so close under the thin, tantalizing clothes, the magnetic mouths and eyes, the smell of them, their electric touch. Watching them touch each other, touch Andy, laughing, vanishing quietly into shared bunks. *What goes on? Can I? My need, my need—*

The power of them, the fierce resentment. . . . Bud muttered and groaned meaningfully despite Dave's warnings. He kept needling Andy until Dave banned all questions. Dave himself was noticeably tense and read his Bible a great deal. Lorimer found his own body pointing after them like a famished hound, hoping to Christ the cubicles are as they appeared to be, unwired.

All they learn is that Myda's instructions must have been ferocious. The atmosphere has been implacably antiseptic, the discretion impenetrable. Andy politely ignored every probe. No word or act has told them what, if anything, goes on; Lorimer was irresistibly reminded of the weekend he spent at Jenny's scout camp. The men's training came presently to their rescue, and they resigned themselves to finishing their mission on a super-*Sunbird,* weirdly attended by a troop of Boy and Girl Scouts.

In every other way their reception couldn't be more courteous. They have been given the run of the ship and their own dayroom in a cleaned-out gravel storage pod. They visit the control room as they wish. Lady Blue and Andy give them specs and manuals and show them every circuit and device of *Gloria,* inside and out. Luna has bleeped up a stream of science texts and the data on all their satellites and shuttles and the Mars and Luna dome colonies.

Dave and Bud plunged into an orgy of engineering. *Gloria* is, as they suspected, powered by a fission plant that uses a range of Lunar minerals. Her ion drive is only slightly advanced over the experimental models of their own day. The marvels of the future seem so far to consist mainly of ingenious modifications.

"It's primitive," Bud tells him. "What they've done is sacrifice everything to keep it simple and easy to maintain. Believe it, they can hand-feed fuel. And the backups, brother! They have redundant redundancy."

But Lorimer's technical interest soon flags. What he really wants is to be alone a while. He makes a desultory attempt to survey the apparently few new developments in his field, and finds he can't concentrate. What the hell, he tells himself, I stopped being a physicist three hundred years ago. Such a relief to be out of the cell of *Sunbird;* he has given himself up to drifting solitary through the warren of the ship, using their excellent 400 mm. telescope, noting the odd life of the crew.

When he finds that Lady Blue likes chess, they form a routine of bi-weekly games. Her personality intrigues him; she has reserve and an aura of authority. But she quickly stops Bud when he calls her "Captain."

"No one here commands in your sense. I'm just the oldest." Bud goes back to "Ma'm."

She plays a solid positional game, somewhat more erratic than a man but with occasional elegant traps. Lorimer is astonished to find that there is only one new chess opening, an interesting queen-side gambit called the Dagmar. One new opening in three centuries? He mentions it to the others when they come back from helping Andy and Judy Paris overhaul a standby converter.

"They haven't done much anywhere," Dave says. "Most of your new stuff dates from the epidemic, Andy, if you'll pardon me. The program seems to be stagnating. You've been gearing up this Titan project for eighty years."

"We'll get there." Andy grins.

"C'mon, Dave," says Bud. "Judy and me are taking on you two for the next chicken dinner, we'll get a bridge team here yet. Woo-ee, I can taste that chicken! Losers get the iguana."

The food is so good. Lorimer finds himself lingering around the kitchen end, helping whoever is cooking, munching on their various seeds and chewy roots as he listens to them talk. He even likes the iguana. He begins to put on weight, in fact they all do. Dave decrees double exercise shifts.

"You going to make us *climb* home, Dave-o?" Bud groans. But Lorimer enjoys it, pedaling or swinging easily along the rungs while the women chat and listen to tapes. Familiar music: he identifies a strange spectrum from Handel, Brahms, Sibelius, through Strauss to ballad tunes and intricate light jazz-rock. No lyrics. But plenty of informative texts doubtless selected for his benefit.

From the promised short history he finds out more about the epidemic. It seems to have been an airborne quasi-virus escaped from Franco-Arab military labs, possibly potentiated by pollutants.

"It apparently damaged only the reproductive cells," he tells Dave and Bud. "There was little actual mortality, but almost universal sterility. Probably a molecular substitution in the gene code in the gametes. And the main effect seems to have been on the men. They mention a shortage of male births afterwards, which suggests that the damage was on the Y-chromosome where it would be selectively lethal to the male fetus."

"Is it still dangerous, Doc?" Dave asks. "What happens to us when we get back home?"

"They can't say. The birthrate is normal now, about

two percent and rising. But the present population may be resistant. They never achieved a vaccine."

"Only one way to tell," Bud says gravely. "I volunteer."

Dave merely glances at him. Extraordinary how he still commands, Lorimer thinks. Not submission, for Pete's sake. A team.

The history also mentions the riots and fighting which swept the world when humanity found itself sterile. Cities bombed, and burned, massacres, panics, mass rapes and kidnapping of women, marauding armies of biologically desperate men, bloody cults. The crazies. But it is all so briefly told, so long ago. Lists of honored names. "We must always be grateful to the brave people who held the Denver Medical Laboratories——" And then on to the drama of building up the helium supply for the dirigibles.

In three centuries it's all dust, he thinks. What do I know of the hideous Thirty Years War that was three centuries back for me? *Fighting devastated Europe for two generations.* Not even names.

The description of their political and economic structure is even briefer. They seem to be, as Myda had said, almost ungoverned.

"It's a form of loose social credit system run by consensus," he says to Dave. "Somewhat like a permanent frontier period. They're building up slowly. Of course they don't need an army or air force. I'm not sure if they even use cash money or recognize private ownership of land. I did notice one favorable reference to early Chinese communalism," he adds, to see Dave's mouth set. "But they aren't tied to a community. They travel about. When I asked Lady Blue about their police and legal system she told me to wait and talk with real historians. This Registry seems to be just that, it's not a policy organ."

"We've run into a situation here, Lorimer," Dave says soberly. "Stay away from it. They're not telling the story."

"You notice they never talk about their husbands?" Bud laughs. "I asked a couple of them what their husbands did and I swear they had to think. And they all have kids. Believe me, it's a swinging scene down there, even if old Andy acts like he hasn't found out what it's for."

"I don't want any prying into their personal family lives while we're on this ship, Geirr. None whatsoever. That's an order."

"Maybe they don't have families. You ever hear 'em mention anybody getting married? That has to be the one thing on a chick's mind. Mark my words, there's been some changes made."

"The social mores are bound to have changed to some extent," Lorimer says. "Obviously you have women doing more work outside the home, for one thing. But they have family bonds; for instance Lady Blue has a sister in an aluminum mill and another in health. Andy's mother is on Mars and his sister works in Registry. Connie has a brother or brothers on the fishing fleet near Biloxi, and her sister is coming out to replace her here next trip, she's making yeast now."

"That's the top of the iceberg."

"I doubt the rest of the iceberg is very sinister, Dave."

But somewhere along the line the blandness begins to bother Lorimer too. So much is missing. Marriage, love affairs, children's troubles, jealousy squabbles, status, possessions, money problems, sicknesses, funerals even—all the daily minutiae that occupied Ginny and her friends seems to have been edited out of these women's talk. *Edited*. . . . Can Dave be right, is some big, significant aspect being deliberately kept from them?

"I'm still surprised your language hasn't changed more," he says one day to Connie during their exertions in the gym.

"Oh, we're very careful about that." She climbs at an angle beside him, not using her hands. "It would be a dreadful loss if we couldn't understand the books. All the children are taught from the same original tapes, you see. Oh, there's faddy words we use for a while, but our communicators have to learn the old texts by heart, that keeps us together."

Judy Paris grunts from the pedicycle. "You, my dear children, will never know the oppression we suffered," she declaims mockingly.

"Judys talk too much," says Connie.

"We do, for a fact." They both laugh.

"So you still read our so-called great books, our fiction and poetry?" asks Lorimer. "Who do you read, H. G. Wells? Shakespeare? Dickens, ah, Balzac, Kipling, Brian?" He gropes; Brian had been a bestseller Ginny liked. When had he last looked at Shakespeare or the others?

"Oh, the historicals," Judy says. "It's interesting, I guess. Grim. They're not very realistic. I'm sure it was to you," she adds generously.

And they turn to discussing whether the laying hens are getting too much light, leaving Lorimer to wonder how what he supposes are the eternal verities of human nature can have faded from a world's reality. Love, conflict, heroism, tragedy—all "unrealistic"? Well, flight crews are never great readers; still, women read more. . . . Something *has* changed, he can sense it. Something basic enough to affect human nature. A physical development perhaps; a mutation? What is really under those floating clothes?

It is the Judys who give him part of it.

He is exercising alone with both of them, listening to them gossip about some legendary figure named Dagmar.

"The Dagmar who invented the chess opening?" he asks.

"Yes. She does anything, when she's good she's great."

"Was she bad sometimes?"

A Judy laughs. "The Dagmar problem, you can say. She has this tendency to organize everything. It's fine when it works but every so often it runs wild; she thinks she's queen or what. Then they have to get out the butterfly nets."

All in present tense—but Lady Blue has told him the Dagmar gambit is over a century old.

Longevity, he thinks; by god, that's what they're hiding. Say they've achieved a doubled or tripled life span, that would certainly change human psychology, affect their outlook on everything. Delayed maturity, perhaps? We were working on endocrine cell juvenescence when I left. How old are these girls, for instance?

He is framing a question when Judy Dakar says, "I was in the crèche when she went pluggo. But she's good, I loved her later on."

Lorimer thinks she has said "crash" and then realizes she means a communal nursery. "Is that the same Dagmar?" he asks. "She must be very old."

"Oh no, her sister."

"A sister a hundred years apart?"

"I mean, her daughter. Her, her *grand*-daughter." She starts pedaling fast.

"Judys," says her twin, behind them.

Sister again. Everybody he learns of seems to have an extraordinary number of sisters, Lorimer reflects. He hears Judy Paris saying to her twin, "I think I remember Dagmar at the crèche. She started uniforms for everybody. Colors and numbers."

"You couldn't have, you weren't born," Judy Dakar retorts.

There is a silence in the drum.

Lorimer turns on the rungs to look at them. Two flushed cheerful faces stare back warily, make identical head-dipping gestures to swing the black hair out of their eyes. Identical. . . . But isn't the Dakar girl on the cycle a shade more mature, her face more weathered?

"I thought you were supposed to be twins."

"Ah, Judys talk a lot," they say together—and grin guiltily.

"You aren't sisters," he tells them. "You're what we called clones."

Another silence.

"Well, yes," says Judy Dakar. "We call it sisters.

Oh, mother! We weren't supposed to tell you, Myda said you would be frightfully upset. It was illegal in your day, true?"

"Yes. We considered it immoral and unethical, experimenting with human life. But it doesn't upset me personally."

"Oh, that's beautiful, that's great," they say together. "We think of you as different," Judy Paris blurts, "you're more hu— more like us. Please, you don't have to tell the others, do you? Oh, *please* don't."

"It was an accident there were two of us here," says Judy Dakar. "Myda *warned* us. Can't you wait a little while?" Two identical pairs of dark eyes beg him.

"Very well," he says slowly. "I won't tell my friends for the time being. But if I keep your secret you have to answer some questions. For instance, how many of your people are created artificially this way?"

He begins to realize he *is* somewhat upset. Dave is right, damn it, they are hiding things. Is this brave new world populated by subhuman slaves, run by master brains? Decorticate zombies, workers without stomachs or sex, human cortexes wired into machines. Monstrous experiments rush through his mind. He has been naive again. These normal-looking women could be fronting for a hideous world.

"How many?"

"There's only about eleven thousand of us," Judy Dakar says. The two Judys look at each other, transparently confirming something. They're unschooled in deception, Lorimer thinks; is that good? And is diverted by Judy Paris exclaiming, "What we can't figure out is why did you think it was wrong?"

Lorimer tries to tell them, to convey the horror of manipulating human identity, creating abnormal life. The threat to individuality, the fearful power it would put in a dictator's hand.

"Dictator?" one of them echoes blankly. He looks at their faces and can only say, "Doing things to people without their consent. I think it's sad."

"But that's just what we think about you," the younger Judy bursts out. "How do you know who you *are?* Or who anybody is? All alone, no sisters to share with! You don't know what you can do, or what would be interesting to try. All you poor singletons, you— why, you just have to blunder along and die, all for nothing!"

Her voice trembles. Amazed, Lorimer sees both of them are misty-eyed.

"We better get this m-moving," the other Judy says.

They swing back into the rhythm and in bits and pieces Lorimer finds out how it is. Not bottled embryos, they tell him indignantly. Human mothers like everybody else, young mothers, the best kind. A somatic cell nucleus is inserted in an enucleated ovum and reimplanted in the womb. They have each borne two "sister" babies in their late teens and nursed them a while before moving on. The crèches always have plenty of mothers.

His longevity notion is laughed at; nothing but some rules of healthy living have as yet been achieved. "We should make ninety in good shape," they assure him. "A hundred and eight, that was Judy Eagle, she's our record. But she was pretty blah at the end."

The clone-strains themselves are old, they date from the epidemic. They were part of the first effort to save the race when the babies stopped and they've continued ever since.

"It's so perfect," they tell him. "We each have a book, it's really a library. All the recorded messages. The Book of Judy Shapiro, that's us. Dakar and Paris are our personal names, we're doing cities now." They laugh, trying not to talk at once about how each Judy adds her individual memoir, her adventures and problems and discoveries in the genotype they all share.

"If you make a mistake it's useful for the others. Of course you try not to—or at least make a *new* one."

"Some of the old ones aren't so realistic," her other self puts in. "Things were so different, I guess. We make excerpts of the parts we like best. And practical things, like Judys should watch out for skin cancer."

"But we have to read the whole thing every ten years," says the Judy called Dakar. "It's inspiring. As you get older you understand some of the ones you didn't before."

Bemused, Lorimer tries to think how it would be, hearing the voices of three hundred years of Orren Lorimers. Lorimers who were mathematicians or plumbers or artists or bums or criminals, maybe. The continuing exploration and completion of self. And a dozen living doubles; aged Lorimers, infant Lorimers. And other Lorimers' women and children . . . would he enjoy it or resent it? He doesn't know.

"Have you made your records yet?"

"Oh, we're too young. Just notes in case of accident."

"Will we be in them?"

"You can say!" They laugh merrily, then sober. "Truly you won't tell?" Judy Paris asks. "Lady Blue, we have to let her know what we did. Oof. But *truly* you won't tell your friends?"

He hadn't told on them, he thinks now, emerging back into his living self. Connie beside him is drinking cider from a bulb. He has a drink in his hand too, he finds. But he hasn't told.

"Judys will talk." Connie shakes her head, smiling. Lorimer realizes he must have gabbled out the whole thing.

"It doesn't matter," he tells her. "I would have guessed soon anyhow. There were too many clues . . . Woolagongs invent, Mydas worry, Jans are brains, Billy Dees work so hard. I picked up six different stories of hydroelectric stations that were built or improved or are being run by one Lala Singh. Your whole way of life. I'm more interested in this sort of thing than a respectable physicist should be," he says wryly. "You're all clones, aren't you? Every one of you. What do Connies do?"

"You really do know." She gazes at him like a mother whose child has done something troublesome and bright. "Whew! Oh, well, Connies farm like mad, we grow things. Most of our names are plants. I'm Veronica, by the way. And of course the crèches, that's our weakness. The runt mania. We tend to focus on anything smaller or weak."

Her warm eyes focus on Lorimer, who draws back involuntarily.

"We control it." She gives a hearty chuckle. "We aren't all that way. There's been engineering Connies, and we have two young sisters who love metallurgy. It's fascinating what the genotype can do if you try. The original Constantia Morelos was a chemist, she weighed ninety pounds and never saw a farm in her life." Connie looks down at her own muscular arms. "She was killed by the crazies, she fought with weapons. It's so hard to understand. . . . And I had a sister Timothy who made dynamite and dug two canals and she wasn't even an andy."

"*An* andy," he says.

"Oh, dear."

"I guessed that too. Early androgen treatments."

She nods hesitantly. "Yes. We needed the muscle-power for some jobs. A few. Kays are quite strong anyway. Whew!" She suddenly stretches her back, wriggles as if she'd been cramped. "Oh, I'm glad you know. It's been such a strain. We couldn't even sing."

"Why not?"

"Myda was sure we'd make mistakes, all the words we'd have to change. We sing a lot." She softly hums a bar or two.

"What kinds of songs do you sing?"

"Oh, every kind. Adventure songs, work songs, mothering songs, roaming songs, mood songs, trouble songs, joke songs—everything."

"What about love songs?" he ventures. "Do you still have, well, love?"

"Of course, how could people not love?" But she looks at him doubtfully. "The love stories I've heard from your time are so, I don't know, so weird. Grim and pluggy. It doesn't seem like love. . . . Oh, yes, we have famous love songs. Some of them are partly sad too. Like Tamil and Alcmene O, they're fated together. Connies are fated too, a little." She grins bashfully. "We love to be with Ingrid Anders. It's more one-sided. I hope there'll be an Ingrid on my next hitch. She's so exciting, she's like a little diamond."

Implications are exploding all about him, sparkling with questions. But Lorimer wants to complete the darker pattern beyond.

"Eleven thousand genotypes, two million people: that averages two hundred of each of you alive now." She nods. "I suppose it varies? There's more of some?"

"Yes, some types aren't as viable. But we haven't lost any since early days. They tried to preserve all the genes they could. We have people from all the major races and a lot of small strains. Like me, I'm the Carib Blend. Of course we'll never know what was lost. But eleven thousand is a lot, really. We all try to know every one, it's a life hobby."

A chill penetrates his ataraxia. Eleven thousand, period. That is the true population of Earth now. He thinks of two hundred tall olive-skinned women named after plants, excited by two hundred little bright Ingrids; two hundred talkative Judys, two hundred self-possessed Lady Blues, two hundred Margos and Mydas and the rest. He shivers. The heirs, the happy pall-bearers of the human race.

"So evolution ends," he says somberly.

"No, why? It's just slowed down. We do everything much slower than you did, I think. We like to experience things *fully*. We have time." She stretches again, smiling. "There's all the time."

"But you have no new genotypes. It is the end."

"Oh but there are, now. Last century they worked out the way to make haploid nuclei combine. We can make a stripped egg cell function like pollen," she says proudly. "I mean sperm. It's tricky, some don't come out too well. But now we're finding both Xs viable we have over a hundred new types started. Of course it's hard for them, with no sisters. The donors try to help."

Over a hundred, he thinks. Well. Maybe. . . . But "both Xs viable." What does that mean? She must be referring to the epidemic. He had figured it primarily affected the men. His mind goes happily to work on the new puzzle, ignoring a sound from somewhere that is trying to pierce his calm.

"It was a gene or genes on the X chromosome that was injured," he guessed aloud. "Not the Y. And the lethal trait had to be recessive, right? Thus there would have been no births at all for a time, until some men recovered or were isolated long enough to manufacture undamaged X-bearing gametes. But women carry their lifetime supply of ova, they could never regenerate reproductively. When they mated with the recovered males only female babies would be produced, since the female carries two Xs and the mother's defective gene would be compensated by a normal X from the father. But the male is XY, he receives only the mother's defective X. Thus the lethal defect would be expressed, the male fetus would be finished. . . . A planet of girls and dying men. The few odd viables died off."

"You truly do understand," she says admiringly.

The sound is becoming urgent; he refuses to hear it, there is significance here.

"So we'll be perfectly all right on Earth. No problem. In theory we can marry again and have families, daughters anyway."

"Yes," she says. "In theory."

The sound suddenly broaches his defenses, becomes the loud voice of Bud Geirr raised in song. He sounds plain drunk now. It seems to be coming from the main garden pod, the one they use to grow vegetables, not sanitation. Lorimer feels the dread alive again, rising closer. Dave ought to keep an eye on him. But Dave seems to have vanished too; he recalls seeing him go toward Control with Lady Blue.

"OH, THE SUN SHINES BRIGHT ON PRET-TY RED WI-I-ING," carols Bud.

Something should be done, Lorimer decides painfully. He stirs; it is an effort.

"Don't worry," Connie says. "Andy's with them."

"You don't know, you don't know what you've started." He pushes off toward the garden hatchway.

"—AS SHE LAY SLE-EPING, A COWBOY

CREE-E-EEPING—" General laughter from the hatchway. Lorimer coasts through into the green dazzle. Beyond the radial fence of snap-beans he sees Bud sailing in an exaggerated crouch after Judy Paris. Andy hangs by the iguana cages, laughing.

Bud catches one of Judy's ankles and stops them both with a flourish, making her yellow pajamas swirl. She giggles at him upsidedown, making no effort to free herself.

"I don't like this," Lorimer whispers.

"Please don't interfere." Connie has hold of his arm, anchoring them both to the tool rack. Lorimer's alarm seems to have ebbed; he will watch, let serenity return. The others have not noticed them.

"Oh, there once was an Indian maid." Bud sings more restrainedly, "Who never was a-fraid, that some buckaroo would slip it up her, ahem, ahem," he coughs ostentatiously, laughing. "Hey, Andy, I hear them calling you."

"What?" says Judy, "I don't hear anything."

"They're calling you, lad. Out there."

"Who?" asks Andy, listening.

"*They* are, for Crissake." He lets go of Judy and kicks over to Andy. "Listen, you're a great kid. Can't you see me and Judy have some business to discuss in private?" He turns Andy gently around and pushes him at the bean-stakes. "It's New Year's Eve, dummy."

Andy floats passively away through the fence of vines, raising a hand at Lorimer and Connie. Bud is back with Judy.

"Happy New Year, kitten," he smiles.

"Happy New Year. Did you do special things on New Year?" she asks curiously.

"What we did on New Year's." He chuckles, taking her shoulders in his hands. "On New Year's Eve, yes we did. Why don't I show you some of our primitive Earth customs, h'mm?"

She nods, wide-eyed.

"Well, first we wish each other well, like this." He draws her to him and lightly kisses her cheek. "Keerist, what a dumb bitch," he says in a totally different

voice. "You can tell you've been out too long when
the geeks start looking good. Knockers, ahhh—" His
hand plays with her blouse. The man is unaware,
Lorimer realizes. He doesn't know he's drugged, he's
speaking his thoughts. I must have done that. Oh, god.
. . . He takes shelter behind his crystal lens, an observer in the protective light of eternity.

"And then we smooch a little." The friendly voice is
back. Bud holds the girl closer, caressing her back.
"Fat ass." He puts his mouth on hers; she doesn't
resist. Lorimer watches Bud's arms tighten, his hands
working on her buttocks, going under her clothes. Safe
in the lens his own sex stirs. Judy's arms are waving
aimlessly.

Bud breaks for a breath, a hand at his zipper.

"Stop staring," he says hoarsely. "One fucking more
word, you'll find out what that big mouth is for. Oh,
man, a flagpole. Like steel. . . . Bitch, this is your
lucky day." He is baring her breasts now, big breasts.
Fondling them. "Two fucking years in the ass end of
noplace," he mutters, "shit on me will you? Can't wait,
watch it—titty-titty-titties—"

He kisses her again quickly and smiles down at
her. "Good?" he asks in his tender voice, and sinks
his mouth on her nipples, his hand seeking in her
thighs. She jerks and says something muffled. Lorimer's
arteries are pounding with delight, with dread.

"I—I think this should stop," he makes himself say
falsely, hoping he isn't saying more. Through the
pulsing tension he hears Connie whisper back, it sounds
like "Don't worry, Judy's very athletic." Terror stabs
him, they don't know. But he can't help.

"Cunt," Bud grunts, "you have to have a cunt in
there, is it froze up? You dumb cunt—" Judy's face
appears briefly in her floating hair, a remote part of
Lorimer's mind notes that she looks amused and uncomfortable. His being is riveted to the sight of Bud
expertly controlling her body in midair, peeling down
the yellow slacks. Oh god—her dark pubic mat, the
thick white thighs—a perfectly normal woman, no
mutation. Ohhh, god. . . . But there is suddenly a

drifting shadow in the way: Andy again floating over them with something in his hands.

"You dinko, Jude?" the boy asks.

Bud's face comes up red and glaring. "Bug out, you!"

"Oh, I won't bother."

"Jee-sus Christ." Bud lunges up and grabs Andy's arm, his legs still hooked around Judy. "This is man's business, boy, do I have to spell it out?" He shifts his grip. "Shoo!"

In one swift motion he has jerked Andy close and backhanded his face hard, sending him sailing into the vines.

Bud gives a bark of laughter, bends back to Judy. Lorimer can see his erection poking through his fly. He wants to utter some warning, tell them their peril, but he can only ride the hot pleasure surging through him, melting his crystal shell. Go on, more—avidly he sees Bud mouth her breasts again and then suddenly flip her whole body over, holding her wrists behind her in one fist, his legs pinning hers. Her bare buttocks bulge up helplessly, enormous moons. "Ass-s-s," Bud groans. "Up you bitch, ahh-hh—" He pulls her butt onto him.

Judy gives a cry, begins to struggle futilely. Lorimer's shell boils and bursts. Amid the turmoil ghosts outside are trying to rush in. And something *is* moving, a real ghost—to his dismay he sees it is Andy again, floating toward the joined bodies, holding a whirring thing. Oh, no—a camera. The fools.

"Get away!" he tries to call to the boy.

But Bud's head turns, he has seen. "You little piss-ass." His long arm shoots out and captures Andy's shirt, his legs still locked around Judy.

"I've had it with you." His fist slams into Andy's mouth, the camera goes spinning away. But this time Bud doesn't let him go, he is battering the boy, all of them rolling in a tangle in the air.

"Stop!" Lorimer hears himself shout, plunging at them through the beans. "Bud, stop it! You're hitting a woman."

The angry face comes around, squinting at him.

"Get lost, Doc, you little fart. Get your own ass."

"Andy is a *woman,* Bud. You're hitting a girl. She's not a man."

"Huh?" Bud glances at Andy's bloody face. He shakes the shirtfront. "Where's the boobs?"

"She doesn't have breasts, but she's a woman. Her real name is Kay. They're all women. Let her go, Bud."

Bud stares at the androgyne, his legs still pinioning Judy, his penis poking the air. Andy puts up his/her hands in a vaguely combative way.

"A dyke?" says Bud slowly. "A goddam little bull dyke? This I gotta see."

He feints casually, thrusts a hand into Andy's crotch.

"No balls!" he roars. "No balls at all!" Convulsing with laughter he lets himself tip over in the air, releasing Andy, his legs letting Judy slip free. "Na-ah," he interrupts himself to grab her hair and goes on guffawing. "A dyke! Hey, dykey!" He takes hold of his hard-on, waggles it at Andy. "Eat your heart out, little dyke." Then he pulls up Judy's head. She has been watching unresisting all along.

"Take a good look, girlie. See what old Buddy has for you? Tha-a-at's what you want, say it. How long since you saw a real man, hey, dog-face?"

Maniacal laughter bubbles up in Lorimer's gut, farce too strong for fear. "She never saw a man in her life before, none of them has. You imbecile, don't you get it? There aren't any other men, they've all been dead three hundred years."

Bud slowly stops chuckling, twists around to peer at Lorimer.

"What'd I hear you say, Doc?"

"The men are all gone. They died off in the epidemic. There's nothing but women left alive on Earth."

"You mean there's, there's two million women down there and no men?" His jaw gapes. "Only little bull dykes like Andy. . . . Wait a minute. Where do they get the kids?"

"They grow them artificially. They're all girls."

"Gawd. . . ." Bud's hand clasps his drooping penis,

jiggles it absently until it stiffens. "Two million hot little cunts down there, waiting for old Buddy. Gawd. The last man on Earth. . . . You don't count, Doc. And old Dave, he's full of crap."

He begins to pump himself, still holding Judy by the hair. The motion sends them slowly backward. Lorimer sees that Andy—Kay—has the camera going again. There is a big star-shaped smear of blood on the boyish face; cut lip, probably. He himself feels globed in thick air, all action spent. Not lucid.

"Two million cunts," Bud repeats. "Nobody home, nothing but pussy everywhere. I can do anything I want any time. No more shits." He pumps faster. "They'll be spread out for miles begging for it. Clawing each other for it. All for me, King Buddy. . . . I'll have strawberries and cunt for breakfast. Hot buttered boobies, man. 'N' head, there'll be a couple little twats licking whip cream off my cock all day long. . . . Hey, I'll have contests! Only the best for old Buddy now. Not you, cow." He jerks Judy's head. "Li'l teenies, tight li'l holes. I'll make the old broads hot 'em up while I watch." He frowns slightly, working on himself. In a clinical corner of his mind Lorimer guesses the drug is retarding ejaculation. He tells himself that he should be relieved by Bud's self-absorption, is instead obscurely terrified.

"King, I'll be their god," Bud is mumbling. "They'll make statues of me, my cock a mile high, all over. . . . His Majesty's sacred balls. They'll worship it. . . . Buddy Geirr, the last cock on Earth. Oh man, if old George could see that. When the boys hear that they'll really shit themselves, woo-ee!"

He frowns harder. "They can't all be gone." His eyes rove, find Lorimer. "Hey, Doc, there's some men left someplace, aren't there? Two or three, anyway?"

"No." Effortfully Lorimer shakes his head. "They're all dead, all of them."

"Balls." Bud twists around, peering at them. "There has to be some left. Say it." He pulls Judy's head up. *Say it,* cunt."

"No, it's true," she says.

"No men," Andy/Kay echoes.

"You're lying." Bud scowls, frigs himself faster, thrusting his pelvis. "There has to be some men, sure there are. . . . They're hiding out in the hills, that's what it is. Hunting, living wild. . . . Old wild men, I knew it."

"Why do there have to be men?" Judy asks him, being jerked to and fro.

"Why, you stupid bitch." He doesn't look at her, thrusts furiously. "Because, dummy, otherwise nothing counts, that's why. . . . There's some men, some good old buckaroos—Buddy's a good old buckaroo—"

"Is he going to emit sperm now?" Connie whispers.

"Very likely," Lorimer says, or intends to say. The spectacle is of merely clinical interest, he tells himself, nothing to dread. One of Judy's hands clutches something: a small plastic bag. Her other hand is on her hair that Bud is yanking. It must be painful.

"Uhhh, ahh," Bud pants distressfully, "fuck away, fuck—" Suddenly he pushes Judy's head into his groin, Lorimer glimpses her nonplussed expression.

"You have a mouth, bitch, get working! . . . Take it for shit's sake, *take* it! Uh, uh—" A small oyster jets limply from him. Judy's arm goes after it with the bag as they roll over in the air.

"Geirr!"

Bewildered by the roar, Lorimer turns and sees Dave—Major Norman Davis—looming in the hatchway. His arms are out, holding back Lady Blue and the other Judy.

"Geirr! I said there would be no misconduct on this ship and I mean it. Get away from that woman!"

Bud's legs only move vaguely, he does not seem to have heard. Judy swims through them bagging the last drops.

"You, what the hell are you doing?"

In the silence Lorimer heard his own voice say, "Taking a sperm sample, I should think."

"Lorimer? Are you out of your perverted mind? Get Geirr to his quarters."

Bud slowly rotates upright. "Ah, the reverend Leroy," he says tonelessly.

"You're drunk, Geirr. Go to your quarters."

"I have news for you, Dave-o," Bud tells him in the same flat voice. "I bet you don't know we're the last men on Earth. Two million twats down there."

"I'm aware of that," Dave says furiously. "You're a drunken disgrace. Lorimer, get that man out of here."

But Lorimer feels no nerve of action stir. Dave's angry voice has pushed back the terror, created a strange hopeful stasis encapsulating them all.

"I don't have to take that any more. . . ." Bud's head moves back and forth, silently saying no, no, as he drifts toward Lorimer. "Nothing counts any more. All gone. What for, friends?" His forehead puckers. "Old Dave, he's a man. I'll let him have some. The dummies. . . . Poor old Doc, you're a creep but you're better'n nothing, you can have some too. . . . We'll have places, see, big spreads. Hey, we can run drags, there has to be a million good old cars down there. We can go hunting. And then we find the wild men."

Andy, or Kay, is floating toward him, wiping off blood.

"Ah, no you don't!" Bud snarls and lunges for her. As his arm stretches out Judy claps him on the triceps.

Bud gives a yell that dopplers off, his limbs thrash—and then he is floating limply, his face suddenly serene. He is breathing, Lorimer sees, releasing his own breath, watching them carefully straighten out the big body. Judy plucks her pants out of the vines, and they start towing him out through the fence. She has the camera and the specimen bag.

"I put this in the freezer, dinko?" she says to Connie as they come by. Lorimer has to look away.

Connie nods. "Kay, how's your face?"

"I felt it!" Andy Kay says excitedly through puffed lips. "I felt physical anger, I wanted to hit him. Woo-ee!"

"Put that man in my wardroom," Dave orders as they pass. He has moved into the sunlight over the lettuce rows. Lady Blue and Judy Dakar are back by the wall, watching. Lorimer remembers what he wanted to ask.

"Dave, do you really know? They're all women?"

Dave eyes him broodingly, floating erect with the sun on his chestnut beard and hair. The authentic features of man. Lorimer thinks of his own father, a small pale figure like himself. He feels better.

"I always knew they were trying to deceive us, Lorimer. Now that this woman has admitted the facts I understand the full extent of the tragedy."

It is his deep, mild Sunday voice. The women look at him interestedly.

"They are lost children. They have forgotten He who made them. For generations they have lived in darkness."

"They seem to be doing all right," Lorimer hears himself say. It sounds rather foolish.

"Women are not capable of running anything. You should know that, Lorimer. Look what they've done here, it's pathetic. Marking time, that's all. Poor souls." Dave sighs gravely. "It is not their fault. I recognize that. Nobody has given them any guidance for three hundred years. Like a chicken with its head off."

Lorimer recognizes his own thought; the structure-less, chattering, trivial, two-million-celled protoplasmic lump.

"The head of the woman is the man," Dave says crisply. "Corinthians one eleven three. No discipline whatsoever." He stretches out his arm, holding up his crucifix as he drifts toward the wall of vines. "Mockery. Abominations." He touches the stakes and turns, framed in the green arbor.

"We were sent here, Lorimer. This is God's plan. *I* was sent here. Not you, you're as bad as they are. My middle name is Paul," he adds in a conversational tone. The sun gleams on the cross, on his uplifted face, a strong, pure, apostolic visage. Despite some intellectual reservations Lorimer feels a forgotten nerve respond.

"Oh Father, send me strength," Dave prays quietly, his eyes closed. "You have spared us from the void to bring Your light to this suffering world. I shall lead Thy erring daughters out of the darkness. I shall be a stern but merciful father to them in Thy name. Help me to teach the children Thy holy law and train them in the fear of Thy righteous wrath. Let the women learn in silence and all subjection; Timothy two eleven. They shall have sons to rule over them and glorify Thy name."

He could do it, Lorimer thinks, a man like that really could get life going again. Maybe there is some mystery, some plan. I was too ready to give up. No guts. . . . He becomes aware of women whispering.

"This tape is about through." It is Judy Dakar. "Isn't that enough? He's just repeating."

"Wait," murmurs Lady Blue.

"And she brought forth a man child to rule the nations with a rod of iron, Revelations twelve five," Dave says, louder. His eyes are open now, staring intently at the crucifix. *"For God so loved the world that he sent his only begotten son."*

Lady Blue nods; Judy pushes off toward Dave. Lorimer understands, protest rising in his throat. They mustn't do that to Dave, treating him like an animal for Christ's sake, a man—

"Dave! Look out, don't let her get near you!" he shouts.

"May I look, Major? It's beautiful, what is it?" Judy is coasting close, her hand out toward the crucifix.

"She's got a hypo, watch it!"

But Dave has already wheeled round. "Do not profane, woman!"

He thrusts the cross at her like a weapon, so menacing that she recoils in mid-air and shows the glinting needle in her hand.

"Serpent!" He kicks her shoulder away, sending himself upward. "Blasphemer. All right," he snaps in his ordinary voice, "there's going to be some order around here starting now. Get over by that wall, all of you."

Astounded, Lorimer sees that Dave actually has a weapon in his other hand, a small grey handgun. He must have had it since Houston. Hope and ataraxia shrivel away, he is shocked into desperate reality.

"Major Davis," Lady Blue is saying. She is floating right at him, they all are, right at the gun. Oh god, do they know what it is?

"Stop!" he shouts at them. "Do what he says, for god's sake. That's a ballistic weapon, it can kill you. It shoots metal slugs." He begins edging toward Dave along the vines.

"Stand back." Dave gestures with the gun. "I am taking command of this ship in the name of the United States of America under God."

"Dave, put that gun away. You don't want to shoot people."

Dave sees him, swings the gun around. "I warn you, Lorimer. Get over there with them. Geirr's a man, when he sobers up." He looks at the women still drifting puzzledly toward him and understands. "All right, lesson one. Watch this."

He takes deliberate aim at the iguana cages and fires. There is a pinging crack. A lizard explodes bloodily, voices cry out. A loud mechanical warble starts up and overrides everything.

"A leak!" Two bodies go streaking toward the far end, everybody is moving. In the confusion Lorimer sees Dave calmly pulling himself back to the hatchway behind them, his gun ready. He pushes frantically across the tool rack to cut him off. A spray cannister comes loose in his grip, leaving him kicking in the air. The alarm warble dies.

"You will stay here until I decide to send for you," Dave announces. He has reached the hatch, is pulling the massive lock door around. It will seal off the pod, Lorimer realizes.

"Don't do it, Dave! Listen to me, you're going to kill us all." Lorimer's own internal alarms are shaking him, he knows now what all that damned volleyball has been for and he is scared to death. "Dave, listen to me!"

"Shut up." The gun swings toward him. The door is moving. Lorimer gets a foot on solidity.

"Duck! It's a bomb!" With all his strength he hurls the massive cannister at Dave's head and launches himself after it.

"Look out!" And he is sailing helplessly in slow motion, hearing the gun go off again, voices yelling. Dave must have missed him, overhead shots are tough—and then he is doubling downward, grabbing hair. A hard blow strikes his gut, it is Dave's leg kicking past him but he has his arm under the beard, the big man bucking like a bull, throwing him around.

"Get the gun, get it!" People are bumping him, getting hit. Just as his hold slips a hand snakes by him onto Dave's shoulder and they are colliding into the hatch door in a tangle. Dave's body is suddenly no longer at war.

Lorimer pushes free, sees Dave's contorted face tip slowly backward looking at him.

"Judas—"

The eyes close. It is over.

Lorimer looks around. Lady Blue is holding the gun, sighting down the barrel.

"Put that down," he gasps, winded. She goes on examining it.

"Hey, thanks!" Andy—Kay—grins lopsidedly at him, rubbing her jaw. They are all smiling, speaking warmly to him, feeling themselves, their torn clothes. Judy Dakar has a black eye starting, Connie holds a shattered iguana by the tail.

Beside him Dave drifts breathing stertorously, his blind face pointing at the sun. *Judas* . . . Lorimer feels the last shield break inside him, desolation flooding in. *On the deck my captain lies.*

Andy-who-is-not-a-man comes over and matter-of-factly zips up Dave's jacket, takes hold of it and begins to tow him out. Judy Dakar stops them long enough to wrap the crucifix chain around his hand. Somebody laughs, not unkindly, as they go by.

For an instant Lorimer is back in that Evanston toilet. But they are gone, all the little giggling girls. All gone forever, gone with the big boys waiting outside to jeer at him. Bud is right, he thinks. *Nothing counts any more*. Grief and anger hammer at him. He knows now what he has been dreading: not their vulnerability, his.

"They were good men," he says bitterly. "They aren't bad men. You don't know what bad means. You did it to them, you broke them down. You made them do crazy things. Was it interesting? Did you learn enough?" His voice is trying to shake. "Everybody has aggressive fantasies. They didn't act on them. Never. Until you poisoned them."

They gaze at him in silence. "But nobody does," Connie says finally. "I mean, the fantasies."

"They were good men," Lorimer repeats elegiacally. He knows he is speaking for it all, for Dave's Father, for Bud's manhood, for himself, for Cro-Magnon, for the dinosaurs too, maybe. "I'm a man. By god yes, I'm angry. I have a right. We gave you all this, we made it all. We built your precious civilization and your knowledge and comfort and medicines and your dreams. All of it. We protected you, we worked our balls off keeping you and your kids. It was hard. It was a fight, a bloody fight all the way. We're tough. We had to be, can't you understand? Can't you for Christ's sake understand that?"

Another silence.

"We're trying." Lady Blue sighs. "We are trying, Dr. Lorimer. Of course we enjoy your inventions and we do appreciate your evolutionary role. But you must see there's a problem. As I understand it, what you protected people from was largely other males, wasn't it? We've just had an extraordinary demonstration. You have brought history to life for us." Her wrinkled brown eyes smile at him; a small, tea-colored matron holding an obsolete artifact.

"But the fighting is long over. It ended when you did, I believe. We can hardly turn you loose on Earth, and we simply have no facilities for people with your emotional problems."

"Besides, we don't think you'd be very happy," Judy Dakar adds earnestly.

"We could clone them," says Connie. "I know

there's people who would volunteer to mother. The young ones might be all right, we could try."

"We've been *over* all that." Judy Paris is drinking from the water tank. She rinses and spits into the soil bed, looking worriedly at Lorimer. "We ought to take care of that leak now, we can talk tomorrow. And tomorrow and tomorrow." She smiles at him, unselfconsciously rubbing her crotch. "I'm sure a lot of people will want to meet you."

"Put us on an island," Lorimer says wearily. "On three islands." That look; he knows that look of preoccupied compassion. His mother and sister had looked just like that the time the diseased kitten came in the yard. They had comforted it and fed it and tenderly taken it to the vet to be gassed.

An acute, complex longing for the women he has known grips him. Women to whom men were not simply irrelevant. Ginny . . . dear god. His sister Amy. Poor Amy, she was good to him when they were kids. His mouth twists.

"Your problem is," he says, "if you take the risk of giving us equal rights, what could we possibly contribute?"

"Precisely," says Lady Blue. They all smile at him relievedly, not understanding that he isn't.

"I think I'll have that antidote now," he says.

Connie floats toward him, a big, warm-hearted, utterly alien woman. "I thought you'd like yours in a bulb." She smiles kindly.

"Thank you." He takes the small, pink bulb. "Just tell me," he says to Lady Blue, who is looking at the bullet gashes, "what do you call yourselves? Women's World? Liberation? Amazonia?"

"Why, we call ourselves human beings." Her eyes twinkle absently at him, go back to the bullet marks. "Humanity, mankind." She shrugs. "The human race."

The drink tastes cool going down, something like peace and freedom, he thinks. Or death.

Nebula Awards, 1975, 1976: Win, Place, and Show

For the listing of Nebula Award winners for the first ten years, from 1965 through 1974, the reader is referred to *Nebula Ten* (Harper & Row); or, for a more complete listing of award-wining science fiction, to *A History of the Hugo, Nebula, and International Fantasy Awards,* published by Howard DeVore, 4705 Weddel Street, Dearborn, Michigan 48125.

1975

NOVEL

Winner: THE FOREVER WAR by Joe Haldeman (St. Martin's Press; Ballantine Books)

Runners-up: THE MOTE IN GOD'S EYE by Larry Niven and Jerry Pournelle (Simon & Schuster; SF Book Club)

DHALGREN by Samuel R. Delany (Bantam)

THE FEMALE MAN by Joanna Russ (Bantam)

NOVELLA

Winner: "Home Is the Hangman" by Roger Zelazny *(Analog)*

Runners-up: "The Storms of Windhaven" by Lisa Tuttle and George R. R. Martin *(Analog)*

"A Momentary Taste of Being" by James Tiptree, Jr. (from *The New Atlantis,* Hawthorn)

"Sunrise West" by William K. Carlson *(Vortex)*

NOVELETTE

Winner: "San Diego Lightfoot Sue" by Tom Reamy *(The Magazine of Fantasy and Science Fiction)*

Runners-up: "The Final Fighting of Fion MacCumhaill" by Randall Garrett *(The Magazine of Fantasy and Science Fiction)*

"Retrograde Summer" by John Varley *(The Magazine of Fantasy and Science Fiction)*

"A Galaxy Called Rome" by Barry Malzberg *(The Magazine of Fantasy and Science Fiction)*

"The Custodians" by Richard Cowper *(The Magazine of Fantasy and Science Fiction)*

SHORT STORY

Winner: "Catch That Zeppelin!" by Fritz Leiber *(The Magazine of Fantasy and Science Fiction)*

Runners-up: "Child of All Ages" by P. J. Plauger *(Analog)*

"Shatterday" by Harlan Ellison *(Gallery)*

"Sail the Tide of Mourning" by Richard Lupoff *(New Dimensions 5)*

"Time Deer" by Craig Strete *(Worlds of If)*

"Utopia of a Tired Man" by Jorge Luis Borges *(The New Yorker)*

"A Scraping of the Bones" by A. J. Budrys *(Analog)*

"Doing Lennon" by Greg Benford *(Analog)*

DRAMATIC PRESENTATION

Winner: YOUNG FRANKENSTEIN, screenplay by Mel Brooks and Gene Wilder

Runners-up: DARK STAR, screenplay by John Carpenter and Dan O'Bannon

ROLLERBALL, screenplay by William Harrison

A BOY AND HIS DOG, from a story by Harlan Ellison

GRAND MASTER AWARD

Winner: Jack Williamson

1976

NOVEL

Winner: MAN PLUS by Frederik Pohl (Random House; Bantam Books)

Runners-up: WHERE LATE THE SWEET BIRDS SANG by Kate Wilhelm (Harper & Row)

SHADRACH IN THE FURNACE by Robert Silverberg *(Analog)*

INFERNO by Larry Niven and Jerry Pournelle (Pocket Books)

ISLANDS by Marta Randall (Pyramid)

TRITON by Samuel R. Delany (Bantam)

NOVELLA

Winner: "Houston, Houston, Do You Read?" by James Tiptree, Jr. *(Aurora,* Fawcett)

Runners-up: "The Samurai and the Willows" by Michael Bishop *(The Magazine of Fantasy and Science Fiction)*

"Piper at the Gates of Dawn" by Richard Cowper *(The Magazine of Fantasy and Science Fiction)*

"The Eyeflash Miracles" by Gene Wolfe *(Future Power, Harper & Row)*

NOVELETTE

Winner: "The Bicentennial Man" by Isaac Asimov *(Stellar 2, Ballantine)*

Runners-up: "Diary of the Rose" by Ursula K. LeGuin *(Future Power, Harper & Row)*—withdrawn by request of author

"In the Bowl" by John Varley *(The Magazine of Fantasy and Science Fiction)*

"Custer's Last Jump" by Steven Utley and Howard Waldrop *(Universe 6, Doubleday)*

"His Hour Upon the Stage" by Grant Carrington *(Amazing)*

SHORT STORY

Winner: "A Crowd of Shadows" by Charles L. Grant *(The Magazine of Fantasy and Science Fiction)*

Runners-up: "Tricentennial" by Joe Haldeman *(Analog)*

"Stone Circle" by Lisa Tuttle *(Amazing)*

"Breath's a Ware That Will Not Keep" by Thomas F. Monteleone *(Dystopian Visions, Prentice Hall)*

"Mary Margaret Road-Grader" by Howard Waldrop *(Orbit 18, Harper & Row)*

"Back to the Stone Age" by Jake Saunders *(Lone Star Universe, Heidelberg)*

DRAMATIC PRESENTATION

NO AWARD

Nominees: HARLAN! HARLAN ELLISON READS HARLAN
ELLISON by Harlan Ellison

THE MAN WHO FELL TO EARTH, based on
a novel by Walter Tevis

LOGAN'S RUN, based on a novel by William F. Nolan and George C. Johnson

GRAND MASTER AWARD

Winner: Clifford Simak

ABOUT THE EDITOR

Born in Edmonston, Alberta, Canada in 1923, GORDON R. DICKSON moved permanently to the United States in 1937. After attending graduate school in the midwest, Mr. Dickson became a full-time writer, and at this point, has over a hundred and fifty short stories, thirty-three novels, including four novels in collaboration, six collections of short stories, and the editing of several anthologies to his credit. His major work is the Childe Cycle, a cycle of twelve novels, three of which are historical, three contemporary and six set in the future. President of Science Fiction Writers of America for two consecutive terms from 1969-1971, and recipient of the World Science Fiction Award ("Hugo Award"), the Science Fiction Writers of America Nebula Award, the E. E. Smith Memorial Award for Imaginative Fiction and the August Derleth Award of the British Fantasy Society, Mr. Dickson is one of the most esteemed members of the science fiction community.